Dear Reader,

I am thrilled to present *The Big Scoop*, my second book for Harlequin, and my first for the Flipside line.

The inspiration for this story came from my own experience as a freelance journalist. Like Jack Gold, I, too, got a little jaded in my approach to researching and writing stories, especially profiles of real people. Bored silly by the truth, I once wrote a fictionalized, outrageously tongue-in-cheek account of a real person's life (her parents were missionaries gifted with ESP; she was born in the jungle with a third eye in the middle of her forehead, etc.), then sat at my computer station, cackling hysterically while at the same time fretting over my diminishing sanity. In the end, I submitted the real story for publication. But I kept the bogus version on my hard drive as a personal reminder to get a new life.

Change, as it turns out, comes in surprising, delightful packages. For me it was a switch from nonfiction to romance fiction. It's impossible to get jaded when you're having this much fun. For Jack Gold it was a "delicious, devious, demented little dairy princess" by the name of Sally Darville.

Jack and Sally change one another forever—and definitely for the best! If you enjoyed reading their story as much as I enjoyed writing it, get in touch with me at sandrackelly@shaw.ca.

Sandra Kelly

"Jack Gold, you're a poor excuse for a Gobey winner."

A monstrous grin lit up his whole face at Sally's comment. "You know about that?"

What an ego! "Of course I know about it. I did *my* homework. I know where you were born and where you went to school. I know that you've been twice nominated—"

"Three times, actually."

"Whatever. The point is..."

"I get the point." He dropped his chin and looked at her thoughtfully. "Normally, I do background research on a story. I didn't in this case because, well, because I usually don't get assignments like this one. I usually get, you know, bigger, ah, I mean weightier assignments. See, after I won the Gobey, I got a little big for my britches." He chuckled as if that weren't really true, but for the sake of argument Sally should accept it as truth. "My editor decided to bring me down a notch."

What? Had he just said what she thought he'd said? "Do you mean to tell me that I'm your *punishment*? For acting like a jerk?"

Sandra Kelly

The Big Scoop

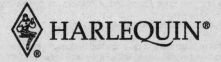

HARLEQUIN®

TORONTO • NEW YORK • LONDON
AMSTERDAM • PARIS • SYDNEY • HAMBURG
STOCKHOLM • ATHENS • TOKYO • MILAN • MADRID
PRAGUE • WARSAW • BUDAPEST • AUCKLAND

ISBN 0-373-44204-1

THE BIG SCOOP

www.eHarlequin.com

Printed in U.S.A.

ABOUT THE AUTHOR

Sandra Kelly has been putting words on paper since she was old enough to lift a pen. Before becoming a Flipside author, she published more than a million words of nonfiction in magazines and corporate publications across Canada. For seven years she taught in the Professional Writing Program at Mount Royal College in Calgary, helping hopeful young writers to realize their own dreams of becoming published. Sandra lives in Calgary with her husband Bob, and two ungrateful cats.

Books by Sandra Kelly

HARLEQUIN DUETS
76—SUITEHEART OF A DEAL

For Jean Molloy
1931–2003
Thanks for the humor, Mom

1

July 10: On the front page of the Peachtown Post

Can Peach Paradise Save Our Town?

Sally Darville, marketing manager for Darville Dairy, is a woman with a mission.

Darville, the twenty-seven-year-old daughter of Dean and Sarah Darville—the fourth generation of Darvilles to own and operate the local dairy—believes that Peach Paradise, their delicious new ice cream, can save Peachtown from ruin.

After three consecutive years of drought, Peachtown's usually thriving tourism industry is hurting. With daily temperatures soaring into the high nineties and fire bans in effect at all campgrounds, people are staying away in droves. Darville believes that Peach Paradise will bring them back.

"We can't make rain, but we can make the world's best ice cream," she said.

The tasty treat, introduced last March, sold out of local stores within a week and has since attracted fans throughout the Okanagan Valley. Now Darville has enlisted the help of *Vancouver Satellite* reporter "Cracker" Jack Gold to spread the word about Peach Paradise across British Columbia's densely populated lower mainland.

Gold, thirty-four, recently won the Gobey Award for uncovering a conspiracy by Vancouver-based Denton Corporation's top executives to launder two million dollars siphoned from the company's employee pension fund. Gold is the youngest reporter ever to win the prestigious international award.

Said Darville, "If Cracker Jack Gold can't help us, no one can."

"HOT ENOUGH FOR YA?"

Fingertips tapping out a steady beat on the chipped white countertop, Jack regarded the too-cheerful customer service clerk with the little patience he had left. "Yes, it is. I wonder if you'd mind taking another look at those records."

The clerk, a lanky youth with a drunk-on-life smile and a giant zit in the middle of his forehead, struck a solemn tone. "I can if you like, sir, but I really don't believe your car was towed. I believe it was moved."

"Is there a difference?"

"Well, yes. You see, sir, there's no record of anyone from this office having towed a candy-apple red 1968 Mustang convertible with the original leather seats plus inlaid mother-of-pearl console *and* the black-and-yellow foam dice once owned by Jerry Lee Lewis. No record at all, sir."

"Then, do you have any thoughts on who might have...moved it?"

The boy shrugged. "I may have."

Jack forced his fingers to be still as he drew a shallow breath. Five years of pounding the backroads for small-town newspapers across the lower mainland had taught him there was no point in losing it with guys like—he glanced at the boy's name tag—Dudley here. The Dudleys of the world, he vaguely recalled from those long forgotten days, couldn't be rushed under terrorist threat.

Back then, Jack had customized a smile for people he had nothing against but hoped never to see again. He flashed it now. "Care to share your thoughts, Dudley?"

The teenager nodded in the general direction of the window separating the tiny impoundment office from Peachtown's main drag. "Well, see, we have these identical twins here in town—Terry and Tommy Trubble? Anyway, they're sorta the town pranksters." He rolled his eyes. "Well, okay, the county pranksters, if you wanna be, you know, real accurate." His voice dropped to a whisper as he leaned closer to Jack. "You won't believe this, but one time they..."

"My car, Dudley?"

"Oh, right. Well, the fact is, sir, they like to move cars."

"Move cars," Jack repeated dumbly. "You mean steal cars."

Shock turned Dudley's zit a singularly unattractive shade of red. "Oh no, sir! They don't keep 'em. They just hot-wire 'em and then relocate 'em." His vacant gaze suggested that no further explanation should be necessary.

"Uh-huh, and just for the record, Dudley, where exactly do they relocate them to?"

The boy cleared his throat. "Well now, that depends on a number of things."

Grasping the counter's edge with both hands, Jack arched his aching back and let his eyelids droop. It was bad enough that he was here. It was bad enough that he was here to cover a story about ice cream. It was bad enough that he was here to cover a story about ice cream because he'd acted like—how had his editor put it?—"a spoiled celebrity." *This* headache he definitely didn't need.

In addition to everything else, he was hot and tired and hungry. The inside of his mouth felt like sandpaper, and his legs were stiff and cramped after the four-hour drive east from Vancouver. The drive he had foolishly undertaken in his prized Mustang. The prized Mustang which was now missing.

Just thirty minutes ago, he'd parked it across the street from Cora's Café and gone into the restaurant for directions. While he stood there nodding like a puppet, a woman he presumed to be Cora had passed a pleasant twenty minutes disagreeing with the restaurant's lone patron about the fastest route to Darville

Dairy. Jack had eventually tuned out the debate and inched toward the door.

They were arguing the merits of highway number seven versus county road nineteen when he slipped outside and saw that the Mustang was gone. For one hellish moment he had stood there gawking at the empty parking space, convinced it was an optical illusion created by the heat. It wasn't.

"So," he said to Dudley. "On what sort of things does it depend?"

Well, it being Saturday and all, Dudley explained, the twins *probably* had relocated the Mustang to the Darville Dairy Bar. Lots of folks would be there today, 'cause of Peach Paradise. The twins *might* have taken the car to the bakery just three blocks from here, which, Jack would want to know, gave out free pastries on Saturdays. Course apple turnovers were no competition for Sally Darville's fabulous new ice cream, and being that you could spot a red Mustang that close—what the heck, you could spot one in a blizzard, couldn't you?—most likely the bakery wasn't the place. Yesterday they *definitely* would have taken it to Peach Pit Park....

Jack squeezed his eyes shut. "Where are they most likely to have taken it today, Dudley?"

"To the dairy bar, sir. That's your best bet."

After getting directions, Jack thanked the boy and made haste for the door.

"Hey, wait a minute!" Dudley called after him. "You're that hotshot reporter from the *Vancouver Satellite*. Cracker Jack Gold, right?"

Pleasantly surprised, Jack turned around. Could his reputation have traveled this far? It seemed unlikely. Then again, it wasn't every day that a thirty-four-year-old reporter won the Gobey Award. To his knowledge, until now no one under the age of fifty had ever won it. So, maybe...

He nodded as humbly as a man headed for stardom possibly could. "I am indeed. I take it you're familiar with my work?"

"Nope, never heard of you. Sally said you were some kind of hotshot, was all."

"Oh," Jack muttered. So much for fame.

Opportunity sprang to life in Dudley's big brown eyes. "So, you're here to get the big scoop on Peach Paradise, right?" He slapped his thigh and cackled merrily.

Jack chuckled along with him. It was pointless to tell the boy he'd already heard that one a dozen times back at the *Satellite*—along with a dozen other stupid jokes involving peaches, cream, sugar, waffle cones and reporters whose heads get swelled by major awards and end up in small towns, writing about dairy fat.

"Well, Sally sure is excited," Dudley gushed. "A feature story in the *Satellite*. Imagine!"

"Yes, imagine. Thanks again, Dudley."

"You be sure to have a nice day, Mr. Gold."

Stepping outside, Jack nearly collided with two apple-cheeked matrons in flouncy dresses. Each wore a straw hat laden with plastic grapes and carried a basket of freshly cut roses. Certain he was about to get nailed, Jack mumbled an apology and tried to sidestep the women. The tallest of the two seized him painfully by the arm. "Hello there. You must be that hotshot reporter from Vancouver. The one who got that—what did Sally call it?—a gopher trophy?"

"Actually ma'am, it was the Gobey Award. And if you don't mind…"

"So it was. Aren't you just the handsomest thing. Isn't he handsome, Elsa?"

"Oh, he *is*, Elvira," the much shorter woman agreed. She had the funniest little Betty Boop voice Jack had ever heard.

"Thank you, ladies, but…"

"What's your name, sonny?" the one called Elvira asked. "Sally told me, but my memory's not what it used to be."

"Jack Gold. I'm sorry, ma'am, but I'm awfully late…"

She drew a sharp breath. "Gold. What an interesting name.

We've got a cousin, Goldfisher Elmont Jackson, but everyone calls him Goldy. That's what's we'll call you. Won't we, Elsa."

"Oh yes, indeed. Goldy. Yes indeed."

"Ah, actually, I prefer Jack. And I really do have to move along."

"We're the Jackson sisters," Elvira said without missing a beat. "Our granddaddy, Elmont Jackson, founded this town. Didn't he, Elsa?" Her grip on Jack's arm tightened.

"Oh yes, he did, Elvira. He certainly did."

"You're here to get the big scoop, aren't you?" Elvira looked at Elsa for confirmation of her comic genius, and together they cackled like two tipsy hens at a barnyard bash.

Jack's arm went numb. "Yes ma'am, I am."

"Well, you must come to dinner. Mustn't he, Elsa?"

"Yes, he absolutely must."

Dinner? Not likely. Jack was getting his car, he was getting what he'd come here to get and he was getting out. "Thank you, ladies, but I'm only in town for a couple of hours."

Elvira snickered. "A couple of hours. Now isn't that funny? That was what Charlie said, wasn't it, Elsa?"

"Oh yes, Elvira. Two hours. Those were his exact words."

Jack smiled politely. Like everyone else in the Vancouver news world, he knew all about Charlie Sacks. Back in the seventies, the once venerable editor of the *Satellite* had tried to pass through Peachtown but somehow got stuck here. Before Charlie knew what had hit him, the poor guy was hitched to that year's Peach Pit Princess and chained to a desk at the *Peachtown Post*, a cheesy little weekly with a circulation no bigger than his wedding invitation list. Around the *Satellite* he was known as Sad Sacks, the fool who squandered a promising career for love.

Nothing could persuade Jack to stick around this sleepy little orchard town in the Okanagan Valley—not love or money or, even famished as he was, a good home-cooked meal. In fact, he couldn't imagine living in any small town. Vancouver was it for him. Or, New York. Maybe even Paris, where his father had once been stationed. The cafés and clubs and shops. The sidewalks that vibrated under your feet. The beautiful women on those sidewalks, looking good just for him.

And the stories—a million of them, all waiting for his magic keyboard.

"I appreciate the invitation," he told the women honestly. "But I'm afraid I'll have to take a rain check. I must get back to work." *Real work, that is.*

"Is that so?" Elvira sounded just like his mother. "Well, it can wait. Sunday dinner. Tomorrow. Seven sharp. We'll make all your favorites."

"I'd love to, ma'am, but...ah, my favorites?"

"Yes, your favorites. Seven sharp. In the meantime, have a flower on us, and have a nice day." She thrust a long-stemmed pink rose into Jack's free hand, the one that still had a functioning circulatory system, and released him.

"Listen, I really can't..."

"Seven sharp," Elvira snapped over her shoulder as the sisters waltzed away. "Twenty-nine Silver Creek Road. Don't be late."

Shaking his head, Jack set off in the opposite direction. He'd forgotten how friendly people were in these little towns. Regardless, he hoped the women wouldn't be too disappointed when he failed to show. It *was* nice of them to extend the invitation, especially to a stranger, but tomorrow night he'd be far from here, in every sense.

Still, there was no reason to hurt their feelings... What the hell, he'd look them up later today and at least beg off nicely.

As he strode toward the dairy bar, his eyes recorded every detail of Main Street. The dressmaker's shop with the vintage Singer sewing machine in the window. The hardware store that, according to its hand-painted marquee, doubled as the town's pizza delivery outlet. The drugstore, the barbershop, the *Peachtown Post*.

And, of course, Cora's Café, scene of the crime.

Glancing through the window, Jack saw that the restaurant was now empty. For that matter the whole town seemed deserted. Curious, that. Next to fruit and wine, tourism was the valley's biggest industry. On a hot Saturday afternoon in late July, Peachtown should have been jammed with sightseers.

It was a pretty place, he'd give it that. Of course, all these little valley towns were picturesque. On the drive in, he'd been blown away by the expansive beauty of the region. The sprawling farms and orchards, the vineyards nestled into the hillsides rising up from the shores of Lake Okanagan, the big country houses with white clapboard siding and dormer windows. It was nice—in a quaint, countrified sort of way. There were none of the usual strip malls and gourmet coffee shops that marred the landscape between Vancouver and the province's interior. Time seemed to have stood still here.

Nobody seemed in a hurry—that was for sure. A pickup truck cruising well below the posted speed limit had tested his patience for nearly fifty miles. Then, a herd of cows had held him up for what felt like a year while they clomped across the asphalt at a snail's pace. A chicken strutting jauntily down the road by itself had given him a good laugh, though.

Somewhere between here and there his own feathers had settled down. He wasn't bitter about this assignment—not exactly. Humiliated was more like it. Imagine a Gobey winner being assigned to write about a brand of ice cream that people said was the best they'd ever tasted. Imagine any reporter with ten years experience getting stuck with covering the story.

For one thing, it wasn't news—it was a classic grab for free publicity. Jack's editor, Marty McNab, had gotten the story lead from a Darville Dairy news release. Little companies like Darville were always trying to get free promotional space in the *Satellite.* Normally Marty ignored them.

For another thing, even if it were news, it would be regional news. Who among the *Satellite*'s sophisticated urban readers would give a tinker's damn about it? Nobody, including Jack himself.

Our subscribers are complaining that all the news we print is bad, Marty had tried to tell him. *We need something light, something fun.*

Yeah, well, he could call it light. He could call it fun. He could call it whatever he wanted, but Jack knew it by its real name: punishment. *He* didn't think he'd acted badly after winning the award. Apparently others disagreed. He cringed, recalling the banter around the *Satellite* newsroom these past few weeks. *Hey, did you hear about the Gobey? They're renaming it the Goldby.* Marty had joked: *You must be exhausted from carrying that ego around. Think of this assignment as a vacation.*

Oh well, at least it wouldn't take long to bang the piece off. A quick interview with Sally Darville. Four hours back to the west coast. An hour on the laptop. End of punishment.

The shops along Main Street eventually gave way to little A-framed houses with big side-yards, every one chafing under the brutal midafternoon sun. Jack squinted up the street. Just ahead was the sign announcing the dairy bar. People were lined up three deep for at least a block beyond the small white building. No wonder the town's other streets were deserted.

Beyond the crowd, something glinted bright red under the sun. The Mustang! Jack took off. Soon the car was in plain sight. Two men were hunched over it, doing God only knew what while a cluster of people watched. Jack's heart started to pound, and not just from the running.

"Hey you!" he hollered when the men were within earshot. They straightened and casually turned to face him. A few feet shy of the car, Jack ground to a halt. Reeling from shock, he glanced from face to identical face. The little thieves were barely five feet tall and couldn't have weighed more than a hundred pounds each. Could they be dwarves? Identical, car-napping dwarves?

"How *old* are you?" he demanded, dripping sweat and gasping for air.

"We're twelve, but we'll be thirteen next week," one of the boys replied with obvious pride.

Flabbergasted, Jack took a moment to absorb that. "Twelve? But...you're not even old enough to drive!"

"We drive very responsibly, sir," the other boy assured him.

"He's right. They do," a man in the group said. Peach-colored ice cream circled his mouth and dripped off his chin onto a dark blue mechanic's uniform with the name Ted stitched across one breast pocket.

"Which one are you?" Jack asked the boy who'd just spoken. The twins had matching dark hair, matching Jughead ears, matching everything.

"Terry, sir."

"I'm Tommy," the other one said. "Nice to meet you."

It was then that Jack spotted the yellow chamois resting atop the Mustang's shiny hood. The boys hadn't been vandalizing his car—they'd been buffing it to a fine polish. Helpless to do anything else, Jack burst out laughing. While the little thieves exchanged frowns, he tossed his head back and laughed until he couldn't laugh anymore.

Sobering, he trained a stern eye on them. "Listen, boys, you can't just go around relocating people's cars."

"Why not?" they asked.

"Never mind." Jack opened the driver's side door and tossed Elvira Jackson's tea rose onto the passenger seat. His cellphone was still there, along with his leather satchel and laptop computer. There was cash lying around, too, but the boys hadn't touched it.

"Hummer car," the man with the messy face said as the twins stepped away from the Mustang, giving it one last, reverent look. "Is that the original paint job?"

Jack ignored him. "Listen, I don't suppose either of you know the way to Darville Dairy?" he asked the twins.

"I do," Tommy answered. "Just take highway seven to..."

"No way!" Terry cut in. "It's a lot faster if you follow Main Street to county road nineteen..."

2

"So Ms. Darville, what gave you the idea for Peach Paradise?"

Sally leaned across the patio table and spoke into the banana Trish held out to her. "Well, actually, Ms. Thomas—um, that is your name, isn't it?"

"Yes," Trish huffed. "How many times do I have to tell you that?"

"Ten more times. There are so many lawyers impersonating reporters around here, it's hard to keep your names straight. Anyway, I got the idea from a peach."

"Fruit talks to you?" Trish started to twitter.

"Yes. Just this morning, this very banana said to me, 'Help! I think someone is going to eat me.'" Sally grabbed the fruit from Trish's hand, peeled it and devoured a third in one fatal bite. Trish bowed her head for a moment of silence and they both collapsed in giggles.

Sally couldn't help herself. She just had to say it again. "Aren't I clever, Trish? Didn't I pull it off beautifully?"

Trish rolled her eyes. "Yes, Sal. For the last time, you are very, very clever. And yes, you did manage to get the attention of the *Vancouver Satellite*. I don't know how you got it, but you did. Still I have doubts about this whole thing."

"Really?" Sally batted her blond eyelashes furiously. "I'm shocked. You never have doubts."

"Ha ha. The thing is, I'm surprised the *Satellite* picked up your news release. This isn't their turf and, frankly, Sal, they usually go after bigger stories than this one."

"Is that so?" Sally returned with faint sarcasm. "Obviously they do think it's a big story."

"Obviously. The question is—why?"

"Because it is, of course. And if you must know, I don't care one bit why they're interested. The *Satellite* has half a million readers. Do you know what that kind of exposure will do for Peachtown? For the entire valley?"

"I know what it will do," Trish replied cautiously. "I'm just concerned that you're being overly optimistic. Let's face it, you don't know what the guy is going to write."

"Yes, I do. He's going to write what I want him to write."

"Really? How do you figure that?"

Sally blinked. "Because it's my story, silly." Honestly, for someone so smart, Trish just didn't get it sometimes.

"Sally, why do I think you're going to steamroll over this poor guy like you steamrolled over the revitalization committee last year?"

"I did *not* steamroll over those people."

"Oh yeah? Then why do most of them have unpublished home phone numbers now?"

Sally sniffed and looked away. As a town councillor, it was her job to question the decisions made by council's various sub-committees. It wasn't her fault if they couldn't handle constructive criticism.

Trish lifted her auburn curls and fanned her glistening neck with that week's edition of the *Post*. "Anyway, I've had lots of experience with reporters. I just don't want you to be disappointed when your big story ends up being ten lines at the bottom of page twenty."

Sally dismissed that possibility with a shrug, but she understood what Trish was saying. If she asked nicely enough, Charlie Sacks would publish her grocery list. But the *Peachtown Post* wasn't the *Vancouver Satellite*. Not by a long shot.

Weary of the argument, Sally rose and took yet another look down the narrow driveway zigzagging from her hillside cottage through a stand of crab apple trees, down to county road nineteen. It, in turn, forked left to Peachtown and right to the city of Kelowna. Depending on what map he'd used, Jack Gold could be coming from either direction.

"I thought you weren't anxious," Trish teased her.

"I'm not." From old habit Sally reached up and smoothed back her dark blond hair, already pulled so tightly into a ponytail it couldn't have come loose in a hurricane.

Trish joined her at the rail surrounding the old stone patio, and together they gazed out over the sun-baked vista to Lake Okanagan, glistening clear blue in the distance. Electricity crackled in the overhead power lines and the bone-dry air resonated with the click-click of a million grasshoppers.

Three consecutive years of drought, Sally thought sadly. Three years and not one drop of moisture to quench the valley's usually rich, fertile earth. The region's farmers and fruit growers were hurting. The small businesses that depended on tourism were all but bankrupt. One more summer of this appalling heat, Cora Brown had told her just yesterday, and she would have to close the café.

Sally knew she'd been a bit zealous lately, but so what? The Darvilles were among the oldest families in the valley. Peachtown was her birthplace, her home. If it wasn't up to her to realize its full potential, then whose job was it?

The thing was, if Peachtown had once been famous for fruit and wine, why couldn't it become famous for something else? Thanks to last month's front-page article in the *Post*, folks from all over the valley were talking about Peach Paradise ice cream. With a little help from Jack Gold, the word would soon be out across the province.

In one swift motion Trish nabbed her briefcase and looked at her watch. "Well, Sal, I've enjoyed this little interlude, but I have to run. I'm meeting with Jed Miltown and Evan Pratford in Kelowna."

"On Saturday? Why?"

"In May, Jed lobbed a bucket of golf balls at Evan's barn. Unfortunately, his prized cow ate them and died. There was a hearing, but the judge couldn't decide if bovine-death-by-golf-ball was murder or suicide, so he dismissed the charge. Now it looks like there'll be a civil suit."

Sally frowned. For twenty-five years, the neighboring farmers had been feuding over one thing or another. Trish, she knew, wasn't crazy about representing either of them, but Peachtown didn't have many lawyers. In fact, it had only Trish.

Between the trees a bright red car lurched into sight. Sally gasped. "He's here!"

"And I'm out of here."

"Not so fast." Sally reached out and seized Trish by the wrist. "Stick around a minute. I lied. I'm very nervous."

"You'll do just fine," Trish said. Even so she lingered, her hazel eyes getting bigger and bigger as the vehicle neared. "Oh my, get a load of the car." She whistled softly.

Oh my, Sally thought as Jack Gold climbed out of the flashy convertible and looked straight at her. *Get a load of the man.* Tall. Tawny hair. Tight jeans. White T-shirt. Black shades. Black jacket. Black boots. For some reason she'd pictured someone rumpled and tweedy, like Charlie. Suddenly her mouth was as dry as the valley air.

"Sally Darville?" Jack Gold was coming her way. Saliva. She needed saliva. Hand signals wouldn't suffice for the interview. He stopped just short of where she and Trish were standing and glanced between them. Up close he was drop-dead intimidating.

When Sally's tongue refused to work, Trish cast her a what's-your-problem? look and shook the man's hand. "How do you do? I'm Trish Thomas."

"Jack Gold. Pleasure. I guess that would make you Sally." He thrust his hand toward her, at the same time whipping off the shades and dropping them into his jacket pocket. His eyes were porcelain blue, like hers.

She gulped. "I see you had no trouble finding us."

He smiled, but it was a cold smile that didn't reach those baby blues. "No trouble at all. Shall we get started?"

"Um, get started?"

"Yes. On the interview. I'm a little pressed for time."

Pressed for time? On Saturday? "Gee, that's too bad. I thought you might enjoy a tour of the dairy barn first."

"The dairy barn?" His expression suggested he couldn't imagine setting foot in such a place.

"Yes." Sally indicated behind her, which was dumb, of course. He couldn't possibly see the dairy operation and her parents' house through the trees. No matter—he didn't bother to look anyway.

"I don't think that'll be necessary. I just have a few questions for you. Shouldn't take more than a couple of hours. Is there someplace we could sit?" His gaze went to the patio table, then back to her.

Sally couldn't believe what she was hearing. "A couple of hours? But you have to stay longer than that! I've planned all sorts of things for us."

A frown etched the smooth, symmetrical lines of Jack Gold's face. Sally recognized the look from her three years away at university in Vancouver. It said, *I'm an important person. Don't even dream of wasting my time.*

"Really?" His frown deepened. "What sort of things?"

"Ahem," Trish cut in. "I'd love to stick around, but duty calls." A smile frozen on her lips, she said how *nice* it had been to meet Jack and how *wonderful* it was that he'd come here all the way from Vancouver to get this *important* story. Turning to leave, she locked eyes with Sally and mouthed the words *I told you so.*

As Trish's SUV vanished in the dust, Jack went to the rail and looked out over the valley. "Beautiful place. Is it always this hot?"

"Not always. And see, that's part of..."

"So, you said something about plans?"

Sally flinched. She wasn't used to conversation without eye contact, she wasn't used to being interrupted and she wasn't used to being addressed in such a curt manner. "Would you excuse me for just a minute?"

Cracker Jack Gold deigned to glance over his shoulder. "Sure."

Despite her growing frustration with his attitude, Sally's gaze was glued to his cute backside as she picked up her cellphone and requested a thermos of lemonade from the dairy kitchen. Her guest looked as though he could use a cold drink. Actually, he looked as though he could use a hot one, to thaw him out.

They sat down together, and she marveled as he pulled a pen and a coil-bound steno pad from inside his snug-fitting jacket. How did he have room in there for such things? He clicked the pen into action and treated her to another frigid smile.

"I thought for sure you'd want to see the barn," she said. "There's the dairy bar, too. I thought we might go there at some point. I've got some photos to show you. Um, if you're interested, that is. And then, Tilly—she's our cook—is making dinner for us tonight. We're having Peach Paradise for dessert."

Jack hesitated and Sally figured she'd scored a hit with something in there. But he said, "To be perfectly honest, I'm not sure that seeing the barn will help the story, and I've already seen the dairy bar. As for dinner, I've got a long drive back to Vancouver."

"Oh." Disappointment settled in the pit of her stomach like a stone in mud. Trish was right. Her story wasn't important to this jerk. So why had he come all this way?

His pen was poised, apparently ready to scribble. "What's your position with Darville Dairy?"

What? He was kidding, right? "Do you mean to tell me that you don't know what I do here?"

The question seemed to catch him off guard. "Ah, no. Not really."

That was odd. The news release she'd issued had given her full name and job title. Surely he'd read it. "I'm in charge of marketing and communications."

Head down, Jerk, er Jack, scribbled away. "Mmm. Sounds like a big job." He managed to sound polite and patronizing all at once.

"It *is* a big job. Darville Dairy is the biggest producer of dairy products in central British Columbia."

Surprised, Jack stopped writing and looked up sharply. "Really? I thought it was just a local operation."

The release also had contained a brief profile of the company and its Web site address. Hotshot investigative reporter Cracker Jack Gold had all of this information right at his fingertips. Annoyed, Sally asked a fair question. "Tell me something. Did you do any research for this assignment?"

"Research?"

"Yes, you know. Background research? About me, about my family's business?"

He stiffened. "Actually, I thought an interview would suffice."

"Is that so? Well then, you must think I have nothing but time." Now he looked guilty. Good!

"I don't think that at all."

"Because if you *had* gone to the trouble of doing a little research, you wouldn't be wasting our two precious hours on preliminary questions."

The faintest of smiles flitted across his pouty, pretty-boy mouth, and Sally felt a slow burn coming on. Did he find this funny? Was it some sort of joke to him?

He started to respond, but she'd heard enough. "It may interest you to know, Jack Gold, that there's more to this story than just ice cream. For your information, this town really took off a few years ago. People moved here for the first time in decades. Lots of companies came here. The Gap and Starbucks and...and...others, too. The point is, Peachtown started to *change*...."

Those GQ lips parted again, and Sally snapped. "I'll thank you not to speak!"

He pretended to zipper his mouth shut.

"Then the drought came and all our orchards dried up, and our farmers started hauling in water by the truckload, and the tourists stopped coming because it's too darned hot, and the chain stores high-tailed it right out of here, and now Peach Paradise may just be the only thing that will save our town!" Sally drew a deep breath and collapsed against the back of her chair. Whew, that felt good!

For the first time, Mister Hotshot Reporter actually looked interested. "Save your town?"

"Yes, save our town." Sally leaned forward and narrowed her eyes. "Jack Gold, you're a poor excuse for a Gobey winner."

A monstrous grin lit up his whole gorgeous face, eyes and all. "You know about that?"

Wow, what an ego!

"Of course I know about it. I did *my* homework." Sally went into her cottage and fetched the file she'd been building for over a month. On return, she spread it open on the patio table, plopped down and began to read aloud from the first document. "Jack Langley Gold, nickname Cracker Jack. Senior business reporter, *Vancouver Satellite*. Thirty-four years old. Honors graduate of the University of British Columbia's Journalism and MBA programs. Twice nominated for the Gobey Award..."

He arched his brows and tapped the table top. "Three times, actually."

"Whatever. Father a general in the Canadian army. Mother an antiques dealer. Born in Vancouver, but lived all over Canada and in Paris, France, for a year while father stationed there on special assignment." She glared at him over the document. "Shall I go on?"

"By all means."

She set the paper aside and picked up the clipping from the June 3rd issue of the *Satellite*. "*Satellite*'s golden boy brings home the Gobey..."

"Okay, okay, that's enough!" Laughing, Jack leaned forward and peered at the file. "What else have you got in there?"

"Never you mind." Sally slapped it shut. "The point is..."

"I get the point." He dropped his chin and looked at her thoughtfully. It registered in Sally's heat-addled brain that he was more than pleasantly good-looking—he was flat-out gorgeous. Too bad she was throwing him out in a few minutes. It would have been nice to keep him around for a while, just to look at.

"Okay," he began carefully. "I can explain. Normally, I would do background research on a story. I didn't in this case because, well, because I don't usually get assignments like this one."

Sally frowned. "I don't understand. What do you mean by 'like this one'?"

"I mean, I usually get, you know, bigger, ah, I mean weightier assignments. See, after I won the Gobey, I got a little big for my britches." He chuckled as if that weren't really true, but for the sake of argument Sally should accept it as truth. "I acted badly, I guess, and my editor decided to bring me down a notch."

What? Had he just said what she thought he'd said? "Do you mean to tell me that I'm your *punishment*? For acting like a jerk?"

Hotshot's smarmy grin collapsed and he sat bolt upright. "Ah no, that's not what I meant at all."

"It's what you said!"

"I know, but it's not what I meant. Not at all. Listen, I—"

In a flash, Sally was on her feet. She didn't need the *Vancouver Satellite*. She didn't need Jack Gold. And she most certainly didn't need to be Jack Gold's two-hour penalty. Hands on hips, she stared him down. "Hit the road, Jack."

There was a rustling in the trees behind them and Andy Farnham, Tilly's kitchen helper, appeared with a thermos in hand. "Here's your lemonade, Sally."

"We won't be needing, it, Andy. Take it back, please."

His bewildered eyes darted from Sally to Jack and back again. "Uh, sure." He turned and headed back up the trail.

"Stay right there," Jack said to Sally, then he sprang to his feet and sprinted for his car.

Despite her fury, Sally's heart sank when he jumped into the flashy thing and pulled away, spitting dust and gravel. Disgusted with herself, she watched the car roar down the driveway and disappear. Terrific. Now there would be *no* story.

A few minutes later, though, the Mustang reappeared. Jack parked it in the same spot as before, emerged into the blazing sunlight and strolled purposefully toward her. He had a wilted pink tea rose in hand.

"Sally Darville?" He handed her the flower.

"Um, yes?"

"Let's start fresh here. How do you do? I'm Jack Gold from the *Vancouver Satellite*. I'm a rotten reporter and a poor excuse for a Gobey winner." He grinned.

Okay, so there was hope for the jerk. Some. "Agreed."

"I apologize for my utter lack of professionalism, Sally. How can I make it up to you?" He took her right hand in both of his and idly caressed her palm with one thumb. An innocent gesture, sure, but she couldn't believe how sensual it felt.

"You can start by taking this assignment seriously."

He nodded. "Done."

"That includes doing all the things I planned for us."

He wasn't so fast off the mark this time. "Ah, okay, done."

"Starting with dinner tonight."

"Dinner? Okay, sure. What time?"

Sally hesitated. Her parents were away until tomorrow afternoon. She had planned to take Jack up to the main house for a light supper with Tilly and Andy. But if the warm human being she'd just glimpsed inside him was real, it might be fun to bring the food down to the cottage and spend some time alone with him. "Seven o'clock. Here. At my place. I mean, um, here."

From his expression, she gathered Jack was calculating the time it would take to eat, wrap up the assignment and get back on the road. It would be well after midnight before he reached Vancouver. "You could stay overnight," she quickly suggested. "The Chelsea Country Inn is just down the road."

He meditated on that for a moment, and she could tell that he'd rather have hot coals poked in his eyes. But that was just too bad. By coming here he'd given her hope, then tried to snatch it back. If she was his punishment for being a tool, he deserved her.

"I guess it wouldn't hurt to stay over one night," he conceded. "I could use a shower and a good meal."

"Good! I'll see you at seven, then."

The moment he was gone, Sally did a little victory dance on the patio, then called Trish and told her what had just happened.

"Well, good for you, Sal. It looks like you'll be getting your story."

"And then some! Oh, and Trish? One more thing."

"Go ahead. Rub it in."

Sally laughed. "I told you so!"

3

WHEN HAD IT HAPPENED?

As he cruised along county road nineteen, scanning right and left for the Chelsea Country Inn, Jack wondered what Sally had meant by "just down the road." He should have asked, of course. To the folks around here, everything was just down some road, or around some corner, when in fact it was a zillion miles away and cleverly hidden to boot.

More importantly, he wondered when, precisely, he had stopped being a caring, conscientious storyteller and become a jaded journalist. Everything they were saying about him at the *Satellite* was true. He was a snob. An egomaniac. A jerk.

As a novice reporter he'd treated every one of his assignments as a learning experience. Every story had given him valuable insight into people—the way they thought, the emotions they felt, the rationales they concocted for the sometimes inexplicable choices they made. Obviously, somewhere along the way he'd stopped learning and had started to assign values to his stories. This one a four, that one a seven. This one an important stepping stone in his career, that one just a waste of his precious time.

All seasoned reporters did the same. Jack knew that. But had he become so jaded that he'd actually forgotten how important a story was to the people involved in it?

Sally Darville was right. It wouldn't have hurt him one bit to do some basic research for this assignment. He also should have done a few quick interviews with the folks in line at the dairy bar this afternoon. He should have gotten a head start on things. Dammit, he should have taken *ownership* of the assignment.

Sally didn't think her story was a four. She thought it was a ten, and she was entitled to think that.

Man, she'd straightened him out in a hurry! A month of relentless ribbing from his colleagues hadn't so much as dented his obviously gargantuan ego. But she'd put him smartly back in his place in less than ten minutes.

She wanted to save her town. How noble. How...decent.

She was a ten. If, Jack supposed, you went for that fresh-faced, blond-haired, milkmaid kind of look. Which he did, apparently. Even so, she was nothing like the women he dated in Vancouver. Any one of them, especially Liz Montaine, would eat her for breakfast.

He chuckled to himself. Then again, maybe not.

Crazily, he wondered how Sally *would* taste first thing in the morning. Sweet, like ice cream. Sweet Sally. Yeah.

Whoa there, buddy, he warned himself as the Mustang cleared a blind corner and the inn came into view. *Don't be thinking sweet Sally. Don't be thinking Sally anything. Do your job, do it right, and get the hell out of here.*

The Chelsea Country Inn turned out to be a tall yellow Victorian nestled in a grove of Ponderosa pines. Gingerbread trim and baskets of parched flowers adorned its wide wraparound porch, and the sun glinted off the stained glass transoms above its many narrow windows.

Jack parked in the otherwise empty gravel lot and let himself in through the open front door. Immediately to the right of the foyer was a small room that must have been a receiving parlor at one time. It had an old potbellied stove, a couple of fussy, overstuffed chairs and an ornate table that obviously served as the registration desk. What it didn't have was a registration clerk.

"Anybody here?" he called out. When silence answered, he ventured a few steps down the hall and peered into a huge country kitchen. Someone had to be home. There was an array of chopped fruit on top of the room's long worktable, along with an open carton of cream. He called out again. Still no response. As he was turning to leave, a big, brassy redhead burst through a door to his right. Seeing Jack, she let out a scream.

"Gracious living, boy!" Eyes bulging, she covered her heart with one plump, bejeweled hand and gulped for air. "You scared the daylights outta poor old Martha!"

Jack apologized for snooping. "I'm looking for a room for the night."

"Well, I don't know. I'll have to see about that."

While he wondered what exactly there was to see about—this was an inn, wasn't it?—she twisted her generous mouth into a grimace and ruminated.

"It's just for one night," he assured her.

"Percy!" she hollered in the general direction of the backyard. "Get your butt in here. We got a guest, maybe."

A tall, stooped man in cut-off denim shorts and work boots but no shirt came in through the back door. He paused at the sink to wipe the sweat from his brow, then loped across the big room. Giving Jack a friendly once-over, his eyes lit up like a jukebox. "Well, whaddaya know? Look, Martha, it's Goldy!"

"Goldy" forced a smile. Obviously news traveled fast around here. "If you don't mind, I prefer Jack."

"You're that hotshot reporter from Vancouver," Martha said.

"Yes, ma'am. I'm Jack Gold from the *Satellite*."

"Didn't you win a—what did Elvira call it, Percy? A gandby, or something?"

"It was the Gobey Award, ma'am." Something told Jack that Elvira Jackson and Martha were the means by which news traveled fast around here.

"Of course it was. She told us all about you, and you know our little Sally Sunshine hasn't talked about anything else for days."

Our little Sally Sunshine? Jack couldn't help it. He smiled.

"Pleased to make your acquaintance," Percy said. "We're the Pittles."

No sooner had they shaken hands all around than Percy treated Jack to a resounding slap on the back, nearly propelling him headlong into Martha's ample bosom. "You're here to get the big scoop, aren't you, Goldy?" They both chuckled merrily.

"Yes, sir. I am."

Percy cleared his throat and turned serious. "Well, see son, the thing is, we'd love to have ya, but we're all tied up here gettin' ready for the annual peach-off. Whole town'll be here for it tomorrow afternoon. Then, first thing Monday morning, Martha and I are headin' to Grand Forks to visit the grandkids and, uh..."

"Now, Percy, don't you be givin' secrets away," Martha admonished him with a stern warning look.

"Oh, right," Percy said as Jack wondered what "secrets" a town like Grand Forks could harbor. "Well anyway, son, we're closed for a week."

Weary to the soles of his feet, thirsty, hungry, sweaty and only mildly curious as to what a peach-off might be, Jack asked if there wasn't some way he could impose for just one night. The prospect of negotiating the valley's dusty roads in search of a bed and bath was unbearable. He'd sooner crawl into the Mustang and die.

"Well..." Martha squinted at her husband. "There *is* the honeymoon suite. Bed's made, at least."

As Jack grew resigned to his impending suicide, the Pittles launched into a lengthy discussion of just whether or not they should be taking on a guest, what with all that was going on and...

"*Squawwwwwwwwk.*"

The screech coming from the far corner of the room gave Jack a jolt. He'd spotted the parrot in the gilded cage soon after entering the room, but had taken it for a stuffed ornament.

"*Squawwwwwwwwk.* Polly wants a martini."

In a stern voice, Percy told the bird it was "too early" for cocktails, then turned to Jack. "Tell you what, Goldy. Martha and I have to run into town and pick up a few things for the party. If you'll keep an eye on this place, we'll give you that suite for the night."

Jack said he couldn't thank them enough, then followed Martha down a long hall and into a bed-sitting room fresh off a Norman Rockwell canvas. Big and bright, it had a quilted sleigh bed, a tea table, a hand-hewn rocking chair and a mess of needlepoint cushions only his mother could love. Actually the room was beautiful—if you liked little pink and green hearts.

Martha told him to help himself to whatever he wanted from the kitchen, then looked him over sadly. "Goldy, did you pack a bag? You're lookin' a little mangy 'round the edges."

The *Satellite* occasionally sent him on overnight assignments, so Jack kept a shaving kit in the trunk of the Mustang, but he hadn't brought a change of clothes along on this trip. "No, ma'am, I'm afraid I didn't."

"Tell you what. There's a robe in your bathroom there. You leave your grubbies outside the door and I'll put 'em in the washer. You'll have to put 'em in the dryer, though. Can you manage that?"

Jack said he could. A cool shower, clean clothes, a snack, dinner with a pretty milkmaid and a comfortable bed. Things were looking up. As soon as Martha left the room, he gave up his clothes and went into the bathroom, only to discover that the "robe" in question was a woman's pink paisley housecoat with a lace collar and satin piping. Nice. His beer buddies would howl.

After the Pittles left, he took a long, cool shower, donned the ridiculous robe and ambled into the kitchen. An apple and a hunk of cheese later, he called Marty McNab at the *Satellite*. "Hey, boss."

"Hey, Jack. How's it going? Did you get the big scoop?" There was the sound of a hand covering a receiver, some muffled chat and a chorus of howls. Obviously Marty had a room full of reporters covering the weekend beat.

"No, I didn't, Marty."

"What do you mean?"

"I mean, I haven't done the interview yet."

"Why the hell not?"

"Well, it's sort of complicated."

Polly let out another squawk. "Polly wants a gin and tonic!"

"Who was that?" Marty asked. "Are you at a party?"

"No. Just so you know, I'm staying here tonight."

"You're kidding. Why?"

"Because I'm going to need more time than I thought, that's why."

From the *tsk, tsk* sound he made, you'd think Marty was trying to reason with an idiot. "Jack, Jack, Jack. There's no story there, and you know it."

"Really, boss? Then why did you send me here?"

Marty chuckled low in his throat.

"Anyway, there is a story here. At least I think there is."

"Oh yeah? What's the angle?"

"I'm not sure yet," Jack said honestly. "Woman saves a dying town with ice cream—something like that." He recalled the flush in Sally's cheeks, the fire in her eyes, the passion in her pitch.

"For crying out loud, Jack. It was a joke. You've served your time. You can come home now." There was more chortling behind Marty. Someone laughed loud enough to induce a coughing fit.

Jack squeezed his eyes shut. "I know it was a joke, Marty. I may be arrogant, but I'm not stupid."

"Then bang off three paragraphs and e-mail them to me tonight. We'll run them tomorrow and that'll be the end of it."

No, Jack thought, surprised by the depth of his own renewed passion. Sally expected—and deserved—more. "That won't be possible. I'm dining with my source tonight."

"Dining? Where are you? Club Med?"

Jack grinned. "Gee, boss, I thought you told me to treat this assignment as a vacation."

Marty grumbled and groused as Jack promised to do the interview during dinner and write the piece tomorrow. "You can run it on Monday."

"Sunday, Monday, whatever. Just remember, Jack, Northern Consolidated and Blain Enterprises are holding a press conference on Monday morning to announce that merger. It's a big story. I need you there."

Jack was well aware of the conference. No sweat. He'd be home long before then. "Don't fret, boss."

There was a moment's silence. "Listen, Jack. Since you're there anyway, do me a favor, would you? Drop in and give my best to Charlie Sacks at the *Post*. We were college roommates back in the day."

"Tomorrow is Sunday, Marty. The *Post* will be closed."

"Then look him up at home. I'm sure he won't mind."

Jack said he would if, and only if, he found the time. Ending the call, he tallied the damage to date: Dine with Sally, do the interview, tour the dairy barn, look at Sally's photos, get some sleep, visit the dairy bar, visit with Charlie Sacks, drive home, write the article, get some sleep....

"How 'bout we have that drink later," he said to Polly, but the bird had nodded off. Seemed like a good idea. Maybe he should grab a nap, too. His watch read four-fifteen.

"AND SO I THOUGHT, well hey, why not? I mean, we've always produced milk and cheese and butter and cream, but never *ice* cream, and all the other big dairies do, so why not us? We have the talent and the equipment. We're perfectly capable. Sooooooo, to make a long story short, we experimented with different recipes, Tilly and I, for months on end. You, know, various ratios of fruit to cream and so on, and then it just became a matter of..."

Seeing Jack's eyes glaze over, Sally trailed off and gave him a rueful look. After his appalling behavior this afternoon, he deserved an earful. But she'd been babbling away at him practically nonstop for three hours now—right through cocktails, appetizers, dinner with wine, coffee, liqueurs and double helpings of Peach Paradise. They were seated together on her sofa now, trying not to touch.

"I suppose you don't need all of this information," she said with a nervous laugh. What was it about this guy that made her schizoid?

Jack shook his head. "Not true. It's an old rule of thumb in feature-writing that more is better. I may not use everything you've given me, but it's good to have it."

Okay, that was sweet. As promised, he was taking her seriously. Frankly, it was a little hard to take *him* seriously in that ridiculous getup—Percy Pittle's baggy denim coveralls and Pretty Peach Party Hardy T-shirt. She'd avoided mentioning it up until now, but couldn't resist any longer.

"Jack Gold, I can't believe you've been in town less than one day and have already sunk to the level of farm fashion. Did Martha dress you, or did you manage this yourself?"

"I'm afraid it's my own doing. If I hadn't overslept, I would have had time to dry my own things. And, actually, these jeans are pretty comfortable. I might just change my look."

"Oh no, don't do that!" Sally blushed furiously. What a dumb thing to say. It was important to keep things professional here. What with the lobster bisque, the ten-year-old chardonnay, her barely-there white minidress and the ravish-me scent she surely must be giving off, Jack would think she was trying to seduce him. Worse, he'd think she was trying to influence him. Oh, yes. Sally Darville, couch-friendly starlet of the dairy set. Willing to exchange favors for favorable copy.

What had she been thinking, sitting this close to him? Everything she didn't want to notice about the guy was right in her face. His silky tawny hair, curling slightly at the edges. His long lashes, blond at the rim, darker at the ends, framing those stunningly intelligent eyes. Oh, and his hands. The man had beautiful hands. She could just imagine them....

Enough already!

"So," her motormouth drove on, "I think we should talk about the story. I'm thinking a full—no, that's excessive—a half-page feature, maybe, as the main article, plus photos, of course, and possibly a sidebar story. A history of Darville Dairy. Or, perhaps, a profile of Peachtown. What do you think?"

Jack stared at her as if she were deranged. Then—what nerve, honestly—he threw back his head and roared. "Tell me something, Sally Darville. Do you always get your own way?"

"Of course not," she lied. "But, this is *my* story." Why did she have to keep reminding people of that?

"Maybe so, but it's my story assignment, and I'll decide how to handle it."

Sally couldn't think of a single good response to that. It was his assignment, but that didn't necessarily mean anything.

They lapsed into an oddly comfortable silence and gazed at one another. Sally tried hard to read Jack's eyes, but they were inscrutable. Darn it, he had to feel the attraction, too. All those lust motes in the air couldn't be hers alone.

"Can I get you anything?" she asked. "More coffee? More Peach Paradise?" *Could I drag you into my bedroom and never let you leave it?*

Jack's hands flew up as if to ward off an attack. "No thanks, Sally. If I eat more of that fabulous ice cream tonight, I'll explode. But if you can spare a pint, I'd love to take it back to the inn with me."

"No problem." Sally went into the kitchen and pulled a carton from the freezer. Setting it on the counter, she grabbed a moment. Whew. Never in her life had she been so physically attracted to a man. And why did it have to be *this* man? First of all, he was a conceited jerk. He might be making nice tonight, but his true colors had been on full display this afternoon. Secondly, he probably had a steady girlfriend in Vancouver—some slick corporate babe with a million teeth and a closetful of stilettos. Thirdly, he was a reporter and she was a source. There was a clear conflict of interest.

Of course, once the story was written, that would no longer apply....

No. It was no good. He'd be writing the article in Vancouver, not here. And once it was written, he'd be out of her orbit forever. She closed her eyes and whispered, "Forget it, Sally. *Not* going to happen."

When she got back to the living room, Jack was on his feet by the front door, looking at something. "This hinge is about to give. If you remind me in the morning, I'll tighten it up for you."

Oh wow, Sally thought, handsome *and* handy. "Great. I'd appreciate that."

He thanked her for a terrific interview and a lovely evening.

Handing him the ice cream, she said, "I'll expect you around nine tomorrow, Jack. I trust that's not too early for you?"

"No problem. I plan to be on the road by noon at the latest."

She feigned ignorance. "You mean I won't get to read the article before you go?"

"No. I'll write it at home tomorrow night. And even if I did have time to write it here, it's strictly against *Satellite* policy to clear copy with sources."

"I wouldn't change a word of it," Sally lied.

"Oh yeah? How many times have I heard that? Anyway, I promise to do the story justice, Sally. You don't have to worry about that." He seemed to recall something then. "Speaking of promises, I told my editor I'd look up Charlie Sacks tomorrow. I expect you know him?"

Sally rolled her eyes. "Everybody knows Charlie."

"Could I impose on you to make the introduction? I only

know the man by reputation, and I generally don't like to bother people at home on Sunday."

"I'd love to! Um, I mean, sure, no problem."

Sally walked Jack to the Mustang, then stood there feeling foolish and girlish and awkward while he fumbled for his keys. Was it just her or did he seem a little nervous, too? What possible reason could he have to...?

Their eyes met. Overhead a million stars twinkled like diamonds on a bed of black velvet. Somewhere in the distance a night owl screeched. Then Jack Gold did something so inappropriate, and so utterly unexpected, it left Sally reeling for hours. Instead of shaking hands, he bent down and kissed her gently on the cheek, then jumped into his car and sped off. Just like that.

She let out a yell. Yes! It wasn't just her! He *did* feel the attraction, too. Mind whirling, she raced inside and called Charlie. It was late, but so what? He owed her.

"Charlie, sweetie, remember that time I baby-sat your five grandkids?"

"Ah, you're not gonna bring that up again, are you?"

"Remember how they ran me ragged for three hours?"

"Oh now, Sally, ragged is a *strong* word...."

"Listen up, Charlie. I need a favor."

4

"SO, WHY ME?"

Sally glanced sideways at Jack. They were cruising along county road nineteen, the Mustang holding tight to the road as the morning sun warmed their skin.

What did he mean by "why me?" *Why do you find me to be the most attractive man who ever lived? Why do you want me to pull over right now and kiss you again, like I did last night, only properly this time? Why...*

"I mean, why me specifically?" he pressed. "My editor said you requested me personally. Was it because I won the Gobey?"

Oh! Oh! He was talking about the *story*.

"Actually, no," Sally said truthfully. "I don't mean to diminish your achievement. It's really something, winning that award. But...it was more the way you won it. Those people in your story, who lost all their pension money to those horrible crooks? You wrote about them as if you really cared about them, as if you really felt their pain and anger."

Jack flashed her a bemused smile and Sally wondered if she'd assumed too much. Maybe he didn't give a damn about those poor people. Maybe he wasn't even capable of feeling that way. Maybe—oh, God—maybe he was just a slick, heartless, egotistical, big-city reporter building his career on the backs of helpless victims.

"I didn't care about them," Jack admitted. "Not at first. But by the time I got around to writing their story, I was angry, too. I guess that came through in my copy."

"Oh, it did!" Mindful of her tendency to gush around the guy, Sally buttoned it and concentrated on the pavement unfolding before them. It was odd, she thought, how comfortable their silences were. They were perfect strangers and they'd gotten off to a bad start. Shouldn't there be some tension between them? Some awkwardness? Instead they both seemed to use their quiet moments to refuel for the next round. It was refreshing, exciting, wondrous even.

"So, how do you know what a sidebar is?" Jack asked. "Yesterday you said you envisioned a sidebar story along with the main article."

Sally sighed. Okay, it was wondrous until hotshot opened his mouth to change feet. "This may come as a shock to you, Jack Gold, but some of us hicks in this here hick town actually went to college."

Grinning, he patted the top of his head.

Sally frowned. "What are you doing?"

"I'm checking my height. I think I just came down another notch."

She laughed heartily. So, he could feel another's pain, and he could laugh at himself. Those were good signs. Two, anyway.

Jack geared down for a steep hill. "Where did you go to college?"

"The University of British Columbia, just like you. I didn't get a master's degree, but I did do undergraduate work in journalism along with my regular courses."

"You're kidding. When did you graduate?"

"Four years ago," Sally said. Long after Jack had come and gone from UBC. She didn't mention that he'd been a minor legend on campus, the one and only former editor of the student newspaper whose editorials were used as the standard by which all such writing should be judged. Jack being Jack, he probably knew that.

"Why didn't you major in journalism?" he asked. "You'd have made an awesome reporter."

Oh wow, what a nice thing to say. Sally knew that, of course, but coming from Cracker Jack Gold it was a true compliment. She almost replied that a degree in journalism would have led to a less than glamorous career at the *Peachtown Post,* but some instinct told her to keep that thought under wraps. Besides, her life had been mapped out long ago.

"I always knew I'd end up doing the job I'm doing. My family has been in this valley for over a hundred years. I have roots here. I can't imagine living or working anywhere else."

It was Jack's turn to clam up now. Sally could just hear him thinking: *I could never live in a backwater like this.* But he surprised her. "I don't have roots anywhere. I was an army brat. Lived in base housing all over Canada, went to a new school every year. Never made any real friends."

"Why did you pick UBC?"

"It had the programs I wanted."

"Okay, why did you decide to stay in Vancouver?"

He cocked an eyebrow. "Hey, who's doing the interviewing here?"

"Just curious."

"The *Satellite* made me the best job offer."

"So, you aren't especially—" Sally searched for a word "—*loyal* to Vancouver then? I mean, do you plan to live there for the rest of your life?"

He shook his head. "I love the West Coast, but I could never be loyal to any one place. Or to any one employer for that matter. It's a good thing, too. Now that I've won the Gobey, I'll be recruited by major newspapers across the country. Probably in the States, too."

Wow, what confidence, Sally thought. Not, I'll *probably* be recruited, but I *will* be. It was true, of course. All Gobey winners had their pick of the best jobs available. Soon Jack would be making a name for himself in Montreal or Toronto or New York. There was no sense in getting excited by the possibility of...of what, exactly? What was she thinking? That he might stick around here? Fat chance!

"Where am I going?" he asked as they approached the junction of the county road and Main Street. As planned, Sally instructed him to turn south, away from town. Charlie lived a few blocks north of the town centre, but there was something she needed to show Jack before he hightailed it out of here, as he so clearly wanted to do.

Anyway, enough personal talk. What business of hers was it where he chose to live? "So, I guess you could never live in a place like this, huh?"

Jack glanced over at her just long enough to show surprise. Dumb question, his expression said. "No, I couldn't. No offense, Sally, but I really don't want to be here one minute longer than I have to."

Ouch. Did he have to be so blunt?

"I'll bet I can guess how you live in Vancouver," she ventured. Why not have a little fun?

He seemed amused. "Oh yeah? Go for it."

"Okay. I'll bet you live in an architecturally correct condo in West Van, with leather chairs and stainless steel appliances and a pleasing, if not exactly spectacular, view of the coastal mountains."

"Wrong." He let a moment pass before casting her a smile. "I live in an architecturally correct *town house* in West Van with leather chairs and stainless steel appliances and a pleasing, if not exactly spectacular, view of the coastal mountains."

"A minor distinction at best. Score—Sally one, Jack nothing. Let me see now. I'll bet your town house is surrounded by all sorts of trendy little shops and cafés, all of which you cite as your reason—make that your justification—for living in crowded, overpriced West Van, but none of which you've ever set foot in." Was she clever, or what? She could have been an FBI profiler.

"Wrong again. I eat out almost every night, at a trendy little bistro four doors down from my architecturally correct town house. I shop in the local stores, and I'm a Friday night fixture at the corner pub. I've got my own stool there."

"Okay. You score one point, even though I suspect you're exaggerating."

He laughed. "Maybe a little."

Actually, Sally could just picture him sitting on that stool, sipping some pricey foreign ale while he read and admired his own copy in that day's *Satellite*. Probably he wasn't alone. Probably he was reading it aloud to someone.

Someone special.

"One last guess. I'll bet you've got a very tall, very thin girlfriend who dresses in black and smokes French cigarettes." That sounded like fishing, but how else was she going to learn anything about the guy? He wasn't exactly gushy about his personal life.

Jack let the question hang there for a moment, and Sally braced herself for the inevitable. Of course there was a girlfriend. Maybe more than one. A guy like him? Educated, gorgeous, soon to be famous. He probably had the world's biggest speed dial.

"Wrong yet again," Jack finally said. "One more strike and you're out."

Sally waited for details, but, clearly, none were forthcoming. Talk about smooth. He hadn't really answered the question at all. His girlfriend might be short with red hair. Or medium with no hair. He didn't ask if she had a boyfriend, either. Come to think of it, he hadn't asked her a single question that didn't relate to the story. Obviously he didn't care.

Oh well, it was time to switch her hormones off, anyway— stop fantasizing about the impossible and get her mind back on the story.

Their turn was just ahead. Following her directions, Jack swung left onto the smooth two-lane blacktop, its centre line a ribbon of bright, untarnished yellow. They passed through a dark tunnel formed by the bowed, sweeping branches of over-grown poplars, then abruptly burst into a sun-dappled meadow.

Sally watched Jack for his reaction to the spectacle ahead.

Obviously stunned, he slowed the Mustang to a crawl, his gaze riveted on the ghostly remains of half-built structures—shops, restaurants and, beyond, a network of empty streets where new homes should have been.

He brought the car to a full stop in the middle of the deserted road and sat there, gawking. Sally gave him a moment to take it all in.

"What do you see, Jack?" She held her breath.

He took a long time to frame his answer. "I see...a vi-sion...wasted."

Yes! She had been so right. Jack Gold was the one and only reporter who could tell her story.

"What happened here, Sally?"

As he eased off the brake and proceeded slowly along the ac-cess road, she explained how several years ago the town had sold the land to a developer with an inspired vision: Build a se-ries of small, independent communities extending south of town—pods, sort of—that would attract young families looking for affordable homes, with schools and shops nearby. The plan had been to recruit a few national store chains and at the same time to presell the homes. Then the drought came and the local economy tanked. The buyers didn't come. "The chains backed out. The developer lost his shirt and, well, this is the outcome."

"I've never seen anything like this," Jack marveled as he cruised through the eerie district, looking all around him. "I've never seen anything so...unfinished."

"That's just it, Jack! There's a standing proposal before town council to recruit another developer, but no one in the valley is interested. And there's no way we can finish the project our-selves, not without raising property taxes through the roof." Sally was ranting again and she knew it, but she just had to get

Jack on board. "Do you know what this would have meant for Peachtown?"

He parked at a curb and turned toward her. "This isn't really about ice cream, is it, Sally?"

"No. Well, yes *and* no. Like I said yesterday, we were positioned for growth and change. For progress, Jack." *Please, please, understand this.*

"You don't really believe that Peach Paradise is going to change all this, do you?"

"Got a better idea?"

"It's not my place to come up with ideas for urban renewal."

"No, but it is in your power to get the attention of the people who will come up with those ideas—"

"Look, Sally." His tone was soft, placating.

"—and then make them happen!"

"Sally…"

"Jack, you promised to do the story justice!"

"I came here to write a story about ice cream, and I will do it justice."

"Yes, but there's so much more to the story than that. Listen, Jack. All of this—" she waved her hands around "—is documented at Peachtown Hall. We could go there tomorrow. I could give you all the background information you need to get started. I…" What the…? Was he *laughing* at her? "What's so funny, mister?"

"You. I've never met anybody like you."

Sally's face heated up. "I'll thank you to take me seriously, Jack Gold. Like you promised."

"And I'll thank you to remember why I came here. I've got an article to write. A short article, and I'm planning to write it tonight, in Vancouver. Besides, I can't be here tomorrow. I'm covering an important press conference first thing in the morning, *in Vancouver.* In the meantime, you and I are going to pay Charlie Sacks a visit. I'll tour the dairy barn with you and I'll look at your photos, as promised. That's all."

Sally folded her arms and worked up her best pouty princess look. Why was he being so difficult? People usually went along with her plans and schemes.

"The pouty thing doesn't work with me, Sally."

Darn. She tried wounded puppy instead.

"That doesn't work, either."

A sigh escaped her. "Oh, Jack."

For all of a second he appeared to weaken. But Trish's comment about her tendency to steamroll over people echoed in Sally's head, and she decided to let the matter drop—for now.

COULD HE FEEL ANY WORSE?

Jack stood beside Sally on Charlie Sacks's front porch, waiting for someone, anyone, to answer the bell. They'd only been there a minute or two, but it felt like a week. The air between them was charged with electricity. Sally was annoyed. No doubt about that. But there was nothing he could do to change it.

What was it about her that made him feel so bad? What power did she have to make him second-guess himself? People usually flattered him—buttered him up to get what they wanted. Not Sally Darville. She could act coy, but ultimately she wanted what she wanted on her own terms. It was sort of...refreshing.

Regardless, he wasn't buckling—no matter how sexy she looked in those little white shorts and that filmy pink blouse with the lacy bra showing through. Her fingernails and toenails were painted a pale pink and her hair was down today, loose and blond and beautiful around her shoulders. And that musky scent she wore—it could lull a man into stupidity.

Was she trying to seduce him? The possibility had struck him last night, and she definitely had been making girly eyes at him this morning. To what lengths would the woman go to get her way? Dammit, he shouldn't have kissed her last night. It had seemed natural, somehow, but it must have given the impression that he *could* be seduced. Which, maybe, he could. But not for a price.

The door finally opened and Jack found himself face-to-face with a tall, handsome woman in, perhaps, her late fifties. She had short dark hair and smiling brown eyes.

"You must be Jack Gold, the famous reporter," she said in a lovely, lilting voice. "I've heard such wonderful things about you." Her handshake was more a caress than an up-down motion. It charmed Jack into a case of instant like.

"It's a pleasure to meet you, ah, Mrs. Sacks."

"Oh please, call me Arlene. Come on in."

Inside the spacious foyer, the women air kissed and agreed that they both looked lovely. While Jack looked around, they chatted about the heat. When would it end? Arlene asked about the dairy. Was business good? And Sally's parents. Were they expecting any company this summer? Here was something else Jack had forgotten about small towns—the endless welcoming chitchat. Vancouver moved at a faster clip.

"Are you enjoying your stay in Peachtown?" Arlene asked him.

Graciousness seemed in order. "Very much, thank you."

"That's good. We pride ourselves on showing people a good time, don't we, Sally?"

"Hmm."

Trailing the women down a long central hall, Jack admired the grand old staircase leading to the second floor, and peered into rooms that looked lived-in and happy. On his own, he would never have thought to look up Charlie Sacks. Who wanted to meet a sad old man who'd wasted his chance? Stuck in a small town. Stuck in a dead-end job. But meeting Charlie's beautiful wife and seeing his comfortable home—well, the man's life didn't exactly look like torture.

Arlene glanced over her shoulder. "I must warn you, Charlie's not in the best of shape today."

"Oh, is it that awful back problem of his?" Sally asked in a cheesy, theatrical voice Jack had never heard her use before.

Arlene gave a sigh. "I'm afraid so." She made it sound like the man was about to draw his last breath.

What was that about? Jack wondered. They sounded like amateur actors reading from a bad play.

They passed through a homey kitchen and into a big, sunny family room. Bookcases crammed with dog-eared books and family photos stood at right angles against two long walls. Matching overstuffed sofas and a sunken easy chair took up the centre of the room. Flat on his back on one of the sofas was a bald, chubby man in agony. His mournful eyes slid toward Jack. "Oh, the pain. The terrible *paiiiiiiiin.*"

Smiling tightly, Arlene addressed him as if he were a toddler. "Now, now, Charlie. You're exaggerating. It's time to get vertical. Our guests are here."

Charlie Sacks made a valiant attempt to sit up, but ended up falling back again. He let out a moan.

Alarmed, Jack rushed across the room. "Here, sir. Let me help you." Arlene offered to get coffee and disappeared. Sally said a chirpy hello and unceremoniously plopped into the chair. Gee, Jack thought as he helped Charlie struggle to an upright position, you'd think the women would have a little more sympathy for the poor guy.

Charlie's baby face contorted with pain as he reached out to shake Jack's hand. "Cracker Jack Gold. It's a pleasure to meet you. Have a seat, son."

"It's certainly an honor to meet you, sir." It was true, Jack realized as he perched on the edge of the other sofa. Whatever his life choices, Charlie Sacks was a legend. His investigative reporting skills were reputedly second to none. He still ranked as the youngest person ever to serve as chief editor of the *Satellite.* In newspaper circles the man was an icon. Or had been.

Charlie chuckled. "I must say, though. I've got mixed feelings about meeting the man who displaced me."

"Displaced you, sir?"

"Please. Call me Charlie. Oh yes, indeed. Until last month I was the youngest reporter ever to win the Gobey." He furrowed his brows until they became one big bush. "Surely you knew that?"

Jack was flabbergasted. In all his ramblings about the late, great Charlie Sacks, Marty McNab had never once mentioned that fact.

"Sir, ah, Charlie, I had no idea."

"Humph, doesn't surprise me one bit. By the way, how is my old friend Marty?"

Jack shrugged. "Marty is...well, he's Marty."

"Enough said. Tell me all about your job. What's up at the *Satellite*? And the Gobey. How did it feel to win?"

Arlene set a tray of steaming mugs down on the coffee table and urged everyone to help themselves. Jack waited for her to sit down, then talked at length about his work—the nature of his assignments, the friendly rivalry among his colleagues, the daily buzz and hum of the *Satellite*'s busy newsroom. Charlie nodded as if he remembered it all fondly, occasionally interrupting to ask a question. At one point, he tried to change position and ended up wincing.

Out of the corner of his eye, Jack caught Arlene and Sally exchanging a funny look. Something was up with the two of them, but what? Suddenly self-conscious, he shortened his speech and gave a self-deprecating shrug. "As for the Gobey, sir, you know what an honor it is to win."

"Oh yes, I do know that. And let me say, son, that I don't think any journalist today deserves it more than you. Your series of articles on that pension scam at Denton Corporation was the best investigative reporting I've seen. Thorough, concise and well written."

"Thank you, sir."

"Nobody knows better than me how hard it is to get a story

like that in the first place. It's like pulling teeth, trying to get into the financial records of those big companies."

Jack nodded. "I confess that I had an informant. A senior accountant with Denton. He didn't have hard facts, but he'd had suspicions for a long time. That was enough to get my interest."

"Well, Jack, I must say, I like what I see. You're a fine young man and a great reporter."

"Isn't he, though!" Sally cried.

Arlene nodded vigorously. "I couldn't agree more."

Jack did his best to look humble. In truth, after Sally's disgust with him last night, the praise heaped on him this past month was finally starting to wear thin. When you got right down to it, he was young and there were a hell of a lot more stories to write. If winning the Gobey at the age of thirty-four was the crowning achievement of his career, he was pretty much washed up now. But praise from Charlie Sacks meant something.

It seemed only polite, so Jack asked about the *Post*. What kind of stories were they covering? Any plans for expansion? He sipped at his coffee, now lukewarm.

Charlie waved a hand wildly in the air, which, curiously, did not induce another spasm. "Oh, I don't want to bore you with all that. It's a good little paper. I've done the best I could with it, but my day is just about over now." He cleared his throat. "As long as we're on the subject, though, I wonder if I could impose on you to do me a little favor?"

"I'm sure Jack would love to do you a favor!" Sally interjected.

Once again, Arlene just couldn't agree more. "I'll bet he'd be delighted!"

Jack frowned in their direction. All they needed was a playing field and two sets of pom-poms. "Ah, sure," he said to Charlie. "What can I do?"

"Well, see, I've got two young reporters on my staff, but

they're both off this week. One's getting married and the other's, ah, ah..."

"On vacation," Arlene supplied.

"Right. On vacation. Anyway, I need somebody to cover the peach party at Percy Pittle's place this afternoon. I realize, heh, heh, that it's a big step down for a Gobey winner, but do you think you could handle it? As you can see, I just can't manage it myself."

Jack held himself perfectly still. Something had told him the favor wasn't going to be little at all. But *this?* It was an outrageous thing to request of someone on such short acquaintance. Under the circumstances, he could understand why the man would ask, but still.

He stole a glance at Sally. There she sat, her perfect little hands folded demurely in her lap, smiling just as sweetly and innocently as an angel. Dammit, how could he possibly refuse with her sitting right there? He'd won her respect only to lose it, then win it back, then lose it again. What would she think if he turned down an old man in horrible pain who had just called him "a fine young man and a great reporter?"

He offered Charlie a lame smile. "I'd be glad to help."

5

TRISH CIRCLED Sally, looking her up and down. "So, what's with the fancy duds? You look like Scarlett O'Hara at the Twelve Oaks barbecue party."

Sally kept her eyes trained on the crowd milling about on the Pittles' sprawling front lawn. "I just felt like dressing up, that's all."

"Oh yeah? I don't recall you dressing up for last year's peach party. Come to think of it, you showed up in cut-offs and a stained tube top. You hadn't even shaved your legs."

So what? Sally thought. Okay, so maybe her dress was a bit much. Certainly no one else at the party was wearing a calf-length Laura Ashley original with a silk underlay, a Peter Pan collar and clusters of seed-pearl embroidery. Plus matching parasol, of course. "What can I say? I've changed."

"Uh-huh. Your clothes, right? About ten times since breakfast?"

"What's that supposed to mean?"

Shielding her eyes from the harsh afternoon sun, Trish looked down the gently sloping lawn, directly at Jack. Notebook in hand, he was frowning as Cora Brown held up a peach and turned it from side to side. "Don't be coy with me, Sally Darville. I saw the way you reacted to you-know-who yesterday, and I see the way you're looking at him now."

"I am *not* looking at him in any particular way, Ms. Smarty Pants."

"Oh yes, you are, Ms. Obvious. I've never seen you look at anyone like that. And by the way, why is he still here?"

In a breezy voice that sounded phony, even to her, Sally explained about Charlie—how indisposed he was, and how shorthanded he was, and how very sweet it was of Jack to pitch in.

Trish's eyebrows shot up. "Since when does Charlie Sacks have a bad back?"

Tired of the conversation, Sally looked around as if she was interested in spotting someone other than Jack. "Mmm, I think it's always given him a little trouble, hasn't it?"

"I think you're stirring up a little trouble. That's what I think."

Sally tried not to sound defensive. "Nonsense. Sometimes things get...stuck. I'm just helping them along a little, that's all."

"Sally..."

Why, Sally fumed, did everyone insist on speaking to her in that patronizing tone of voice? You'd think she was a shameless schemer or something. "I'm not stirring up anything that doesn't need stirring up."

"Get a grip, Sal. The guy is a snooty jerk. Ted Axton said he met him yesterday at the dairy bar, and that he was rude to everybody."

"For heaven's sake, Trish, the Trubble twins had stolen his car!" Jack had told Sally about the incident this morning, on their way back to her place from Charlie's. "Besides, you only spent two minutes with Jack yesterday. You don't know him."

"Oh, and you do?"

"I'm getting to know him. I've been with him almost constantly since he got here, and I've enjoyed every minute." It was true, Sally realized. They'd only been apart long enough to sleep and change clothes. She'd never been able to spend that much time with anyone without getting bored and restless.

"Yeah, well, two minutes was all I needed with the guy."

Sally glared at her old friend. "Don't you have something to do, Trish?"

"Yeah. Oh, and speak of the devil."

From far across the lawn, Jack strolled toward them, twins in tow. They were tugging at his jacket sleeves and yaking non-stop at him, but his eyes were trained on Sally. Her stomach fluttered. The more she saw of him, the more she wanted to see of him. Trish was wrong about Jack. Sure he was snooty—on the surface. But there was a better man below.

Way below, mind you.

Damn him anyway! What would it take to get through to him? He'd already told her he was planning to "bang off" Charlie's story right after the party, deliver it in person, then head straight for Vancouver. Presumably he would then "bang off" her unimportant little story and grab a good night's sleep before forgetting about her—er, about Peachtown—altogether.

What would it cost him to blow off that dumb news conference and stay here just one more day? Surely if he squeezed a measly few hours out of his oh-so-busy schedule to review those records, the reporter in him—the Cracker in the Jack—would get interested in the real story.

This morning she'd been itching to tell him there were unfinished urban renewal developments not just in Peachtown but all over the valley. It was a much bigger story than even she had let on. But the timing had felt wrong. Why overwhelm the poor guy?

How to stall him? How? Frankly, she was running out of ideas. Impassioned pleas didn't work on Jack. Anger was useless, too. He just ignored it. Short of sedating the man and tying him to a chair, what was left?

Jack came up to them, smiling vaguely at Trish. "Ah, hello again." Obviously he'd forgotten her name.

"Hi, Trish!" Tommy Trubble grabbed her right arm while Terry commandeered the left one. "Wanna see a fruit with a monster bruise on it?"

"Nice to see you again, Jack," Trish lied just before the little beasts dragged her away.

Jack beamed down at Sally. "I meant to tell you earlier how pretty you look."

Surprise all but overwhelmed her. "Why, Jack Gold, that's the first truly nice thing you've said to me."

"Yeah, well, nice isn't my specialty." He gazed out over the crowd, shaking his head. "I confess, I don't get the point of all this, Sally. I mean, isn't one peach pretty much the same as another peach?"

"Of course not," she teased. "There's color and texture and taste to consider. And size and shape, of course. Last year, Tawny Trubble's entry was almost perfectly round. The judge said it looked like a cue ball with fuzz."

Jack laughed. "Okay. So, help me out here. What, exactly, am I supposed to report?"

Honestly, for someone so smart, he could be truly daft.

Without thinking about it, Sally linked her arm through his and began to steer him through the crowd, toward the display and food tables. "Okay. Once again, Mister Gobey winner. Look around and tell me what you see."

"Okay. I see...more food than I've ever seen in one place in my entire life. I see...a lot of people. Is the whole town here?"

"Not everyone." Sally did a quick survey. She didn't see the Jackson sisters. Other prominent people were absent, too. It made a sad statement about the kind of year Peachtown was having. The drought. The heat. The poor crops and fruit yields. People just weren't in the mood to party.

"Over there—" Jack pointed to the judges' table "—I see a row of nearly identical peaches undergoing harsher scrutiny than any one little peach should ever be subjected to."

It was Sally's turn to laugh. She attended this event every year, mostly because she felt obligated to, but seeing it through Jack's eyes really drove home its value. It was silly. It was fun. It was pointless, and that *was* the point.

"Okay, hotshot, what do you see overall?"

"I see a bunch of people having a good time."

"Bingo! So you'll report on some of the folks who were here, and what a splendid time they had. And on the contest, of course. There'll be first, second and third prizes."

Jack seemed amused. "Do I have to report that Miss Sally Darville of Darville Dairy wore..." He squinted down at her.

"A Laura Ashley dress."

"A Laura Ashley dress with, ah..."

"Seed-pearl clusters? No, Jack." Sally rolled her eyes. "We're not *that* corny here in the hinterland."

Blue eyes brimming with mirth, he reached around and placed his free hand over hers. For one wildly unimaginable moment, they stood still, gazing fondly at one another. Their bodies were touching, and the heat they generated had nothing to do with the weather. Jack's gorgeous face was just inches away from hers. He parted his lips slightly and Sally did likewise. Her breath shortened.

"Goldy!"

Percy Pittle loomed over them, peach juice dripping off his chin. Jack released Sally and took a few awkward steps away from her. He stuffed his hands in his jacket pockets while she blushed clean through to her sandals.

"Percy. How are you?"

"Never better, Goldy. Didja get the big scoop yet?"

"Not just yet. I seem to be working for Charlie Sacks today."

"So I heard." Percy did a double take at Sally's outfit. "Well, my, my, sunshine. Aren't you the southern belle."

"Mmm." She made a mental note to lose the dress. Today.

"Nice party," Jack commented when Percy showed no sign of moving on.

"Not too shabby, huh? I kinda wish we'd had a better turn out, though. You young people will have to eat up all this food before you go."

"No problem there."

Percy nodded toward the judges' table. "Goldy, come on

over here and have a look at these entries. I'm judgin' this year, and I just can't make up my mind."

Jack smiled wistfully over his shoulder as Percy led him away. Watching his long, lean legs in motion, Sally tried hard to shake the fantasy that was starting to consume her. It was critical that she stay focused on Jack's real reason for being here.

But, the truth was, her attraction to the guy had nothing whatsoever to do with her story. If Jack were here for any other reason, she would want him just the same. He was smart and confident and attractive, and he could be almost human. And despite what he surely must think, she hadn't been trying to seduce him in exchange for more column space. He was tempting her all on his own.

But...could she seduce him and still maintain a professional relationship with him? Still get the copy she wanted? Still achieve her ultimate goal of saving the valley from economic ruin? Maybe Trish was right. Maybe she was begging for trouble and overlooking the consequences. But how was she supposed to stop being attracted to Jack? Giving up sleep would be easier.

Oh God. He was leaving in a few hours' time, and there was nothing she could do about it.

Despair setting in, she roamed the grounds aimlessly for a while, chatting with friends and neighbors without hearing a word they said. Bored with that, she wandered into the house. Martha and Percy wouldn't mind. Since childhood she'd dreamed of living in the big old mansion, and the Pittles had promised her first dibs on it, should they ever decide to sell. Of course she'd always envisioned other people living with her in the house. A husband and children. Then grandchildren, coming to visit. In her fantasy, there was laughter in the kitchen. Parties on the lawn. Quiet evenings on the porch.

It was starting to feel like a pipe dream.

In the wide entry hall she assessed her reflection in Martha's antique beveled mirror. Twenty-seven and no prospects in sight. Why? She was reasonably attractive. She could hold up her end of a conversation. Trish said it was because she was too pushy, but what could Sally possibly do about that? Pretend to be meek and obedient just because flies were attracted to honey? No way. The man who took her on would have to take *all* of her.

Turning around, she noticed two big suitcases, packed and standing at attention in the front parlor. What the...? Oh, right. The Pittles were going away tomorrow. Martha had said something the other day about visiting with family.

Sally took a leisurely tour of the rest of the house, then went back outdoors and wandered through the crowd. Jack finally got free from Percy and found her flirting with self-pity by the arts and crafts kiosk.

He searched her eyes for clues to her obvious mood change. "Say, did you hear the one about the horse who goes into a bar, and the bartender asks him, 'Why the long face?'"

A laugh erupted in Sally's throat. *Please, Jack,* she thought, *don't turn into a full-fledged human being on me. Not now.* "I think the heat is getting to me," she mumbled.

"Me, too." He wiped his forehead with the back of his hand. "By the way, I meant to ask, where are your parents? Wouldn't they attend something like this?"

Sally nodded. "Normally, yes. But they're at an antiques road show in Cranbrook."

"Are they interested in antiques?"

"My mother's been collecting them for years, but she doesn't know much about them. She just buys what she likes."

"My mother is an antiques dealer."

"I know." Sally grinned. "It's in your file."

"Right. I forgot about my file."

Sally poked him gently in the ribs. "If you were here tomorrow night, you could meet them."

"Sally..."

There it was again—that *tone.*

"You know, you did promise to do everything I had planned for us, Jack. That included meeting my parents."

"C'mon, Sally, cut me a little..." Something behind her caught Jack's attention and his eyes widened. "Oh no..."

"What?" Sally looked over her shoulder. Striding toward them at their usual breakneck pace were Elvira and Elsa Jackson. "What, Jack? What is it?"

"It's the Jackson sisters. They invited me to dinner tonight. I was going to call and cancel, but I completely forgot about it!"

Sally didn't inquire when or where or how the eccentric sisters had managed to rope him in. Who cared? Right now she could just kiss the old darlings!

"Goldy!" Elvira Jackson barked. Elsa was right on her heels, huffing and puffing. "How nice to see you again. Need we remind you about dinner?"

Jack's pretty-boy lips parted, but nothing came out. Sally glared at him, daring him with her eyes to just try to weasel out of it. But his shoulders slumped as weary resignation set in.

"Of course not, Elvira. I've been looking forward to it all day."

Sally choked back a howl as Elvira gave her a scathing once-over. "Oh my, dear. I believe you've put Jezebel on notice."

"Thanks, Elvira. It's lovely to see you, too." Desperate to snag an invitation, Sally flashed her eyes wildly at the woman, but she didn't catch on.

"Are you all right, dear? Is there something in your eye?"

Jack came to the rescue. "Would it be okay if Sally came along?" he asked the sisters generally. "Would it be any trouble?"

Elvira, God love her, said it would be no trouble at all. Elsa declared it would be charming, just charming, to have both young people at their dinner table tonight. Without further ado, they marched off into the crowd, leaving Jack disgusted and Sally giddy with joy.

"Don't say a word," he warned her. "Not one word."

"Oh, I wasn't planning to say anything," Sally lied. "Except, maybe, how *sorry* I feel for you, having to drive *all* the way back to Vancouver tonight in the dark." She clasped her chin and gazed at the sky. "Let me see now, if dinner wraps up at ten and you hit the road soon after, you should be able to make the West Coast by about, mmm, 2:00 a.m. Of course, if you were to stay over, just one more night..."

"I can't, Sally. For one thing, I don't have a place to sleep tonight."

"Ladies and gentlemen," Martha called out from the front porch. "If I could just get your attention, please. The judging is about to begin."

On the way to the judges' table, Jack protested in harsh whispers and Sally pooh-poohed in soothing, almost maternal tones. He wasn't to worry his head over details. Something would be worked out. In the meantime, he had a job to do. She dumped him, still grumbling, at the head of the table, then hustled across the lawn and cornered Percy while she still could.

"Percy," she whispered. "I need a word."

"JACK, YOU PROMISED!"

Jack brought the Mustang to a screeching halt outside Sally's cottage. He hadn't planned to go inside, but when she jumped out of the car and sprinted for the door, he had no choice but to follow.

"Listen, Sally," he said to her back, "I did not promise to fix that broken hinge. I offered to."

She threw open her front door—didn't anyone around here ever lock their doors?—and went inside. Jack stayed hard on her heels.

"Explain to me, Jack, the difference between a promise and an offer." She dropped her parasol on the sofa, then planted her hands on her gorgeous little hips and stared him down.

"Okay," he said after a moment's thought. "A promise is carved in stone, but an offer is...flexible."

"Aha! So you admit that a promise is not flexible."

Damn. She had him there. "Sally, it's almost five o'clock. I've got less than two hours to get back to the inn, shower, wash my clothes *again,* write the *Post* article, deliver it to Charlie, swing by here and pick you up, then drive out to the Jacksons' place."

She smiled like a little girl. "I know. For our date."

What? Oh, she was over the line now. Well over it. "Sally, we are not going out on a date."

"Is that so? If my memory serves me correctly, you invited me out to dinner. In my books, that's a date."

Jack weighed his response carefully. He didn't want to hurt her feelings. Far from it. "I asked only because it seemed polite. It was courtesy. Nothing more."

She nodded agreeably. "Fine. You call it what you want, and I'll call it what I want."

"Fine."

A tense moment later they both cracked up. He wouldn't dream of telling her—why give ammunition to the enemy?— but to himself Jack acknowledged the truth: she was sly and sneaky and manipulative and bossy and pushy, but Sally Darville was also sweet and sexy and a lot of fun. Trouble was, he didn't want fun. He wanted to finish the job here and get back to the *Satellite.* Soon there would be a dozen offers from major dailies sitting on his desk. One of them would hold his future.

And okay, maybe it hadn't been just courtesy. Maybe he wanted to spend a little more time with her. But only a little. The woman was a deadly net. The deeper you sank into her, the harder it was to climb out.

Why did she have to look so good? Standing there in her pretty dress, with her pretty blue eyes and pouty pink lips. Why did she have to smell so good? Every time she walked past him, he wanted to reach out and...

"It will only take you ten minutes to fix that hinge, Jack. Relax and I'll get you a screwdriver."

Too hot and tired to argue further, Jack sank into the sofa and closed his eyes. Minutes later he heard Sally on the phone, requesting a screwdriver from the main house. Great. How long would that take? It didn't make sense, but she seemed to be stalling him. Why? It wasn't like he was leaving town in the next two hours.

Then he heard the shower running. Assuming she had stepped into it, he ambled into the kitchen and rummaged in the fridge for a cold drink. But she came into the room behind him, wearing nothing but a short silky robe. White with satin trim. Very sexy.

Jack struggled to keep his eyes level with hers. But they wandered anyway, over her small breasts, clearly separated by the satin lapels, and down her tummy to the tops of her legs. They were beautiful legs—slender and firm. A man could stare at them all day.

"Um, you know, you could shower and wash your things here," she said quietly. "You could, um, write Charlie's article here, too." Tiny beads of moisture danced across her upper lip. Jack had a vicious urge to bend down and lick them off.

"I don't think that's a good idea." He searched her eyes, silently pleading, *Don't do this to me, Sally. Please.*

"Why not?" She reached up and smoothed down her hair. That and the "um" thing were nervous habits, Jack had observed. She was uncertain right now. Shy and a little scared. Not nearly the vixen she believed herself to be.

Against his will, Jack felt a stirring in a place where he didn't want to feel anything for her. He didn't want to feel anything for her anywhere. "Why not...what? Oh. Because..."

"Sal?" a male voice called out from the front door. "Are you here?"

Jack lingered behind the fridge door just long enough to cool things down, then went into the living room. The young man who'd turned up yesterday with a thermos stood on the threshold of the front door, screwdriver in hand. His eyes darted from

Jack to Sally and back again. "Ah, do you need help, Sal?" He pretended not to notice her skimpy robe.

"No, Andy, I'm fine. Thank you." She yanked the tool out of his hand and motioned to close the door.

The loose hinge caught the boy's attention. "I can fix this for you, no problem."

Sally said she had all the help she needed, thank you very much, and shut the door in the poor kid's face.

Jack threw back his head and roared.

Flushed and pretty and looking just about as guilty as a person could look, Sally spun around. "What's so funny?"

"All the help you need? Isn't that the truth!"

Fuming, she marched into the bedroom and slammed the door behind her.

6

WHEN JACK got back to the inn, the catering staff were busy cleaning up after the party. Cardboard boxes overflowing with crumpled linens were strewn around the lawn, and most of the serving tables had been stacked by the company's van. Martha and Percy were nowhere to be seen.

Mindful of the clock, he went straight to his room, undressed, donned Martha's ridiculous housecoat, then raced down to the laundry room and threw his things in the washer. It was five-thirty. If he remembered to put them in the dryer, they'd be ready just in time for him to head back to Sally's place. He sprinted back to his room, grabbed a quick shower and looked around for his laptop computer. Damn. It was on the back seat of the Mustang. Past caring about appearances, he raced outside and retrieved it while the delighted workers looked on. He ignored their snickers.

Back in his room, he set up the machine and looked around for his notes from the peach party. Damn. They were in the car, too. He ran back outside and got them. His audience got bolder.

"Hey guys, look. Blanche Dubois is back."

"Ooh, I *love* a man in paisley."

"Gimme a break." As Jack bounded up the porch steps, the sash on his robe came loose, and he flashed a little thigh. That sparked a round of wolf whistles.

Sweating already, he plopped down on his bed and took a breather. What the hell was he doing here? He should be at home right now, relaxing with a cold brew while he prepared his questions for tomorrow's press conference.

After he'd fixed her door, Sally had tried to stall him even fur-

ther. She'd neglected to give him the latest quarterly sales reports for Peach Paradise. Did he want to review them now? No,
he didn't. How about touring the barn? He was fast losing out
on that opportunity. And the photos. He'd promised to look at
those, hadn't he?

What was she up to? And what was that nonsense about
them going out on a date? Under other circumstances he
wouldn't hesitate to ask Sally out. But his future was set and
Peachtown wasn't in it. Besides, she was a source. Dating her
wouldn't constitute a serious breach of ethics—lots of reporters
had dated sources. Some even married them. But only *after* their
stories were published. He'd been in Peachtown for twenty-
eight hours and had yet to write a single word.

Mulling over that little problem, Jack padded down to the
kitchen in search of the cold drink he still needed. Polly was fast
asleep in her cage, and the room had been hastily cleaned. A
deep silence pervaded the house. Where were the Pittles, anyway?

The suitcases they'd packed and placed in the parlor this
morning were gone. Come to think of it, their big old Chevy
wasn't in the parking lot, either. Back in the kitchen, he spotted
a white envelope propped against the toaster. It was addressed
to Goldy.

Dear Goldy:
We had planned to start our trip tomorrow morning, but
something came up and we had to leave early. Please take
good care of Polly while we're gone. She gets fresh water
and birdseed every morning. If she asks for liquor, just put
her off by promising to get some later. There is no charge
for your room, and don't worry about answering the
phone. Much appreciated and see you next week.
Martha and Percy Pittle

"What?" Jack said aloud. He read the note again, convinced
it was a joke. What could possibly have come up on such short

notice? And who in their right mind would just take off, leaving a perfect stranger to care for their home? It was downright stupid. The Pittles didn't strike him as stupid.

Polly stirred in her cage. "*Squawwwwwwwwk*. Polly wants a Black Russian!"

Jack nearly jumped out of his skin. "For the love of... Do you have to scream like that?"

The crazy bird repeated her request.

"Sorry, Polly, it's, ah, it's Sunday. The liquor store is closed."

Terrific, he thought, catching his flowery reflection in the stainless steel refrigerator door. Twenty-eight hours in the valley and look what you've become: a cross-dressing dupe who talks to a bird with a substance abuse problem.

Laughing—what else could he do?—Jack spread his hands wide on the workstation and shook his head. Was there any doubt about what had actually come up? No, sir. It was official. There were no limits to what Sally would do to keep him here. *Don't worry about a place to sleep, Jack. Something will be worked out.* The question was, how had she convinced the Pittles to play along?

It was crazy—he should be disgusted. But he actually admired her. The woman had more gumption than anyone he'd ever met, and that was saying something.

He paced the room for a while, thinking. Sally's methods might be suspect, but her goal was solid. She had a story to tell, and she needed someone to tell it. When you got right down to it, he should be flattered that she'd picked him. But the story she wanted was entirely different than the one he'd come here to get. And, in all likelihood, Marty would be no more interested in a stalled rural development project in central British Columbia than he was in a new ice cream. Jack had no control over that.

A picture popped into his head—of a flushed and frantic Sally pleading for his understanding as she showed him the unfinished development. Such caring. Such commitment.

After tonight, he wouldn't see her again. Ever.

Wondering why that suddenly mattered, Jack poured himself a glass of ice-cold lemonade and gazed out the window into the Pittles' sun-drenched backyard. What was the harm in just taking a quick look at those records? It would mean a lot to Sally, and if the *Satellite* wasn't interested in the bigger story, well, that would be his ticket out of here. He could squeeze one more day out of Marty. There was a way. After that, Sally could take care of Polly and keep an eye on this place. She'd orchestrated this little disaster and she could bloody well take responsibility for it.

Before he could change his mind, he fetched his cell phone and called Marty at home.

"Jack, what a surprise. Why are you disturbing me during Sunday dinner?"

Jack apologized and did his best to explain the situation.

"So, let me get this straight. You're still there and you haven't written a word."

"Nope. Not a word."

"And you're working for Charlie Sacks."

"Well, I'm not exactly working for him. I did him a favor, that's all."

"Uh-huh. And you're dining out again."

"Yup. With the Jackson sisters. They promised to make all my favorites."

"And you're—correct me if I misheard you—baby-sitting a parrot for someone named Percy Pittle?"

"Technically, it's bird-sitting."

"Jack, get in your car this minute and go home. You've got a job to do first thing in the morning."

"C'mon, Marty, it's a note-taking exercise. Give it to Sheldon or Marie. Anybody can handle it."

"I want *you* to handle it."

He wasn't going to give. That was unfortunate. Jack had no choice now but to play his ace. "Tell me something, Marty. How come you never mentioned that Charlie Sacks won the Gobey?"

The line went silent.

"Boss?"

Marty grumbled like a bear gazing into an empty garbage pail. "I should have known he'd tell you that. Any chance to brag, any chance at all."

Jack smiled. His instinct had been right. "Could it be that you were up for that award, too?"

"Yeah well, it's nice to be nominated."

"Sure it is. I can't help wondering what my colleagues would say if they knew their esteemed boss lost out to old Sad Sacks. Could be hard on a man."

"Now, Jack..."

"Course, I could be persuaded to keep that information under my hat."

"That's blackmail."

"Think of it more as incentive. C'mon, Marty, cut me some slack. One day. That's all I'm asking for."

"Oh, all right. Take your damn day. But I'll see you in my office first thing Tuesday morning."

Jack ended the call and turned his attention back to Polly. "Well, my friend, it's time to go to work. Tonight, I'm going to have a little fun, though. With Ms. Sally Darville."

"MORE CASSEROLE, GOLDY?"

"Why, I don't mind if I do." Jack smiled graciously as Elvira ladled another serving of the mysterious concoction onto his plate. For the life of him, he couldn't figure out what it was. Tomatoes, maybe, with tuna and pine nuts. Some kind of sauce. It was barely edible, but what did he care? He was having a great time.

Sally, on the other hand, looked as though she was about to pass a gallstone. He gazed across the big, ornate dining room table at her. God, she was beautiful tonight. Her hair was pulled back into a—what did they call it? A French braid?—and diamond studs sparkled at her ears. Her lips and nails were cherry-red and she wore a sleeveless black minidress that flattered her every curve. If it weren't for the look on her face, she could have been this month's *Vogue* cover.

Twice on the way here she'd asked him if anything was new. No, he'd responded both times. What could possibly be new in the scant two hours they'd been apart? The bewilderment and frustration in her eyes had been priceless. Jack could just hear her wondering how the Pittles possibly could have screwed up.

Minutes after they'd arrived here she had excused herself to use the bathroom—a pathetic ruse if ever he'd seen one. Jack knew for a fact that she was frantically calling the inn to find out if Percy and Martha were still there. She would have gotten their answering machine, of course, and been no better informed than before the call.

"So, Goldy, how long are you going to be with us?" Elsa asked in that funny little voice of hers. She giggled after every question, Jack had noticed, as if she anticipated a sly, naughty response.

"Jack is going home tonight," Sally said before he could speak for himself. "Aren't you, Jack?" She glared at him.

"That's right, Elsa. I'm planning to drive Sally home, then head straight for the highway."

Elsa's fleshy lips formed a little O. "Noooooo. You're not serious, are you? Why, you just got here!"

Enjoying himself immensely, Jack gave a solemn nod. "I know, but I can honestly say, Elsa, that I feel like I've been here forever." Out of the corner of his eye, he saw Sally's mouth fall open.

This was way, way too much fun.

"Oh, I know exactly what you mean. We're so welcoming here in the valley, perfect strangers just feel right at home. Don't they, Elvira?"

"They certainly do. Which reminds me..."

Elvira launched into another story from the sisters' colorful past, which, like all the other stories she'd told tonight, had no connection whatsoever to the conversation immediately preceding it. Jack gave her his full attention. He loved stories and

Elvira had some real doozies. Who would have guessed by looking at them that the sisters had lived and worked all over the world? That they'd raised eleven children, welcomed twenty-six grandchildren and buried no fewer than five husbands between them?

A couple of times Elvira had alluded to great wealth. Looking around, Jack wondered where it had gone. The sisters' bungalow was huge and must have been something in its day, but it was a beater now. Worn hardwood floors, droopy ceilings, doors and mouldings that had been painted too many times. From where he sat right now, he could see five things that needed fixing.

Elvira finished her story and started another. Jack sensed Sally watching him. At the risk of seeming rude, he took his eyes off Elvira and looked straight at her. She was giving him her wounded puppy look now. With the muted overhead light falling softly on her hair, it made her look less like the scheming she-devil she was and more like a sad little girl.

It struck him like a bolt of lightning then. The nervous way she'd flirted with him this afternoon. Her assertion that they were dating. Sally wanted her story, sure. But she also wanted him. For himself. Oh, man...

"Sally." Elsa cut her sister off, snapping Jack back to attention. "Why don't you show Goldy the grounds? Elvira and I will clean up here, and we'll have our dessert later."

Sally frowned. "Are you sure? I don't mind helping."

"Me, either," Jack was quick to add.

"I wasn't quite finished," Elvira huffed.

Elsa hauled her considerable bulk to a standing position and began to clear the table. "Yes, you were, dear. Let the young people go."

"But..."

"Let them *go*, dear."

As Elvira grudgingly relented, Sally led Jack through the sisters' cluttered kitchen and out the back door. She held her head high and walked smartly. Jack got the feeling she'd rather show him the road than the grounds.

The Jackson house may have been a wreck, but the yard was spectacular. Or would have been, he thought, if it weren't for the water-use ban in effect throughout the valley. The sisters had excepted a few rose bushes, but all of the kidney-shaped flower beds dotting the grounds had been plowed under for lack of moisture. The shrubs were dry and scrubby looking, the grass parched.

It was a gorgeous night, though, warm but not stifling. The evening light was different here than on the coast. Softer, and faintly golden. Strolling a comfortable distance away from her, Jack stole a glance at Sally. Beautiful night. Beautiful woman. It was enough to make a dirty rotten scoundrel repent. Almost.

They walked in silence for a while, the air between them crammed with unspoken thoughts. Sally inquired how he had ended up wearing Percy's coveralls again.

"Don't ask."

More silence. Somewhere in the distance a car backfired. Then a dog barked in a series of short, staccato bursts before falling silent at the sound of a human command.

"Our hosts are very nice," Jack commented.

Sally glanced at him. "Mmm. They're sweethearts, aren't they? They're a little off-center, but that's part of their charm."

"Definitely." Jack realized that until now he and Sally hadn't made much small talk. There was no need for it. They had so much more going on.

"So," he ventured. "How do you like our date so far?"

"It's not a date," she reminded him stiffly. "It's a courtesy."

"Gee, I don't know about that. I've never met a courtesy who looked as good as you." The second the words left his mouth, Jack regretted them. If she really was hot for him, caution was critical. The last thing he wanted was to give the impression that he felt the same way. Even if he did. In his dreams last night he'd made hot, sweaty love to her for eight straight hours. But this was reality.

A faint smile crossed her lips, then vanished in a flash. *I have no further use for the likes of you,* she seemed to be saying. Jack wasn't fooled. If sometime in the next ten minutes she came up with a fresh strategy for holding him hostage, she'd put it to work right away.

"Tell me what you're planning to do with my story," she demanded.

Jack swatted a fly away from his face. "Pretty much what we talked about. I think I have enough material for a short feature. I don't know about that sidebar, though. Could be a stretch."

"Humph. And I suppose you'll write it tomorrow, for print on Tuesday?"

He gave a lazy shrug. "I suppose so. Maybe not, though. I've got kind of a busy day tomorrow."

Blue eyes blazing, she stopped cold and threw her hands in the air. "Jack Gold, I can't believe you're walking out on the best story in the world! I picked you because I thought that you and only you would see it for what it is. I thought you were a visionary. But you're not. You're just a...a...a big disappointment!"

"Ah, c'mon, Sally. I'm sure you can do better than that."

"Damn right I can. You're worse than a poor excuse for a Gobey winner. You're a poor excuse for a human being!"

"Ah now, that's harsh." He grinned.

"What's so funny, mister?"

"It's your ears. I'm waiting for steam to come out of them."

She drew a sharp breath. "Un-bloody-believable."

Somehow they'd wandered onto the driveway winding from the house down to the rural road. Cursing under her breath, Sally turned and began to march down it, toward the Mustang. Where did she think she was going?

"Hey," Jack called out. "We haven't had dessert yet."

Her arms flew up again and she looked skyward, shaking her head. When the heel of her strappy sandal sank into a crack in the asphalt, she lost her footing and nearly took a tumble. Trying not to laugh, Jack ran to steady her.

"Get your hands off me!" She shook him off and continued past the car and down to the road. With nowhere left to go, she sat her shapely tush on the guardrail and crossed her arms. Jack sat a few feet away from her, spread his feet wide on the road and gripped the rail with both hands.

They stared across the road, into the trees.

He sighed, just for fun. "Let me guess. This is the part where you remind me about all the things I promised, right?"

"Yes, and that a promise is carved in stone."

"Touché. Well, I wouldn't want to leave you thinking that I'm a man who doesn't keep his word."

"What?" She frowned at him.

"Sally, you know that I didn't have enough time today to tour the barn and look at your pictures."

She nodded. "So?"

Jack played it straight. "So, I was thinking that, if I manage my time well, I should be able to fit those things in tomorrow."

Her pretty red mouth flew open. "Tomorrow? But..."

"See, I figure if I take a look at those records first thing in the morning, I should be able to spend some time with you midday. Can you get free then?"

In a flash, she was on her feet, stomping all over the road and wagging one bright red fingernail at him. "You! You've been playing me."

He let out a snort. "Oh now, that would be the pot calling the kettle black, wouldn't it?"

"You've got a lot of nerve, Jack Gold!"

"Yeah well, I'm learning from the master. That was pretty sneaky, setting me up to house-sit for the Pittles."

Right before his eyes she went from ranting hothead to innocent waif. "I have no idea what you're talking about."

Jack shook his head and chuckled. Oh, she was fun. Too much fun for one man.

Suddenly all sugar and spice, Sally came slinking toward him. Jack's shield went up. What the...? Before he knew what was happening, she positioned herself between his legs and draped her slender arms around his neck. His eyes came level with her breasts—a dangerous place for them.

She smiled sweetly down at him. "Oh, Jack. I take back all those nasty things I just said about you."

"One day, Sally. That's all I'm giving you, and I am not—repeat, not—making any promises. I'll review those records, and if I think there's a story there I'll pitch it to my editor. But I'm telling you right now, he's a tough sell. Understand?"

She ignored every word he'd just said. "And if you must know, Jack, I couldn't ask you to stay with me. My parents wouldn't approve, and I knew you wouldn't accept anyway."

"You're right. I wouldn't have."

Her gaze traveled from his eyes to his mouth, and for one heady moment Jack thought she was going to kiss him on the lips. But she bussed his cheek instead.

"Hey," he joked nervously. "No smooching allowed."

Her second kiss landed soft and wet on his earlobe. Jack felt a major stirring this time. This was bad. It had to stop.

"Why not?" she whispered into his ear. "You kissed me."

"That was different."

"No it wasn't. This is different." She touched her lips lightly to his. At first Jack froze, then he weakened—c'mon, he was a man—and let her kiss him properly. His hands circled her trim waist and the kiss deepened.

She kissed like a goddess. She smelled like heaven. She felt right.

A pickup truck careened around the bend and Sally peeled her mouth off Jack's just long enough to glance at it. Jack caught a fleeting glimpse of the driver. A man he'd seen yesterday at the dairy bar, and again this afternoon at the party. He couldn't recall the guy's name, but something told him the guy would remember his. Great. Just great.

Flushed and a little glassy-eyed, Sally licked her lips. "Where were we?"

Jack held up his hands. "Sally, I can't do this."

Reading his mind, she stepped back and planted her hands

on her hips. "Oh, Jack, this isn't investigative journalism. There's no serious breach of ethics here, and you know it."

"Maybe not, but it's still frowned upon. I'm in the news, Sally. If word got out that I was fooling around with a source, it would reflect badly on me *and* on the Gobey. It's not just an award. It's a responsibility."

She worked up a pout. "Either that, or you're just not interested."

Uh-oh, dangerous territory. Jack racked his brain for the right response. His hormones were definitely interested, but saying so would open the door to all kinds of trouble. Besides, they had a short attention span and Sally was nobody to trifle with. On the other hand, if he lied and said he had no interest at all, that would close the door forever. Then again, why did he want to leave it open?

He opted for a compromise. "I didn't say that."

Sally beamed like she'd just won the lottery.

Damn. Wrong answer.

"Let's go in and have that dessert," she suggested.

As if nothing had just happened between them, she linked her arm through his and led him back to the house, talking a mile a minute. Tomorrow was a workday, but she didn't have to work all day. Jack could go to Peachtown Hall in the morning, then meet her for lunch at Cora's Café. They could both work in the early afternoon, then tour the dairy barn and look at her photos. Then, of course, there was dinner with her folks....

"Whoa, Sally, you're assuming I'll be here tomorrow night. That may not be the case."

"Hmm."

As they ascended the rickety steps leading to the Jacksons' rear deck, the wooden handrail came off in Jack's right hand. Then his right foot plunged clean through the top step. The only thing that spared him from injury was the thrice-folded bottom legs of Percy's coveralls. Sally yelped and lunged forward, scraping her left hand across the deck's rough surface. Jack winced in sympathy. He could just feel the splinters breaking her skin.

The sisters came out the back door and rushed to their aid. "Oh my," Elvira cried. "I'm so terribly sorry!"

Jack told her not to worry. "Are you okay?" he asked Sally.

"I'm fine." She helped him ease his foot up and through the rotted, jagged planks. He climbed onto the deck and helped her up. Ignoring her protests, he held her sore hand up and examined it. It wasn't too bad—mostly surface damage.

Elvira seemed on the verge of tears. "I just don't know what to do. Things are falling apart all over this old place."

"Jack is handy," Sally volunteered. "Aren't you, Jack?"

"Well..."

"Oh my." Elsa giggled. "Handsome *and* handy. Imagine that."

As usual, Sally didn't know when to quit. "He fixed my door today and did a terrific job. Didn't you, Jack?"

Jack hesitated. The last thing he needed was to become the Jacksons' on-call handyman. Still, here they were, a couple of sweet old ladies with no money and no one to help them out. "Got a hammer, Elvira?"

"I do indeed, Jack. And while I'm at it, I'll get you a tissue for that lipstick."

Puzzled, Jack looked at Sally. Her lipstick was long gone. While she stood there laughing, he reached up and touched his cheek.

His fingertips came back cherry-red.

7

THE NEXT MORNING Sally sat in her office, daydreaming. Bulging files and sales reports and telephone messages on little pink slips littered her desktop. She had a lot to do if she wanted to leave early today. Right now, all she could think about was Jack.

He was interested. He'd said so, hadn't he? Okay, maybe not in so many words, but at least he hadn't flat-out rejected her. With so much at stake, it had been foolish and reckless to kiss him like that, but she couldn't help herself! Just standing next to the guy got her hormones tuned.

Feeling sort of loose-limbed and lazy, she got up from her desk and gazed out the window at her parents' house. They'd be home late this afternoon, and if she played her cards right, Jack would be at their dinner table tonight.

So, he was determined to play by the rules. It was understandable, really. The *Satellite,* like all the major dailies, would have a strict code of ethics for its employees. Reporters couldn't use close friends as sources. They couldn't pay for information, and they couldn't accept gifts of any kind. Dating sources was a gray area in the code—Sally knew that from Ethics 101. But Jack's reluctance to go there only meant that he was a straight-arrow kind of guy. She might not like it, but it spoke well of him.

Mmm, that kiss. It had kept her up half the night, staring into the darkness and licking her lips until the taste of him was just a memory. She'd wanted badly to kiss him again when he dropped her off at home, but had decided not to push it.

Anyway, so what if he couldn't kiss her without getting in trouble? She could kiss him, couldn't she? There was no code holding her back. As for more, clearly that was out of the question until after her story was written. Jack had said he planned to write it in Vancouver, but that was just a minor glitch. She'd simply change his mind about it.

A chill ran up her spine. Whew, sometimes her confidence alarmed even her.

Sally heard the main door open, followed by soft footsteps down the hall. She waited to be surprised. Her dad had given the dairy staff the day off, and no visitors were expected.

Ooh, maybe it was Jack, dropping in to say hello. She smoothed down her hair and tried to look casual. Trish, who didn't look a bit like Jack, appeared in the doorway, in her boating clothes. She dispensed with small talk. "So, His Lordship is still in town, and rumor has it that you're in trouble."

Sally smiled like a flight attendant. "Good morning to you, too."

"Speak to me, girlfriend. I'm in a hurry."

"Why aren't you at work?"

"I'm taking a mental health day. Speaking of which."

Stalling for time, Sally sat down at her desk and began to organize the mountain of stuff on it. What should she tell Trish right now? And how soon would she have to eat her words? "What makes you think I'm in trouble?"

Trish dropped into the chair across from her and tapped her chest with all eight fingertips. "I personally am having a hard time believing this, Sal, but Ted Axton says he saw you kissing Jack Gold on the highway last night."

Sally rolled her eyes. What was Ted anyway? A paid informant? "So?"

"So, what were you thinking, letting that guy hit on you? He's a reporter, for heaven's sake." She made *reporter* sound like *rapist*.

"For your information, Ms. Thomas, I kissed him. And it was wonderful."

"Sally..."

Fed up, Sally pointed her letter opener at Trish's nose. "For the last time, do not use that tone with me."

"C'mon, Sal, Jack Gold is here to get your story—that's all." Trish leaned forward and arched her brows. "You remember the story, right?"

"Of course I do, silly."

"So stick with the program. And watch your heart. A hunk like that's gotta have a busload of babes."

"He *is* a hunk, isn't he?" Sally giggled.

"Yeah. I'm not blind. I just don't want you to end up feeling used."

"Jack's not like that," Sally insisted. It was true. If he'd wanted to take advantage of her, he could've done so last night. In a heartbeat. "Trish, I really, really, really like the guy. He's not like any man I've ever known. Check this out. He doesn't get mad at me. And he doesn't give in, either. He outsmarts me."

"Yeah, well, from where I'm sitting, that doesn't look too difficult."

"Oh, puhleeze."

Real worry clouded Trish's eyes, and she softened her tone. "Be realistic, Sal. Where can it go? A guy like that's not going to stick around here. Are you planning to move to Vancouver?"

"Of course not." Sally grinned. "I'm a valley girl."

"Then..." Grimacing, Trish held her hands up. "No, never mind. I don't want to know what kind of scheme you're cooking up."

Good thing, Sally thought. 'Cause right now her brain was too tired to cook up anything. Stalling Jack was hard work. Besides, a certain amount depended on him now.

As always, she thanked her old friend for caring. "You don't have to worry about me, Trish. I'll be fine."

"Well, just be careful, that's all."

As Trish rose to leave, Sally realized that all they'd talked about was Sally and Jack, then Jack and Sally. Apparently lust made her self-absorbed. "Tell me, how did the meeting with Jed Miltown and Evan Pratford go?"

"Badly," Trish admitted. "I prayed they'd reach an out-of-court settlement, but they didn't, of course. Now there'll be a trial."

Sally shook her head sadly. When would that silly feud end?

"Why don't you take the rest of the day off?" Trish bent down to pull up her socks. "I'm going sailing with my mom. You should come."

Sally said she was having lunch with Jack, but thanks anyway, and began to sort through her phone messages.

Trish hovered.

"What?"

"May I be perfectly honest with you, Sal?"

"No. That would be out of character for you."

"Very funny. Okay, here goes. I don't think you're going to get the guy."

Sally flinched. "We'll see about that."

"Are you at least going to get the story you really wanted?"

Of course, Sally told her indignantly. In fact, Jack was at Peachtown Hall this morning, doing the research he needed to get started. She looked at her watch. "He should be there right now."

After Trish left, Sally had a moment, wondering if her old friend was right. With so much riding on their working partnership, could she and Jack have a romance, too? It was complicated, but they were adults. They should be able to manage it—shouldn't they?

They? Hah! What was she thinking? Forget Jack. Somehow *she* would have to find a way to incorporate a personal relationship with him into her overall plan, and to keep it separate from their other dealings. Because the idea was in her head now, and it definitely wasn't leaving.

"DUDLEY. What a surprise. It's, ah, nice to see you again."

The gangly teenager beamed at Jack from behind the reception counter of the Peachtown Hall records department. The blemish on his forehead had faded to pink, but he still had the monstrous grin and the don't-rush-me demeanor. "Thank you, sir. It's nice to see you again, too."

Jack glanced around the musty old room with its glaring fluorescent lights and neat rows of dark green file cabinets. Little wooden boxes crammed with notepapers stood like bookends on either side of the long service counter. Behind it an antiquated microfilm machine sat next to a computer that not even Bill Gates would remember.

"What are you doing here?" he asked Dudley. "I thought you worked at the impoundment office."

"I do, sir. That's my Saturday job. This here is my Monday job."

"I see." Jack dared not ask what he did the rest of the week. Instead he reached into his jacket pocket and pulled out the list of documents Sally had scribbled on the back of a blank check last night in the car.

Dudley took his time reading it. "Well now, there may be a little problem with this."

Jack waited for an explanation, then remembered who he was dealing with. "How's that?"

"See, most of these documents are attached to the minutes of town council meetings."

"And that's a problem because?"

"Well, sir, those minutes are not a matter of public record."

"I beg to differ. Town council minutes are always open to the taxpayers."

"That is correct," Dudley stated as if Jack had just aced the daily double on *Jeopardy*. "But with all due respect, sir, you're not a citizen of Peachtown, so technically you're not the tax-payer that these particular minutes are open to."

Hmm, he had a point. Jack drummed his fingertips on the countertop and debated what to do. Sally hadn't said a word about meeting minutes, but that was okay—he should have known. Finally, he asked if Dudley had any idea how he could get official approval to proceed.

The boy shrugged. "I may have."

"I'm all ears."

Well now, Dudley explained, *if* Jack were to follow proper procedure, he'd have to get in touch with the records depart-ment manager, but she was in Kelowna this morning getting a root canal, and even if she *were* available, chances were she wouldn't give her approval over the phone, especially to an outsider and a newspaper reporter at that....

"Cut to the chase, Dudley."

"I'll call the mayor." He motioned for Jack to hang tough and picked up the phone. "Hi, Charlie," he said moments later. "How are you?"

Jack blinked. Charlie?

He shifted impatiently from one foot to the other while Dud-ley and Charlie made endless small talk—about the weather and what they'd done that weekend and how their families were doing and what their summer vacation plans were and blah, blah, blah. When Jack tapped his watch, Dudley cut the chat short and explained why he'd called. A minute later, he hung up. "Mr. Sacks says to give you everything you need, sir."

"Charlie *Sacks* is the mayor?"

"Sure is. Three terms running now."

Jack shook his head. "Well, what do you know." While he stood there chuckling, Dudley disappeared into a side room. At the same time, a woman who looked vaguely familiar came down the hall and got in line behind Jack. She had a friendly smile.

"Hi, Jack," she said while he struggled to recall her name.

"Ah, hi there."

"I'm Tawny Trubble, the twins' mother? We met briefly yesterday at the party."

"Oh, right. How are you?"

"Fine, thanks." She touched his arm lightly. "Listen, I never got the chance to say how terribly sorry I am about the other day. We've told those boys a thousand times that it's not nice to steal people's cars."

Jack shrugged. "No harm done."

"How is Sally?" she asked as if the two of them were an old married couple. Jack assumed she was teasing him, but she seemed perfectly serious.

"She's fine, I guess."

Dudley reappeared with a grocery-size cardboard box filled to the rim with files. Jack couldn't believe his eyes. Real estate generated a lot of paper, sure, but one little housing project wouldn't produce anything close to this kind of tonnage.

"What *is* all this stuff?" he asked.

"These here are the background files on all the unfinished real estate developments in the central region. Altogether there are—" Dudley peered at a sheet of paper taped to the side of the box "—fourteen of them."

"Fourteen? But I thought... Why would you keep records for the entire region?"

"Well, sir, these particular records are all related. See..."

"Never mind," Jack muttered. "I'll figure it out for myself."

He reached into the box and rifled through a stack of thick file folders, scanning their labels. *Revelstoke. Kelowna. Cranbrook. Osoyoos.* The names of towns and cities scattered across British Columbia. Sally had told him the project included a series of communities, but he'd assumed they were all in and around Peachtown.

Damn. He had expected a few simple documents, which he could have reviewed with her over lunch. At the inside, it would take him three hours to read all this stuff, determine if there was anything worthwhile there, then give her his verdict. It seemed only fair to do that in person, so that would mean meeting with her again late this afternoon. At this rate he wouldn't be on the road until five.

Driving west. The setting sun in his eyes. Sally in his head.

Jack stared at the box. Something told him that if he pulled even one piece of paper from it, he'd never set eyes on the West Coast again. It wasn't a box. It was a trap.

Jack in the box, he thought hysterically. *That's me now.*

THE SECOND Trish left her office, Sally scolded herself for saying too much, too soon. Declaring that Jack was in hot pursuit of the story. How stupid was that? Sure he had agreed to look at those records, but what if he was doing it just to be nice?

Mmm, no, that couldn't be it.

More likely he had made a false promise just to get her off his back. For all she knew, he might be pulling his things together right now with no intention whatsoever of going to Peachtown Hall, or calling his editor, or doing anything other than gassing up his flashy car and hitting the road. In the end she would get exactly what Trish had said she was going to get—ten lines at the bottom of page twenty. Well, that just wouldn't do.

What a fool she had been! Lusting around after Jack the Hunk, letting her hormones distract her from her real mission. It was time to get her brain out of the bedsheets and get back on track. As for really, really, really liking him, if Jack didn't think her story was worthwhile, she didn't want to know him anyway.

So that was it, then. She would meet him for lunch and make one final throw-out-all-the-stops pitch. But not to the hunk. Somewhere inside that guy was a world-class reporter. Surely *he* would come around.

Of course, a little insurance wouldn't hurt.

Sally chewed her lower lip for a while, then reached for the phone.

GRUNTING, JACK DROPPED the box of files into the Mustang's trunk, then climbed into the driver's seat and coaxed the engine to a purr. He had an hour to kill before meeting Sally at Cora's Café—not enough time to go back to the inn, but too much time to drive around in the heat. After a moment's indecision, he eased into the light morning traffic on Main Street and headed for the restaurant.

At the first red light he encountered, a pedestrian called out to him from across the street. "Hey, Goldy, how's it going?"

Jack had no idea who he was, but he waved anyway. "Great. Thanks."

"How's Sally?" the guy shouted.

What? Again? Jack waited for the guy to start laughing, but apparently he, too, was serious. "She's fine," he shouted back. What was going on here? Were he and Sally suddenly an item?

Luckily there was a free parking space right in front of the café. Jack glanced in the rearview mirror, then scooped it before the car behind him could. Why take any chances? If the mother bear was close, the thieving cubs couldn't be far off, right? He hauled the box out of the trunk and headed for the restaurant door. Might as well get started.

Cora Brown hastened to let him in. Fiftyish, she had dove-gray hair swept back into a roll and lively green eyes framed by laugh lines. Some worry lines, too, Jack noticed.

"Jack!" she cried. "How lovely to see you again."

"Likewise," Jack said, and dropped into a booth by the window—all the better to watch his car. He asked for coffee, and while Cora fetched the pot he looked around. The restaurant was half-full, with every eye trained on him.

Cora poured his coffee and dropped not one, but two menus on the table. Amazing, Jack thought. She knew he was meeting someone for lunch, and he'd bet his house and car that she knew who it was, too.

"How's Sally?" she asked, right on cue. Every ear in the room perked up.

Jack sighed. Why fight it? "Sally's fine. She's great."

"Isn't she just? And how was dinner at the Jacksons' last night?"

That launched a round of whispers, which Jack took in stride. In Vancouver you could scarcely get the waiter's attention, much less that of the patrons. But small towns were different. "It was...interesting."

"No doubt." Cora bent down and lowered her voice. "Was the food edible?"

Sensing it was a test, Jack gave the right answer. "It was delicious."

She cuffed him playfully on the shoulder. "Oh, aren't you nice. For that, you can have all the free coffee you want until Sally gets here. How's that?"

He thanked her, then turned his attention to the box.

The top file was labeled Valmont Developments. Scanning its contents, he saw that Valmont was a consortium of developers from across the province. No surprise there. With projects of this scope, no single builder ever took the risk of going it alone. There was strength in numbers—and power, especially when it came to borrowing money. The file contained the company's certificate of incorporation and some regular correspondence. Yawning, he set it aside and reached for the next one.

It turned out to be a summary of the individual developments—their various locations and sizes. There was a profile of each builder in the consortium, along with a list of tradespeople and suppliers. Curiously there was a valid survey for each site, but no accompanying photograph.

The contents of the town and city files were pretty much what he expected. Municipal government documents. Sealed bids on the various land sites. Some tedious financial data, which on its own didn't reveal the big picture. Nothing too interesting.

Three thick files at the bottom of the box were labeled *Peachtown Council Meeting Minutes*. They presented more reading than Jack cared to do now, but he opened the first file anyway.

Stapled to its inside cover was a directory of town councillors, in alphabetical order. Sally's name leaped off the page.

Jack couldn't help but smile. Sally, a town councillor? What was she—twenty-five? Twenty-seven? The woman was amazing. Educated, with a solid career. Involved in politics. Fighting the good fight to save her town. She was a pain in the ass, but his respect and admiration for her grew by the minute.

Frustrated, Jack shoved the box against the wall. There was nothing in it that said "feature article." A feature needed a beginning, a middle and an end. It had to be cohesive. Two days he'd been here and all he had so far was a bunch of pieces that didn't form a puzzle. There was Sally with her hot head and her ice cream. There was the drought and the sinking economy. The tourism issue and the land deals. What could he do with all that? Call up Marty and say, "Hey boss, I've got a mountain of information here that doesn't add up to a hill of beans. Whaddaya say?"

He had no choice but to let Sally down.

Cora broke his train of thought with a refill and a concerned look. "Are you okay, Jack?"

"I'm fine. Thanks."

She cleared her throat and gestured toward the other diners. "Jack, I think I speak on behalf of all of us here when I say how thrilled we are that you came all this way to write Sally's story. You know...our situation. You know how desperate we are and, well, we just want to say that we think the world of you."

"Damn straight," a voice called out.

"You're the man, Jack," someone else declared.

Jack felt like a heel. It was one thing to have Sally counting on him, but the whole town? He mumbled his thanks and watched Cora walk away.

Wait a minute. What had Cora just said? That it was *Sally's story?* Funny, that was what Sally had called it, too. As if she owned it, somehow. As if it was as much about her as anything else.

Of course! That was it!

8

SALLY TOOK A DEEP BREATH and stepped into Cora's Café. This was it. The final showdown. And she was ready.

Head high, shoulders in check, she looked around for Jack. He wasn't there. Humph, it was just as she'd thought. The lying weasel had skipped town without so much as a phone call. Well, he could just...

A few people waved hello to her and she waved back. At the same time she spied Jack's black jacket draped across the back of her favorite booth. His cell phone and spiral notebook were on the table, along with two menus and a coffee cup. A box of files stared accusingly at her from the seat. The records, obviously.

Guilt overwhelmed her.

"Coffee?" Cora asked Sally as she sat down. She declined. The last thing she needed was a stimulant. Rolling her eyes, Cora nodded toward the men's room. "Jack's had four cups. I finally had to cut him off."

"Mmm." Sally opened the menu she'd memorized ten years ago and pretended to scan it. She was in no mood for small talk.

Jack slid into the booth, across from her. "Hi there."

"Hi." She searched his eyes for some indication of what was to come, but he was impossible to read. She set the menu aside, gathered her wits and plunged in. "Jack Gold, I've got something to say, and you owe it to me to listen."

As usual, he was blunt. "I don't think so, Sally. There's really nothing to talk about." He looked out the window as if his mind was already halfway home and his body just needed to catch up.

Sally flinched. How dare he be so nonchalant about something so important! She should have known better than to think him capable of compassion. She should have sent him packing two days ago.

"I..." Oh, what was the use? The fight drained out of her and she slumped against the back of the booth. *Enough* already.

Jack dropped his chin and gave her one of those smug little smiles he reserved for times when he knew something and she didn't. "Guess what, Sally, I've got the story."

She blinked. "You do?"

"I do." He pointed at her. "It's you. You're the story."

"Me? But..."

He shook his head as if thoroughly disgusted with himself. "It just came to me, and even without this—" he gestured toward the box "—I can't believe I didn't see it until now." He leaned toward her, more animated than she'd ever seen him. "Think about it. A young woman on a mission to save her town. Passionate. Dedicated. Relentless. It's not just a good story. It's a great story."

"But...excuse me, but what exactly did you mean by relentless?"

He sighed. "Sally..."

"All right, all right. But why would the *Satellite* be interested in me?"

"We've got a regular feature called 'People on the Move.' Usually we profile CEOs or politicians with some connection to business, but I think I can sell Marty on you. First of all, there's a business angle here. Secondly, there's a political angle. You're a town councillor." He furrowed his brows. "By the way, why didn't you mention that?"

"I didn't think it was important!"

"It is now. It really helps our case. And, finally, if ever there was a person on the move, it's definitely Sally Darville."

"Oh, Jack." Tears welled up in Sally's eyes. How could she possibly have doubted him? He was Cracker Jack Gold, wasn't he?

"Hey," he said gently. "You're not going to get all mushy on me, are you?"

She was. "Jack Gold, you're my hero."

That seemed to scare him. "Whoa, don't get carried away, Sally. Right now, this is just between you and me. I haven't pitched the idea to Marty yet, and I can't promise you that he'll bite. Most of the people we profile live in Vancouver, or at least have some current ties there. You don't. But I'm sure I can still get him interested."

Obviously having eavesdropped, Cora came over and asked if and when they might get interested in some food.

"Cora," Sally cried. "Guess what? I'm the story!"

"You are? That's wonderful, hon. Now what'll you folks have?"

Sally was too excited to eat now, but she ordered a chef's salad anyway. Jack did the same and they waited politely for Cora to leave. The second her back was turned, Jack picked up his phone. "Let's call Marty right now."

Watching him key in the number, it was all Sally could do to keep from leaping across the table and kissing him. Wow, she was the story! Not really, of course. She knew enough about journalism to grasp that she was mainly a selling tool for Jack, a way for him to package all the information he'd gathered and present it to his editor. But that was just peachy fine. She couldn't care less how her story got pitched, so long as it got published.

And, oh, Jack would be sticking around now. Yes!

"Marty," he said in the unnatural tone everyone used for voice mail. "Jack here. Give me a call." He snapped the phone shut just as Cora set their salads down on the table. Neither of them picked up a fork.

Beside herself with joy, Sally rubbed her hands together. "So, what happens now?"

There were three aspects to the story, Jack said. First of all there was Sally herself. He needed to know everything about her—family history, schooling, hobbies, ambitions, loves and hates—everything.

"Oh sure." She rolled her eyes. "*Now* you want to know more about me."

Jack frowned. "What does that mean?"

Oops. "Never mind. Keep going."

Then there was the business angle. The records weren't enough. He'd have to interview a rep from Valmont Developments, someone who could fill in the blanks and serve as the company's spokesperson for the story. It wouldn't hurt to talk to some of the individual builders, either. There were no site photos, so he'd have to take some of his own. Some travel would be necessary.

Sally's libido smelled an opportunity. "I'll go with you, Jack."

He seemed alarmed. "Ah, that shouldn't be necessary."

Gee, what was he afraid of—that she would try to seduce him on the road? She would, of course, but he needn't worry his pretty head about that now. "Don't be silly, Jack. I've had, um, previous dealings with Valmont. I know the territory."

It was a sound argument and he had no choice but to concede. "Good point. Plus, I can interview you while I drive. Kill two birds with one stone, as it were."

Mmm, Sally thought, *plus I can have you all to myself, away from all these eyes and ears.*

"So, how long will you be here?" she asked.

"I'll book off the rest of the week. Can you get some time off for travel? It would only be a day or two."

"Of course! If ever I had a reason to take time, this is it."

Finally, Jack continued as Sally fought the urge to jump over the table and kiss him, there was the government-slash-tourism angle. "Does Peachtown Council have a subcommittee responsible for rural development?"

She told him that there was a revitalization committee chaired by Elvira, but for some mysterious reason most of its members had unpublished home phone numbers. She'd have to get him a council directory.

His eyebrows shot up. "Elvira?"

"Uh-huh." Sally leaned forward and whispered, "Known to her fellow committee members as Stonewall Jackson."

While they shared a guilty laugh, Cora came over and, without saying a word, tapped her watch, scooped up their untouched salads and went to wrap them. Sally looked at her own watch. It was almost one. "Jack, I have to go back to work, but I can probably get off around three."

"Great. I'll take a more thorough look at these records, then I'll head for your place. We might as well get started."

They thanked Cora for wrapping their food, gathered up their other things, and spilled out onto Main Street. After the relative cool of the café, it was like walking into a furnace.

Sally stood by awkwardly while Jack stashed the box of files in the Mustang's trunk. She wanted desperately to throw her arms around him, but knew he'd be horrified. There were people on the street, not to mention the snoopy eyes behind the café's plate glass window. Thanks to that blabbermouth, Ted Axton, they were all waiting for a show. But poor Jack didn't know that.

She settled for smug satisfaction. "So, I guess this means you'll be having dinner with me and my parents after all, huh?"

He laughed. "It looks like you win this one, Sally."

And the next one, too, she thought with glee. *I'm getting my story, Jack Gold and, no matter what Trish says, I'm getting you, too. Hold on to your shirt!*

JACK WATCHED Sally get into her Jeep and drive away. He couldn't explain it if he had to, but it felt wrong to just let her leave without some kind of contact—a peck on the cheek, or a hug, or something. But, hey, the last thing they needed was to fuel a rumor.

He inhaled deeply the fresh valley air and marveled at the clear blue sky. For the first time in days, he actually felt good about himself. Whether it was because he'd finally gotten the big scoop or because he'd made Sally happy, he wasn't sure. Whatever the reason, it felt damn fine.

As she vanished around a corner, he decided to stroll down to the dairy bar and get a Peach Paradise sundae. He didn't need the empty calories, especially in an empty stomach, but it would be a good time to do some of those on-the-spot interviews. For the story, for color and interest.

Hell, he just wanted the ice cream.

Passing the *Peachtown Post*, he was shocked to see Charlie inside, hunched over a desk, talking on the phone. You'd think he'd be off today, nursing that back. Jack hesitated. Should he go in and say hello? People did things like that in small towns. Plus, it seemed only courteous to thank the man for his help that morning.

Charlie registered surprise when he entered the office, and quickly covered the receiver. "Well, look who's here! Just give me a second." Dropping his voice to a whisper, he mumbled something into the phone. Jack thought he heard Sally's name, but that couldn't be. Why would she be calling here?

Without bothering to say good-bye, Charlie hung up, then flinched as the phone immediately rang again. "Holy jumpin'...!" He motioned for Jack to bear with him, and took the call, speaking loud and clear this time. Based on his responses, Jack could tell it was a subscriber calling with a complaint. He rolled his eyes. Apparently newspapers were the same everywhere.

While Charlie soothed and placated, Jack took a look around. Like all main-street stores of the Victorian era, the converted office was narrow but deep. Its outer walls were red brick, eroded by time and covered now with bulletin boards and framed articles and photographs. At the back door, bundles of newspapers awaited delivery. There was no printing press, of course. All weeklies farmed that job out now.

Rustic was the word that came to mind as Jack took in the furnishings. There were three metal desks in the room, probably dating back to the forties. Atop each was a computer terminal of roughly the same vintage as the one Jack had seen at Peachtown Hall. A monstrous metal box with porcelain knobs and levers stood against one wall. Jack couldn't believe his eyes. A typesetting machine? In this day and age?

The call ended and Charlie wheeled his chair around. "Jack, what a pleasant surprise. I was just, uh, just thinking about you." Attempting to stand, he let out a sharp cry.

Jack helped him to ease back down on the chair. "What the hell are you doing here, Charlie? You should be at home." He straddled the corner of one of the spare desks. It was clean. For that matter, so was the other one. Only Charlie's desk displayed the usual newsroom clutter.

"Somebody's gotta run this show," Charlie grumbled. "Such as it is."

"Hmm, and the big show, too. I understand you're the mayor."

"Yeah, well, I'm glad somebody understands it."

Jack chuckled as he nodded toward the typesetting machine. "Please tell me, Mayor Sacks, that you're not laying out this paper manually."

"I'd love to be able to tell you that, but it just ain't true. The new desktop publishing equipment is a little outside my budget. Besides, I'm a relic. I work faster the old way."

Jack was stunned. He'd been joking.

"I'll tell you though, Jack, it's leagues beyond the equipment Marty McNab and I learned on."

"I didn't realize you were in the same class," Jack said. He knew the pair had been roommates at UBC, but that was all.

"Yup. For three long years." Charlie wagged a finger at him. "For the record, I graduated top of that class."

"Hmmm." Jack wasn't sure what to say to that. If it was true, the man should have ended up somewhere other than here.

"I'll bet you were top of the heap, too, huh Jack?"

"I was, in fact. Seems like a hundred years ago."

Wincing, Charlie reached behind him and came up with a copy of the *Post*. He handed it to Jack. "Take this home with you, son. Fine job you did on the peach party piece. Fine job. You can work for me any day."

"Thanks." Jack glanced at the front-page headline and set the paper aside. In his wildest nightmare, he couldn't imagine working for a paper that considered a fruit contest to be front-page material.

He remembered his manners. "Oh, and thanks for letting me have those records, Charlie. Much appreciated."

"No problem." Charlie sighed as if the weight of the world was on his shoulders. "Course I had to violate standard procedure to do it. Hoo boy, old Janie'll have my hide when she hears about it."

Old Janie, Jack assumed, was the records department manager with the bad tooth. Surely, as mayor, Charlie had the authority to override her? Of course, maybe he just declined to exercise it. One thing Jack knew for sure about small towns was that the power machine operated differently. Whatever the rules, people took things a lot more personally.

Charlie made a big show of clearing his throat, then offered a wan smile. He seemed on the verge of saying something, but was having trouble forming the words. Jack's feeling of goodwill vanished. Something was coming, and he had a pretty good idea of what it was.

"Jack, seeing as how I did you a little favor, I wonder if you'd be kind enough to do me one?"

Yup. Another little favor. "What's that, Charlie?"

"Well, see, we've got these two farmers—Evan Pratford and

Jed Miltown? They've been feuding for twenty-five years and nobody but the two of them knows why. Now Evan is suing Jed. Things don't usually get that far out of hand, so I'm thinking it's time we did a piece on 'em. Nothing too fancy, you understand, just the usual who, what, where, when and why. Take Sally along. She can fill you in on the details.''

I'll just bet she can, Jack thought. Why did he suddenly think that old Janie wouldn't give a red rat's butt whether Charlie released those files or torched them? Why did he also suddenly think that Charlie didn't have a back problem? That his only problem, in fact, was a delicious but devious little blonde by the name of Sally Darville?

Yesterday his gut had told him there was something fishy about the two of them. His gut never lied.

A courier arrived with an envelope for Charlie, giving Jack a moment to think. Another delay. Dammit, at this rate, he would never get around to writing Sally's story. He would never get out of here, period. And the last thing he needed was to get between two feuding farmers. Situations like that could be explosive.

What the hell, there was no sense in calling Charlie out. No matter what half-baked, Sally-bred scheme the man was involved in, Jack needed his cooperation during the next few days. As mayor, he'd be one of the sources for her story.

"When do you need it?" he asked when the courier was gone.

"Tomorrow, if that's possible."

"Tomorrow!"

"I know. It's awfully short notice, Jack, but I already had an interview with Evan Pratford scheduled for four this afternoon. As you can see…"

"I know, I know. You just can't manage it."

"You're a good man, Jack Gold."

Jack tucked the *Post* under his arm and reached out to shake Charlie's hand. "Tomorrow it is." He worked up a look of deep concern. "In the meantime you be sure to take care of that back."

Charlie promised he would.

ALONE IN HER OFFICE, Sally waited the half hour she'd been told to wait, then called the *Post* again. "Charlie, you hung up on me!"

"I had to, Sally. Jack was here."

"That was Jack? What did he want?"

"To say hello."

"You're kidding? Jack? Anyway, I called to say I don't need your help anymore. I really appreciated it, but everything is okay now."

"Too late. I assigned him the Pratford-Miltown piece."

"Oh, Charlie, we don't have time for things like that!"

"I thought you *wanted* me to keep him busy."

"I did, but...I don't anymore."

"Why not?"

"Um, well..." Good grief, what could she say? *I need straight-arrow Jack to hurry up and write my story so he won't be at risk of breaking any rules, so I can drag him into my bedroom and ravage him until he begs for mercy and becomes my helpless love slave and can never leave me?* It was absurd.

"Call it off, Charlie."

"No."

"What do you mean, no?"

"I'm retiring in a couple of months."

"So?"

"Soooo..."

They both fell silent.

"Are you thinking what I'm thinking?" Charlie asked.

Sally's head started to spin. Jack as a replacement for Charlie? Holy cow, not even Mata Hari could pull *that* off. "It's too much, Charlie. I've got enough on my plate, just trying to..."

"*Quid pro quo*, Sally."

She sighed. "My Latin's a little rusty. Care to translate that?"

"*Quid pro quo.* I give you something. You give me something."

Oh, puhleeze. She didn't owe him a thing. The score was even and he knew it. Besides, it just plain didn't work. The more work Jack did for Charlie, the less time he would have to work on her story, and the longer it would be before she could drag his scrumptious butt into bed.

Oh, wow. Two agendas at war. Things were getting out of hand.

"Sorry, Charlie, I can't play right now. Maybe later. Okay?"

HALFWAY TO THE DAIRY BAR, Jack's cell phone rang. Great. That would be Marty. He tapped the talk button without bothering to check his call display. "Marty, thanks for calling me back."

"Marty?" Elvira Jackson barked into the phone. "Who's Marty?"

Elvira? How had she gotten his number?

Jack kept walking. "Elvira. How, ah, nice to hear from you."

"Goldy, I've got a leaking shower head here. I need you to come and have a look at it."

"Ah, well, I'm a little pressed for time…"

"There's water everywhere, Goldy. I'll expect you in half an hour, no later. Elsa will make a pot of tea. And that casserole you liked so much? I saved some just for you."

Resignation setting in, Jack glanced at his watch. It was one-thirty. He had planned to get his sundae, then go back to the inn and get started on Sally's story before tackling Charlie's story, but what was the use in planning anything? His life wasn't his own anymore.

"Goldy, are you there?" Elvira snapped.

"Give me a second, Elvira."

Okay. The Jackson house was twenty minutes away. Assuming that no parts were required, it wouldn't take him more than ten minutes to fix a leaky shower head. Thirty minutes in total.

That would give him another thirty minutes to eat and chat with Elvira about the revitalization committee—might as well double up there—before meeting Sally at three. That left a full hour before he had to interview Evan Pratford.

It could be done.

Already pining for that ice cream, he slowed to a stop in the middle of the street. "Elvira, I'd be happy to help. And I look forward to that casserole. Tell you what, I'll even bring a salad."

She enthused over his thoughtfulness, then warned him not to be late.

Retracing his steps back to the Mustang, Jack wrestled with the idea of calling Marty again. Without a firm go-ahead, it was foolish to do any interviews. Why get everybody's hopes up? He'd already gone too far with Sally. Course, one word of encouragement was all it took to turn *her* into a bulldog with a steak bone.

Nah, there was no point in leaving a second voice mail message. Marty always returned calls. Probably he was swamped and just couldn't get around to it. Jack had already suggested there might be a story here, and sure enough there was.

It was an awesome story. Marty would want it.

How could he not?

9

ON THE ROAD AGAIN.

Never had Jack seen so many backroads. Never had he passed so many pickup trucks, or dodged so many potholes, or inhaled so much dust. Of course, never had he had such a delectable backroads companion.

With her pink-ribboned ponytail, black, zircon-studded shades, white tube top and pink shorts, Sally looked like Lolita on a tear. For the past hour, Jack had made a game of trying *not* to picture her tanned, slender legs wrapped around him. He wasn't winning.

"So," he said, stealing another glance at them. "Tell me everything you know about Evan Pratford and Jed Miltown."

Sitting pretty in the Mustang's passenger seat, Sally uncrossed those legs and crossed them again, the other way. Damn. Did she have to do that?

"There's not much to tell, Jack. They're retired gentlemen farmers. They grow vegetables and keep a few cattle. They're both in their sixties, I think, and they're both widowed with kids and grandkids. They live next door to one another, and they've been fighting for as long as anybody can remember."

"About what?"

"No one knows. Something must have happened before they moved here. They're not locals."

Jack frowned. "Charlie said they'd been here for twenty-five years. Wouldn't that qualify them as locals?"

"In the valley? No. Including me, my family has been here for five generations. *We're* locals."

"Good God, how long does it take to get citizenship around here?"

Adorably, Sally touched her chin with her index finger. "Hmm, about five generations."

That made him laugh. *She* made him laugh. Jack couldn't recall the last time a woman had done that for him. Liz Montaine, his occasional Saturday night date, was interested in his fame, not his funny bone. As for the others, well, they were interested in something else altogether.

The moment seemed right for a little fun. "You know what, Sally? I'm concerned about Charlie. His back was giving him serious trouble today."

"Gee, that's too bad." She gazed off into the trees.

Jack smiled to himself. The little sneak was utterly without shame.

"So, when do we start my interview?" she asked in what he decided was a pathetic attempt to distract him. "I'm dying to tell you all sorts of things about me that you obviously don't want to know on your own."

"Ouch. Tomorrow, Sally. I'm a little busy today."

"Tomorrow? Why can't we get started tonight?"

"We've got dinner with your parents. Remember?"

"I was thinking we could do it afterwards."

Jack decided to let that suggestion hang. There were lots of things he could imagine doing with her after dinner tonight, but interviewing wasn't one of them.

She turned petulant on him. "You weren't too busy to interview Elvira this afternoon."

He shot her a questioning glance. "How did you know about that?"

"I know everything, silly."

"Evidently. And, while we're on it, how did Elvira get my unpublished cell phone number? Not even you have it."

She dodged the question with her usual finesse. "I'm afraid I can't answer that."

"Never mind. And, for your information, I wouldn't exactly call what I did with Elvira 'interviewing.' It was more like standing under a waterfall, fighting with a plumbing fixture while you eat unrecognizable food and say 'Yes, ma'am' a lot."

A laugh came from deep within Sally, rich and hearty and full of life. It was the loveliest sound Jack had ever heard. He liked making her laugh. He liked her. Period.

Wiping joyful tears away, she instructed him to turn right, onto a steeply pitched, single-lane dirt road. The Mustang climbed higher and higher, then leveled out on the crest of a hill. A breathtakingly beautiful meadow stretched out before them, ending where the road separated into two driveways. They in turn led to two nearly identical white clapboard farmhouses, situated within spitting distance of one another. The barbed wire fence between them seemed more symbolic than practical.

"Oh, Jack, let's stop for a minute!" Sally cried. "This is one of my favorite places."

Reluctantly, he brought the Mustang to a halt and climbed out. They'd stopped once before, at a tourist lookout, and it had turned into a wrestling match—Sally subtly trying to kiss him and Jack wrestling with the urge to let her.

He leaned against the car and adjusted his sunglasses. Shielding her own eyes against the brutal sun, Sally walked past him, to the edge of the road, and gazed out over the meadow. Jack realized that until now he hadn't had a chance to really look at her—not without getting caught anyway.

She was sheer perfection. Narrow shoulders. Slender, tapered back. A tantalizing little butt held up by, oh yeah, those legs. Jack wasn't all hung up on a woman's looks, but he appreciated beauty when he saw it.

Glowing, Sally turned around. "Isn't it beautiful, Jack!"

"Yes," he said quietly. "It is."

No dummy, she read his mind and moved toward him. Jack issued a cry and raised his hands to ward her off.

"Very funny." She slipped her arms under his and around his back. "Jack Gold, when are you going to stop fighting this? Life would be so much easier if you just admitted that you find me attractive."

Having nowhere else to park them, Jack put his own arms around her shoulders. "Okay. I find you attractive."

She nestled against him, and he struggled with the urge to slide his hands down her back and over that luscious bottom. How much longer *could* he go on fighting this? He was a man. He was weak. On occasion, he could even be stupid. "What am I going to do with you, Sally Darville?"

"Mmm," she murmured against his neck. "I can think of a few things."

"Sally..."

She sighed. "I know, I know. Ethics."

It was more than that, Jack thought. It was two separate destinies with no possibility of joining. Sally was every man's fantasy, and he'd give his eyeteeth to make love to her, but she wasn't his future. Montreal was his future. Or Los Angeles. Would she give up her job and family and friends to go with him? Not likely. She'd already said that she couldn't imagine living or working anywhere but here.

And even if she did go with him, it was a bad scenario. They'd be happy for a while, then she'd start to resent him for taking her away from everyone and everything she loved.

Then again, if their own love was strong enough... Oh, man. Love. It was dangerous even to *think* that word around her.

He spoke softly. "Sally, I'm trying to be a good guy here."

"You could be a *little* less good." She nibbled his earlobe.

"Uh-huh. How little are we talking?"

She stepped away from him and dredged up her haughty look, one of many in her vast arsenal. "I think we should agree that kissing is okay." Her eyes challenged him to disagree.

Jack feigned confusion. "Kissing, huh? Excuse me, but are we bound by some sort of agreement, you and me? 'Cause the last time I checked, we didn't have a contractual relationship that included negotiations."

She crinkled her nose. "You like being kissed by me."

"Is that so? Tell me something, Sally. Have you always been this confident?"

"Ooh, now *that* would be the pot calling the kettle black."

Jack laughed. By now he should know better than to give her an opening like that. "Sally, I love being kissed by you. Honestly I do. But I'm not going to be here next week. Do you understand what I'm saying?"

She looked him up and down as if he were toxic waste. "What makes you think I want you to be here next week?"

"Point taken. All I'm saying is that I can't make you any promises."

"God, you are conceited. I didn't ask for any."

"Yeah well, you have a way of asking for things without saying a word."

Eyes narrowed, she walked slowly around him, obviously giving serious thought to some half-baked proposal. "What if I said 'no strings attached'?"

Jack tapped his right ear several times. "Excuse me, but did I just hear the puppet master of the universe say 'no strings attached'?"

"Oh you!" She swatted his chest. "The way you speak to me. Honestly."

No strings? Jack had serious doubts about that. But, once again, he was impressed with her genius. By making the offer, she was granting him leverage—the freedom to touch her. It had nothing to do with strings. It was just a clever way for her to gauge his interest.

"Should I bother to argue?" he joked.

"Of course not, silly. Resistance is futile."

"All right then, you win this one. Kissing is allowed. But that's all. Got it?" Jack briefly closed his eyes. Had he actually just warned a smart, sexy blonde to go easy on him?

Sally clapped her hands like an excited kid. "Okay. You go first."

Suddenly self-conscious, he took her in his arms again and lightly touched his lips to hers. She sighed with disgust. "Jack Gold, my mother kisses better than that."

"So go kiss your mother!"

In an instant her little face crumpled and her lower lip started to tremble. Jack cursed himself. He hadn't meant to sound so harsh. "Sally, I..."

She burst into a grin. "Gotcha!"

"For chrissake, Sally."

"Oh, puhleeze, Jack. Do I look thin-skinned to you?"

"Well, now that you mention it." He was laughing when his mouth claimed hers for real, and it took a moment for the kiss to establish itself. When it did, it turned out to be different from their other kisses—softer, sweeter, more intimate. Sally had a gorgeous mouth, and Jack wallowed in the freedom to explore it. He circled her tongue with his own. He gently sucked her lower lip, and then her upper, before smothering her mouth again. Sally moaned.

Uh-oh. Body parts standing at attention again. Heart pumping this time. Skin heating up. Blood pounding through his veins.

As they separated, then lightly kissed once, twice, three times more, Jack realized with gut-wrenching certainty that by buying into this "no strings attached" nonsense, he'd done more than open the door to trouble. He'd opened the floodgates, and now there would be no closing them.

A SHOTGUN BLAST shattered the moment.

Half-crazy with desire, Sally forced herself away from Jack and squinted at the twin farmhouses up the road. There, standing tall and stubborn against the horizon, were Jed Miltown and Evan Pratford, two guys with grudges.

Jed had the gun. Facing Evan across the fence separating their properties, he pointed it skyward and fired off another ear-splitting round. Seconds later, Evan fired up an acetylene torch and raised it high above his head. Jed shouted something at him, but Sally couldn't make it out.

"What the hell?" Jack cried. "Sally, get in the car. I'll call the police."

She waved her hand dismissively. "Oh, don't worry about them, Jack. They fire guns all the time. They trash things. They burn things. Sometimes they even blow things up."

"Are you sure?"

Sally laughed. Obviously things like this didn't happen in West Van. "Believe me, Jack, I'm sure. C'mon, we'll go and see what they're up to."

Her lust subsiding, she took Jack by the hand and all but dragged him toward the Mustang. Silently she damned the farmers. How was she supposed to convince Jack that Peachtown was a great place to live if those two nut jobs were going to act this way? He would think that everyone around here was this crazy, which, admittedly, a lot of people were. But it was the heat that was causing it, not some indigenous genetic disorder.

Rattled, Jack stopped in the middle of the road. "Maybe we should leave the car here and walk up."

He was worried about his *car?* Oh, please. "It'll be okay, Jack. Trust me."

They drove slowly up the dirt road. When they came to the fork that split off into two driveways, Jack brought the car to a stop. Undoubtedly he'd reasoned that choosing one driveway over the other might falsely indicate loyalty. Sally gave him points for smarts.

"Hey, guys." Climbing out of the car, she waved at both farmers. Jack got out and came around to stand beside her, obviously to protect her from harm. How valiant!

"Hey, Sally," Jed drawled. He was a ridiculously tall man with wispy gray hair and sharp facial features. Evan, by contrast, was short and squat, with a mop of dark curls. He bore an astonishing resemblance to Elmer Fudd.

Glaring at Sally, Evan nodded toward Jack. "Who's the pretty boy?"

"Evan, this is Jack Gold. Jack, Evan Pratford." She pointed at Jed, who was rumbling like a bear. "And this is Jed Miltown."

"Pleased to meet you both," Jack said.

Jed pointed his gun at the Mustang. "Nice car. Is that the original paint job?"

"I'm afraid not. I had it redone about five years ago."

"Pity. What's she got in her?"

Sally made a show of looking at her watch. At this rate, Jack wouldn't get around to writing her story until Christmas.

"A 289," he said with pride. "She moves."

"I'll bet she does!"

Evan narrowed his dark eyes. "Gold. You're that hotshot reporter from Vancouver, aren't you? You won some sorta award—a goldfish, or something." He lowered the torch so that its hissing flame came perilously close to his right pant leg. *Terrific*, Sally thought. *He'll set himself on fire, and then we'll have a real spectacle.*

"It was the Gobey award, and I wouldn't call myself a hotshot, sir."

"You're here to get the big scoop, aren't you?" Evan cackled as if he were the cleverest man on the planet.

"I sure am," Jack said cheerfully. "In fact, it's getting bigger by the day." He shot Sally a grin. Pleased to see him calm and in good humor again, she decided not to smirk at him.

"That's the dumbest joke I ever heard," Jed bellowed. Evan pointed the torch at him and waved it about wildly. Jed burst into song. "C'mon baby, light my fire..."

Enough was enough, Sally decided.

Selecting her words carefully, she informed Jed that Jack was here to interview Evan, and that he was on deadline for the *Post*.

"So, if it's okay with you, we'll just go inside with Evan and do that. Then we'll come and sit a while with you."

Before Jed could respond, hotshot opened his mouth and made a stupendous error. "What are you planning to do with that torch?" he asked Evan.

Sally cringed. As an outsider, Jack couldn't possibly know it, but with this pair it was best not to ask questions that might, er, inflame the situation.

"I'm gonna burn that thing down." Evan pointed the torch at a rickety old shed on Jed's lawn, near the fence. "Just had a new survey done. Damn thing's two inches inside my property."

"Hmmm." Jack turned to Jed. "And what are you planning to do with that gun?"

Sally held her breath. Maybe he was onto something, but what?

Jed sneered. "Whaddaya think? I'm gonna kill him right after he burns it down."

"I see. So, what we're shooting for here—excuse the expression, gentlemen—is a torched shed and a dead man. Is that right?"

Both farmers seemed to consider the insanity of that outcome, but Sally remained cautious. You never knew what was going on in those heads.

"Shall we go inside?" she tried again.

"Actually, I have a better idea." Jack walked over to Evan, but wisely kept his attention focused on Jed. "Mr. Miltown, do you have a lawn chair?"

"Why? We havin' a picnic?"

"No. We're going to have an old-fashioned sit-down."

The farmers looked at one another as if to say: Finally, someone who's crazier than we are.

"Best idea I've heard all day," Sally declared. Beaming at Jack—the man was a genius!—she fetched three lawn chairs off Evan's front porch and brought them to where Jack and Evan stood. Grumbling, Jed dragged an old metal chair across his own lawn and parked it a few feet away from the barbed wire fence.

Everybody sat down.

Jack flipped his notebook open and snapped his pen to attention. "So, let's start with this civil suit. Mr. Pratford…"

"Humph, might as well call me Evan, since you're sittin' on my favorite chair."

Sally prayed for patience as Evan accepted Jack's immediate offer to trade seats. Christmas? Easter was more like it.

"Thanks," Jack said when he was comfortable again. "Evan, Mr. Miltown is alleged to have killed one of your cows with a golf ball…"

"Call me Jed."

Evan sneered. "Golf *balls*. A whole bucket of 'em."

"So what?" Jed huffed. "At least somebody around here's *got* balls!"

"For cryin' out loud, Miltown, there's a lady present!" Wild-eyed and ranting, Evan sprang to his feet and looked around for his torch. He'd leaned it against his chair, but Sally had furtively slid it closer to hers. She grabbed it and held on for dear life. At the same time her chair tipped over backwards and she let out a yell. In a flash, Jack was on his feet, helping her up. Jed sprang out of his chair and roared, "That's it. I'm outta here!"

"Sit down!" Jack shouted. "Everybody…just…sit…down."

Dumbstruck, the battling farmers did as they were told. Sally gaped at Jack. Wow, talk about balls.

Jack took his seat and shrugged as if to get a heavy coat off his shoulders. "Okay. Now Jed, why exactly were you lobbing golf balls at Evan's barn?"

He muttered something under his breath.

"Speak up. We can't hear you."

"I said I don't know!"

"I doubt that very much." Jack turned to Evan. "And why exactly are you suing Jed? We gentlemen resolve our differences in private, do we not?"

Talk about smooth, Sally thought.

Evan mumbled something and Jack demanded that he speak more clearly.

"For cryin' out loud, he used a five-iron! Look at that pitch." Turning to face his barn, Evan traced an arc from its hayloft to Jed's backyard. "I ask you, who uses a five-iron for a shot like that?"

Sally sighed. Easter? Thanksgiving, maybe.

Jack shocked everyone by hurling his pen and notebook across the lawn. He held up his hands. "No notes, gentlemen. We're off the record now, and we're going to get to the bottom of this. Why have the two of you been fighting all these years? I'm not leaving here until someone tells me."

The farmers automatically folded their arms and stared at the ground as if it would freeze over before either of them said a word. When the silence became unbearable, Evan nodded toward Jed. "He stole my woman." He said the words calmly.

Sally's jaw dropped.

"I didn't steal her," Jed said just as calmly. "I kissed her, that's all."

"Humph. Might as well have stolen her. Things were never the same again."

"Okay, I want the whole story," Jack said. "Here are the rules. You'll talk in turns. No one will raise his voice. No one will interrupt the other. You will both tell the absolute truth. Got it?"

The men nodded.

"Okay. Jed, you go first."

Sally listened, spellbound, while Jed told an incredible tale. Long ago, before moving here, he had spotted a woman walking down the street in Prince George, a city far to the north. She was the most beautiful woman he'd ever seen, but he didn't know her name and he never saw her again—until he moved here, that was. She turned out to be Evan's wife, and he fell madly in love with her.

He cared about his own wife, but what he felt for Greta Prat-ford was nothing less than the deep, all-consuming love that only a few are privileged to find. She was his perfect match, his true soul mate, and she felt the same way about him. They couldn't act on it, of course, so they soldiered on in miserable silence, raising their families and running their farms and doing their best to avoid one another. Then, one day they weakened. There was a kiss, one passionate kiss that Evan witnessed. It tainted both marriages from that day on.

All the while he'd been speaking, Jed had kept his eyes downcast. Now he looked straight at Jack. "Can you imagine what it's like to be that close to a woman you want and not be able to have her?"

To Sally's utter astonishment, Jack's own eyes sought hers and held them for a moment. "I think I do."

Her heart went straight to heaven.

While Evan told his side of the story, she stole furtive glances at Jack, hoping to catch his attention again and transmit her own feelings. But he was in his element—listening, being a reporter, doing the job he was born to do.

Evan told pretty much the same story, with a few contradictions, of course. When he was through talking, Jack rose to indicate the sit-down was over. He looked at each person in turn. "What was said here today stays here. Are we all in agreement on that?"

Everyone nodded, including Sally. Poor Jack. He really had no idea where he was.

"Good. There will be a story in next week's *Post*, but the story will be that, after careful reconsideration, Evan Pratford dropped his lawsuit against Jed Miltown. And, after twenty-five years of feuding, the men have agreed to resolve their differences and get on with their lives. Got it?"

"I guess so," Evan muttered. Jed followed with something equally noncommittal, but at least the pair made eye contact.

Jack retrieved his pen and notebook, then touched Sally's

arm. "Let's go." As they were strolling to the car, he stopped and spoke to the farmers again. "You know, it strikes me that the two of you don't have enough to do. You're both widowed, right?"

Jed nodded. "Two years now."

"Three for me," Evan confirmed.

"That has to change. There are two widows in this county, Elvira and Elsa Jackson, who might enjoy dinner out one night. Give that some thought."

Jed flinched. "Stonewall Jackson?"

"Never mind. It was just an idea."

As they drove back down the dirt road, it was all Sally could do to keep from smothering Jack with affection. No longer would she be concerned about fawning over him. Cracker Jack Gold deserved to be fawned over! He was amazing! Incredible! Wonderful! He was every bit the man she knew he could be, and more.

"That was really something, what you just did, Jack."

He gave her a gentle warning look. "I meant what I said about keeping this to ourselves, Sally."

"Okay, city boy, let me tell you what will happen now. Within a matter of hours, those two guys will start telling the story themselves. Each will tell his own version. Each will embellish his version over time, so that in ten years nobody will have the slightest idea of what actually happened. Your role will get bigger every year, and eventually you'll be a legend in the valley."

Jack's eyebrows shot up. "Really? A legend? I like that."

"Don't get too cocky, hotshot. And tell me something. Is my imagination in overdrive, or was that 'sit-down' thing a not-too-subtle reference to a bunch of thugs sitting down to negotiate terms and make deals?"

Jack's grin was positively devilish. "Does your mind work along the same sorry lines as mine?"

"Does a chicken have feathers!"

"Does the Pope wear a pointy hat!"

"Does a bear sh—"

"Whoa! Stop right there!" Laughing, Jack reached across the console and clasped her hand. Sally was dazzled. He'd never done that before. She waited for him to release it, but he held on.

Oh Jack, she thought as their fingers intertwined, *you* are *human.*

10

WHAT A DAY!

After dropping Sally off at home and kissing her the way a beautiful woman should be kissed, Jack floated into the inn on a cloud. He couldn't recall a time when he'd felt this good about himself. Graduating top of his class at UBC. Getting hired at the *Satellite*. Winning the Gobey. Nothing compared.

Replenishing Polly's food and water, he called up the day's highlights. Number one: Making Sally happy. The look on her face when he'd told her she was the story. Awesome! *My hero*, she'd called him. Jack couldn't believe it. He'd been called many things over the years, but hero wasn't one of them.

Number two: Brokering a reconciliation between two foolish, feuding farmers. It wasn't the men themselves he cared about. Frankly, if Jed Miltown and Evan Pratford squabbled until Armageddon, it would be no sweat off his butt. It was something else. Without knowing it, they'd put him back in touch with what it really meant to be a journalist.

An idealist at university, Jack had believed the job was about more than just gathering facts and putting them into words. It was about working with, and for, people. It was about being part of the family of mankind, with all the give and take that entailed. He might not have gotten a publishable story from Jed and Evan today, but copy wasn't everything. Human lives were everything. Somewhere along the way he'd forgotten that.

Cracker Jack? Jaded Jack was more like it.

Number three: Becoming a legend. It was corny but, hey, it was cool corny.

Even helping Charlie and Elvira made him feel good. At home no one required his help. No one *needed* him. And so what if Sally was behind the curtain, pulling the strings. A good deed was still a good deed, wasn't it?

Famished suddenly—Elvira's casserole hadn't quite cut it—Jack peered into the fridge. Hmmm, stores were getting low. He'd have to buy some food. For now, an apple and a piece of cheese would do.

As he fetched a paring knife, the red blinking light on the Pittles' answering machine caught his eye. In their note they had told him not to worry about calls, but who could resist that light? He hit the message button, and Martha's gravelly voice came up. "Goldy, are you there?" Behind her was the sound of adults visiting and kids making a ruckus. "Gracious living, Goldy, if you're there, pick up."

Between slices of apple, Jack spoke to the machine. "Trust me, Martha, I'm not there."

"I sure hope you get this message, Goldy. We called your cell phone this afternoon, but you didn't answer. Anyway, we just wanted you to know we're stayin' here another week. Bein' here has reminded us of just how much we miss our kids and grandkids, so we're goin' to look at some condos. You're welcome to stay there as long as you like, but if you have to go, Arlene Sacks will take care of Polly."

There was the sound of a receiver being covered, followed by some hurried discussion between Martha and Percy. Then she came back on the line. "Oh, and Jack. Do us a favor and don't say a word about this to Sally. Not just yet, anyway. Give our love to Polly and y'all have fun now!"

Jack checked his own voice mail. Marty still hadn't called, but sure enough there was a message from the Pittles. They must have called during the sit-down.

Why, he wondered, would Sally care if they moved away? They were friendly, but surely she wouldn't be devastated. And did that mean this house would be for sale? If so, at what price?

Compared with Vancouver, real estate was cheap in the valley. In fact, his town house was probably worth twice as much as this place, with maybe a third of the square footage. It was mortgaged, but there was still enough equity there to...

Hold on. What was he thinking?

"Mom and Dad send their love," he called out to Polly.

"*Squawwwwwwwwwk*. Polly wants a martini!"

"Sorry, my feathered friend. There's no vermouth in the house. If you're good, I'll get you some tomorrow."

As he sliced a hunk of cheese off the block, Jack's thoughts went back to Sally. Was she serious about there being no strings attached? When Liz Montaine said no strings, she really meant it. But Sally wasn't Liz. Both women were smart and strong-willed, sure, but Sally was also sweet and vulnerable.

Or was she? Admittedly, Jack had no talent for calling that one. Some women looked fragile to him, but turned out to be rock-solid. Others looked sturdy, but folded at the first sign of trouble. When you got right down to it, how well did he know Sally? Barely three days worth, that was how well.

Hell, for all the affection she lavished on him, maybe she had no special interest in him at all—just a thing about sleeping with reporters. Maybe she used Peach Paradise to lure a new one to town every year. Stranger things were true.

Whatever, she was definitely itching to seduce him. But as far as she knew, that couldn't happen until after her story was written. Jack, of course, had no intention of writing it here. He could just imagine the wheels in her splendid brain spinning faster and faster as she worked on that little problem.

All he could think was, she must want him pretty badly. And hey, why not? He was worth it.

He finished his apple and went to the fridge for another one. Oh, the trouble little Sally Sunshine was in. Obviously she'd conspired with Charlie to keep him here so that she would get her story published. Talking with Elvira this afternoon, Jack had begun to suspect that Sally also had solicited her help. That, of course, would have been yesterday or this morning, before he'd offered to stay. ·

He chuckled. She was probably on the phone right now, trying to call off her dogs.

What a blast! If he volunteered to help Charlie and Elvira, it would frustrate her to no end. It would be loads of fun for him, and no less than what the little schemer deserved. Alas, there was no time for fun and games. Saturday he was out of here.

Saturday. No later. Absolutely.

Anyway, as much as his aching hormones loved the idea, there wasn't going to be any seduction. No way would he violate ethics.

"Polly," Jack said to his lush of a roommate. "I've got every man's sexual fantasy throwing herself at me, and unless I'm prepared to compromise my integrity, there's not a damn thing I can do about it. What would you do in my situation?"

"*Squawwwwwwwwwk.* Polly wants a gin and tonic!"

"God, you're self-absorbed. What about my problems?"

Chuckling, Jack glanced at the kitchen clock. It was after six, and still no call from Marty. It would have been nice to get a firm go-ahead before meeting with Sally's folks tonight, but it wasn't critical. There was no question he would get it.

The real question was: Why was he so nervous? If he wanted to profile Sally as part of the overall story, it was essential that he meet her family. It wasn't a date, no matter what she thought, and it wasn't a social outing. It was research.

So how come it felt like Meet the Parents night?

Right on cue, his cell phone rang. Jack scrambled to fish it out of his jacket pocket, confident it would be Marty.

It was.

WHAT A WOMAN IN LOVE DOES...

First, she takes a long, hot shower, shaving her legs not just up to the knee, but *aaaallll* the way up. Then she towels off and coats her entire body with fragrant oil, paying special attention to certain zones. While her skin absorbs the oil, she reviews her collection of perfumes, wondering which one will make a man forget about ethics.

Next, she brushes her teeth until their enamel is practically gone. Then she blows her hair dry, one strand at a time until it is shampoo-commercial perfect. She plucks her eyebrows. She applies mascara and blush. She paints her nails with Winter White and thrusts them into the freezer—how appropriate!—for quick drying.

Mission accomplished, she slips on her silk robe, then hauls all her summer dresses out of the closet and drapes them over her bed. Shoes—sixteen pairs in total—she arranges in a line across the floor. She opens her lingerie drawer, which sticks from lack of use, and rifles through it.

She tries on earrings. She considers belts and bracelets.

With nothing more to do, Sally drew a calming breath and called Elvira Jackson to say how very grateful she was for her help with that, um, little matter, but things had changed. Jack was going to be super busy in the coming days, so all in all it would be best if the Jacksons hired a real handyman.

Elvira disagreed. "I'll decide what's best for us, young lady. For your information, Elsa and I enjoyed ourselves this afternoon. It's not often that we mature women see a young stallion in our shower stall."

"Hmm, I know how you feel, Elvira. But see, the thing is—"

"Back off, Sunshine!"

"Yes, ma'am."

"We've got quite a few things that need fixing around here, and it's none of your beeswax who fixes them."

"Yes, ma'am."

"I'll ask for Goldy's help whenever I feel like it, and you won't interfere. Is that clear?"

"Yes, ma'am." Sally sighed. She should have known. In any game of chance, Elvira was always the wild card.

"And one more thing. I have no idea what you're up to, young lady, but I've known you your whole life, and I'll bet it's some sneaky business that will bring consequences. You're familiar with those, aren't you?"

"All too, ma'am."

"What, exactly, *are* you up to?"

"Trust me, Elvira, you don't want to know."

"The hell I don't! Whatever it is, you just go easy on our boy."

Much to Sally's surprise—two visits in one day?—Trish let herself into the house just as Elvira was slamming the receiver down. Trish was lightly sunburned and had the disheveled, wind-whipped look of a person who'd been out on the water too long. She seemed utterly bewildered. "Evan Pratford just called and instructed me to cancel his lawsuit against Jed Miltown."

Sally tightened the sash on her robe. "Really? That's great!"

"It's wonderful. But here's what I don't get. He said he's doing it because Jack Gold made him do it—at gunpoint. Can you explain that to me?"

Wow, it had to be a record. Barely an hour had passed, and version number one of the Legend of Jack Gold was already out. Discretion was a joke now, so Sally told Trish the real story, detail for astonishing detail. "You should have seen him, Trish. He was *amazing.*"

Obviously unimpressed, Trish crinkled her nose and sniffed. "Is that musk oil I smell?"

"Sure is. Come with me." Sally motioned for Trish to follow her into the bedroom, where she selected two dresses and held them up for inspection. "What do you think? Yellow or fuchsia?"

Frowning, Trish took in the mess. "What's going on here? Have you got a date with the Vancouver Canucks?"

"Better, my friend. I've got a date with the most incredible man in the world." Sally shook the dresses. "Help me. Which one?"

"Oh, I don't know. The...pink one, I guess."

As Sally laid the dresses back down, Trish took in her hair, her nails, her shiny skin. "Just look at you, girl. You didn't hear a word I said this morning, did you?"

Sally shrugged. It was really none of Trish's business, what she chose to hear or not hear. She picked up her little black cocktail dress. Hmm, no. Too formal.

"Sally, Jack Gold isn't the right guy for you."

"I never said he was. I just find him...attractive. And, you know how they say opposites attract? Well, guess what, Trish? It's not true for everybody. We're a lot alike, Jack and me."

"Uh-huh, except that he's not living in a dream world."

Sally made a big show of checking her bedside clock. It was time now for all beloved skeptics to beat it. "If you don't mind, Trish, I'm rushed. We'll have to continue this discussion later."

"You can count on that!" On her way through the living room, Trish grudgingly called out, "Go with the yellow. It looks great on you."

Sally smiled. Sunshine-yellow. An excellent choice.

"OOH, LA LA."

Sally drew a sharp breath and batted her eyelashes furiously. "Why, Mother, I thought you were happily married."

The women were standing side by side in the Darville's cheery kitchen, spooning out servings of Peach Paradise. Tilly McMahon, their cook, stood behind them, scrubbing pots and pans.

"I am," Sarah Darville said. "But if I was single, I wouldn't turn *that* away." She nodded toward the dining room, where Sally's dad was busy boring Jack with his stamp collection.

"But Mother," Sally teased. "What about the age difference?"

Sarah snorted. "Who would care? He's so good-looking, and so articulate. Wouldn't you agree, Tilly?"

Up to her elbows in soapy water, Tilly spoke over her broad shoulder. "I couldn't agree more. Such a looker! He could use a little fashion advice, though. Frankly, Sally, he's got worse taste than Percy Pittle."

"Tilly, those *are* Percy's clothes. Jack didn't bring any of his own."

"No matter," Sarah said. "I'm still smitten."

Sally stood tall, as if to give a speech. "How could you not be? He said, and I quote, 'Mrs. Darville, you are even more beautiful than your daughter, and I wouldn't have thought that possible.'" She giggled. She'd been giggling all night and just couldn't seem to stop.

Sarah winked. "Are you kidding? He had me at 'Mrs. Darville.'"

Happiness overwhelmed Sally. Suddenly everything she took for granted was wonderful. Her health, her job, her friends and family. Sweet, bubbly Tilly, who was like a second mom. Her *life*. What a privileged life it had been, thanks to Sarah and Dean Darville. They were great parents, and she was proud to show them off.

Sarah looked lovely tonight. Her blond hair, so much like Sally's, was swept back into a roll, with one loose tendril curling around her chin. Very chic. In keeping with her good fashion sense, she wore a long khaki dress, accented by a simple gold pin and matching earrings. Even Dean, who hated to dress up, had donned tailored pants and a crisp white shirt. He had rugged, working-man looks, but he cleaned up pretty good.

Sally so wanted them to like Jack, and much to her delight he seemed intent on making a good impression on them. All night he'd been nothing less than completely charming.

At eight o'clock sharp, he'd shown up with a bouquet of pink roses for Sarah and a bottle of red wine for Dean. The wine was of vintage class, from one of the nearby wineries. Such genius! Everyone in the valley supported the local winemakers, especially in times like this. Dean, a tough nut to crack, had been quietly impressed.

Then, all through dinner—Tilly's scrumptious beef stew with dumplings—Jack had chatted informatively with Dean about stocks and bonds and market fluctuations. Sally's dad had a way of hogging people, which none of her boyfriends—make that *previous* boyfriends—had been strong enough, or clever enough, to resist. But Jack made a point of including Sally and her mom in the conversation.

They'd all talked about the story, of course, and Jack's job at the *Satellite.* The dairy. The weather. The usual stuff.

Sarah set the dessert bowls aside and put the scoop—the big scoop, Sally thought with a smile—into the dishwasher. "Tell me something, daughter, is it just me, or are you a little smitten yourself?"

Sally groaned. "Please, Mom, don't ask."

"Because, if I didn't know better, I'd swear you were pregnant. You're positively glowing."

"Pregnant? Hah! For that you need action."

Jack came into the kitchen carrying the dinner dishes. Right behind him was Dean, with the cups and cutlery. Mother and daughter exchanged a look. Dean put in ten-hour days at the dairy and did most of the yard work, but he flat-out refused to lift a finger in the house. Jack must have shamed him into it.

"Sarah," Jack said as she took the plates from him. "Is there anything else I can do for you?"

To Sally's delight, her mother actually blushed. "Well, since you asked so nicely, Jack, you can take this ice cream into the living room. Sally and I will bring the coffee."

Jack said it would be his pleasure to do that, then trained

his baby blues on Tilly. "Ma'am, that was the best stew I've ever had. Anything you want to cook, I'll be glad to eat."

Tilly giggled like a schoolgirl. "I like a man with an appetite."

Why, Sally, wondered, was Jack in such good spirits? He could be charming: that she now knew for a fact, but why was he so buoyant? So...happy?

Gracious as a geisha, Jack scooped up two of the four dessert bowls and strolled out of the room. Dean, mouth all twisted out of shape, muttered something unrepeatable and grabbed the other two. "Don't say a word," he warned all three women. They waited until he was gone, then cracked up.

"Sometimes I envy you girls," Sarah commented. "It's a whole different game for your generation."

Sally grinned. "Mom, you have no idea."

"Let me do that," Tilly said as Sarah picked up the coffee tray. "And I'll see to these dinner dishes, too."

"Don't be silly, Tilly." It was an old family joke and they all laughed. "We'll finish up. It's awfully late for you to be here. You should head home before it's too dark to see the road."

Tilly agreed, and Sarah and Sally went to join the men. As they sat around in the living room, eating their ice cream and chatting, Sally stole a peek at her watch. It was getting late and she hadn't perfumed her thighs for nothing. Besides, Jack looked tired. Poor guy. He was supposed to be on assignment, but all he'd done since getting here was run around and help people.

She wanted him awake tonight. Very awake.

Just as she was considering a move, the old floor radio in the corner caught Jack's attention, and he gestured toward it. "I recognize that radio," he said to Sarah. "It's a rare Marconi. They only made fifty of them."

She looked impressed. "Do you know antiques, Jack?"

He shrugged. "I know a little about them. Not as much as my mother, though. She's a dealer, in Vancouver."

"Really?" Sarah set her bowl down. A bad sign. "How interesting. Tell me then, how old is the darned thing? I bought it at a garage sale, and the owners didn't know."

Together Jack and Sarah got up and went over to have a closer look at it. "All fifty of them were made in 1936," he told her. "So they're not genuine antiques. In order to qualify for that status, they'd have to be at least a hundred years old."

Sarah gasped. "Now, see, I didn't even know that. Did you hear that, Dean?"

The next thing Sally knew, Dean was on his feet, steering Jack toward the old cabinet he used to store his stamp books. "What about this piece, Jack? We picked it up at a roadside sale last year."

Sally tapped her foot restlessly on the carpet as Jack opened the cabinet and pointed to something inside it. "Okay. See these tongues and grooves?" Sarah and Dean nodded.

What about my *grooves?* Sally wondered.

"There are no nails in the joints. That's standard prairie construction. In the early days of farm settlement, they had to make their own nails, and it was too much work. I'd guess this piece is circa 1875."

"Well, I'll be." Dean shook his head. "Listen, Jack, at the antiques road show yesterday, they advised us to catalogue all our pieces and have them appraised. But the closest appraiser is in Kelowna. I don't suppose you'd be willing to help us?"

Sarah clapped her hands like a kid. "Oh Jack, would you?"

Sally sighed. Great. Another delay. "Mom, Jack is too busy for that. He has more important things to do."

Mister Too Nice for Words disagreed. "Actually, I'd be delighted to help. But not tonight, if that's okay. I'm pretty tired."

That was all Sally needed to rise and start searching for her purse. She faked a yawn. "Me, too. Let's go."

At the door she kissed her folks goodbye, then vibrated on the spot while Jack took a century to say how nice it had been to meet them, and what a lovely evening it had been, and how he understood so much better now why Sally was smart and ambitious and passionate. Finally the door closed and they stepped onto the path leading to her cottage.

It was a warm, moonlit night. A night for howling.

As they headed down the path, Sally took Jack's arm and squeezed it. "What is with you, tonight? You're acting very strange."

Without a word he took her in his arms and kissed her like he'd never kissed her before. Then he caressed her cheek with the back of his hand. "I haven't had the chance to tell you how fabulous you look tonight, Sally."

Flabbergasted, she gazed up at him. "Omigod, who are you and what have you done with Jack?"

He answered by kissing her again, and Sally wondered if that generous but slightly bogus offer she'd made earlier was behind his dramatic mood change. Hah! Not likely. Most guys freely assumed there were no strings attached. Why would Jack Gold be an exception?

"Jack, please tell me why you're so happy."

"I talked to Marty this afternoon, that's why."

Marty? No wonder! They had their go-ahead. Delirious, Sally clasped his arms and shook them. "Oh, Jack. What did he say? No, wait! Tell me, what were his exact words?"

"His exact words?"

"Yes!"

"You're fired."

11

"Fired!"

Jack steered Sally to the circle of chairs on the stone patio outside her cottage, and made her sit down. Otherwise she'd run around like a person on fire. "Relax, Sally. It's no big deal."

"No big deal! But why? Why did he fire you?"

Jack sat down across from her and propped his elbows on his knees. "Okay. Here's what happened. I pitched your story. I gave it everything I had, Sally. I want you to know that. But he rejected it. He said it's not *Satellite* material. I questioned his judgment, he blew up, then I blew up, and things pretty much went downhill from there."

"But your job! My God, Jack you've been fired!"

Should he tell her the truth? He didn't want her to feel guilty, and he definitely didn't want her to read too much into it. Oh, what the hell, it was a no-win thing. "Actually, he didn't fire me, Sally. I quit."

In a flash, she was on her feet again, ranting. "You quit! How could you do that?"

Jack squeezed his eyes shut. "Sit down, Sally."

"But..."

"Sit!"

Dumbfounded, she sat.

"If you must know, I quit, then he said I couldn't quit because it would deprive him of the privilege of firing me. So, I quit *and* got fired, I guess. But I quit first."

Sally gawked at him as if he were not just irrational but unstable, too. "You quit your job...because of *me*?"

"Basically, yes. I think you're a great story. And if Marty doesn't think you're a great story, I don't want to work for him anymore."

"But...I don't get it, Jack. Why are you so happy about it? You should be in panic mode."

Jack nodded. For at least an hour after talking to Marty, he had been panicked. But then he'd realized it really wasn't a big deal. For one thing, he hadn't planned to stick around the *Satellite* much longer anyway. For another thing, he'd have more time now to devote to Sally's story—to do it justice, like he'd promised. His hormones had pushed the scenario a little further than that, but right now the story had top priority.

Finally, he just plain felt relieved.

He told Sally all of that, except, of course, for the part about his hormones. "I know it sounds crazy, but I feel as if a huge weight has been lifted off me. I feel free."

Sitting there with a halo of moonlight around her pretty head, Sally looked like she didn't know whether to laugh or smash his face. "That's great for you, Jack, but what about my story? I don't have a publisher now!"

Like he always did when making a pitch, Jack got up and moved around, gesturing with his hands. "See, that's the beauty of it. We're free now, you and me, to shop the story around. I made a list of news and business publications this afternoon that might want it. I think—don't break out the champagne just yet—but I think I can even get *Maclean's* magazine interested."

"You said you could get Marty interested!"

Damn, he had said that, hadn't he? *Maclean's*, a national news magazine, suddenly felt like a stretch. But, hey, he could do it. *They* could do it. "Have faith in us, Sally."

That must have been verbal overkill because her jaw almost hit the patio. "Faith—in us?"

"Yeah. You and me. We're a team, right?"

The next thing Jack knew, she was on her feet, sashaying toward him. A languorous smile had replaced her frown, and she had that loosey-goosey manner that told him trouble was imminent.

As always, the transformation was amazing.

"Oh, Jack." Eyes shining, she backed him up to the rail surrounding the patio and put her arms around his neck. "You gave up your job for little old me."

He rested his butt on the rail and drew her close. "Don't be so self-centered, Sunshine. Not everything is about you."

She faked a pout. "It isn't?"

Jack laughed. She was so much fun and so pretty tonight, in her flouncy yellow dress, with her yellow hair all aglow. A golden goddess, glorious in the moonlight. And she smelled like sex. A long hot night of it. He could lose himself in her scent alone.

She caressed the back of his neck with tantalizing fingertips. "So what happens now? Do we have to get another publisher before you start work on the story?"

"Why?" Jack teased. "Are you in a hurry for some reason?"

"Of course not, silly. Why would I be in a hurry?"

"I can't imagine why."

Both of them knowing exactly why, they gazed into one another's eyes—searching, wanting, fearing. Their mouths met for a long, slow, sexy kiss.

Sally moaned.

Jack actually trembled.

It was too much, so they eased apart.

Her lips found the sweet spot on his neck. "Jack?"

"Yes?" Slowly, his hands slid down her back and over her gorgeous little tush, to the tops of her legs, and back again. His breathing slowed.

"It occurs to me that since you no longer have a job..." Sally took his earlobe in her mouth and sucked it gently.

Jack smiled inside. Here it came. "Yes, Sally?" He raked his fingers through her hair, at the same time pulling her toward him for another kiss. He'd wanted to do that for days. The kiss went on for a long time, then Sally slid her mouth across his cheek, so she could whisper in his ear.

"And since you haven't really started work on my story just yet..."

"Uh-huh?" Nuzzling her silky neck, Jack wondered how much longer he could do this. Ten, maybe twenty hours.

But not tonight.

"We have..."

He helped her out. "A window?"

"Yes, a window. We could..."

The mindless, throbbing thing between his legs couldn't believe that Jack was about to do this, but he was. Carefully, he maneuvered Sally so that they were both leaning against the rail, side by side. He put his arm around her. Bewildered, she followed suit.

"Okay. Here's the deal, Sally."

She sighed wearily. "Great. Here comes the deal."

"Listen to me. First of all we don't have a window. We're going ahead with the story, starting tomorrow. I'll read those files, word for word. I'll interview you, for your part of it, and Charlie for his part. The revitalization committee meets tomorrow, and I'll probably attend that meeting. I'll try to book an interview with Valmont Developments and a couple of those builders, for sometime tomorrow. Do you still want to come along?"

"Yes!"

"Okay. So, for now you and I still have a working relationship. The usual rules apply."

"Rules, schmules." Huffing, Sally slipped free and began to wander around the patio. Jack followed her with his eyes. She was pretty when she was frustrated.

"Gimme a break, Sally. If I'm to write well about you, like it or not I have to remain objective. If you and I go to bed, that will be impossible."

She made a sour face. "Bed? Who says I want to go to bed with you?"

Jack howled. "Sally, Sally, Sally. Sometimes I wonder who you think you're talking to. You're dying to take me to bed."

"How dare you!"

"And I'm dying to let you."

She blinked. "You are?"

"Yeah, but you know what I realized this afternoon? I don't know you." Jack pointed up the hill. "Tonight, in your parents' house, I learned that you've got two older brothers, both geologists, both living in Calgary. I learned that you were a straight-A student all through school, and that you won medals in four collegiate sports. I learned that you were thrown from a horse once, and spent four weeks in hospital.

"Call me old-fashioned, Sally, but even without ethics I think a man and a woman should know something about each other before they jump into the sack."

That got her hot. "Is it any wonder you don't know me, Jack? You've been here three whole days and haven't asked me a single question about myself that didn't relate to ice cream!"

Jack closed his eyes and nodded. It was true. And he'd been aware of it every minute of those three days. But what could he have said? *I don't want to know you? I don't want to get close to you? I don't want to...love you?* Hardly.

Sally crossed her arms and pouted—adorably. "So does this mean we *are* going to bed?"

"That depends on you. Did you mean what you said today about no strings attached? 'Cause I'm wondering if you're that strong."

Her eyebrows shot up. "Are you that strong, Jack?"

Hmm, fair question. "I don't know," he answered honestly. "I've got a proposal for you. I think we should wait until after the story's written, then review the idea. Renegotiate, as it were."

"Does that mean you'll be writing the story here?"

Jack tried not to smile. Undoubtedly, Sally was thrilled not to have to sweat over that problem anymore. "Sure, why not? There's no reason for me to rush home. And, besides, freelancing is different. It may be a while before we hear back from the publishers I have in mind, and whoever takes us on will probably want to see the finished article before committing to it."

"How long will it take?"

"For me to get home?"

"No, silly. To write the article."

Grinning, Jack looked her up and down. "Why, Sunshine? Are you desperate to get into bed with me?"

"Don't push it, hotshot."

He nodded. "I'll write it sometime next week. Maybe later. It depends on how much I get done in the next few days."

Obviously intrigued, Sally took a while to think his proposal over. "All right, Jack. But in the meantime our current agreement stands. Kissing is okay." It was a flat statement of fact.

Jack breathed a sigh of relief. The deal was struck, and now it was time to leave. He had a plan in mind that involved a lot more than just kissing, a lot sooner than next week, but one more minute alone in the moonlight with sexy Sally and he might just forget it.

ON TUESDAY MORNING, the dairy was in full swing. All the staff were back at work, the service counter was swamped and the noise level was back to its usual pitch.

Sally was ecstatic. Hard as she tried, she simply could not concentrate on her work. Files stared accusingly at her from atop her desk. Numbers swam before her eyes. Twice, on the phone, she mistakenly called a sales agent Jack, only to be reminded that his name was Harold. Not even close!

Things were working out even better than planned. She tallied her accomplishments to date. Convincing Jack that she had a worthwhile story: mission accomplished. More than accomplished—she *was* the story. Convincing Jack that she was a good lover: mission almost accomplished. It was just a matter of time. Convincing Jack that she would be a good wife: Hmm, that one posed a challenge, but no biggie. She thrived on challenges. Besides, if hotshot couldn't see it, he wasn't half the observational genius he believed himself to be.

There was one little problem: Charlie. Should she try to help him with his plan? There wasn't a whole lot she could do to persuade Jack that he should be running the *Post*—not without being blatantly obvious. But she certainly didn't want to discourage him. If Jack was staying in Peachtown, he would need a job.

Whichever, it would all work out just fine. In the meantime, could she possibly admire him more? Wanting to know her better before they did the dirty deed. Such decency! Most guys tried to get her clothes off before the check arrived. And while Jack was adamant about not making promises, the others had promised her all kinds of things.

She'd had a moment last night, thinking once again that Jack was just trying to put her off, but it passed. A man who trembled in your arms was definitely game.

Jack. Oh, he could be so frustrating! Ethics. Objectivity. Tomorrow he'd probably stick her with integrity. But that was Jack. A straight arrow aimed at her heart.

He could be clever, too. Somehow he'd twisted everything around so that he was Mister Good as Gold, while she was an incorrigible sex fiend. It wasn't true! Lots of men wanted to sleep with her—Matt Caldwell of Valmont Developments had even offered to give up oxygen if she'd go to bed with him, but had she taken him up on his offer? No!

Anyway, she *did* want to tear Jack's clothes off, but nymphomania wasn't exactly the kind of image she wanted to project. He bore watching, Jack did.

Dean poked his head in the door, breaking her train of thought. He was in management mode this morning, his craggy features frozen into a don't-give-me-problems-just-give-mesolutions stare. "I like that young man, Sally. Your mom says you like him, too."

"I like him a lot, Dad."

"Well, it's probably too soon to be saying this, but if he turns out to be the guy, that'll be fine with me."

Happy? Sally thought her heart would burst. No one had ever gotten her dad's endorsement. No one had even come close.

Dean vanished and moments later Sarah took his place. Overdressed for a Tuesday morning, she looked suspiciously flushed and pretty. "Hi, Sally. Guess what? Jack is on his way here. He's going to help me with the antiques catalogue. I offered to take him shopping for some clothes, too, and then out to lunch. I just wanted you to know."

Shopping? Lunch? Gee, at this rate, Jack would never get around to writing her story. They would never get to know one another, and they would never get to bed. They'd end up old and feeble, their body parts rusty from lack of use.

"Mom, if I didn't know better, I'd swear *you* were dating Jack."

"Don't worry, you're safe. But I will say that having him around has inspired me. Your father and I had, shall we say, an interesting night last night."

Sally covered her ears. "Yuck, that was more information than I needed!"

Sarah laughed, a light, tinkly laugh that signaled happiness. "Anyway, I have to run. You have a nice day."

"Mom," Sally said before she could get away. "I need to ask you something."

Intrigued, Sarah came into the room and closed the door. "Shoot."

"What makes a woman a good wife?"

"That's easy. Two things. Food and sex, though not necessarily in that order. Oh, and golf. How's your short game?"

"Terrible. What if I said sex and golf were temporarily out of the question?"

"Ooh, pity. That would leave food. Men love food. It gives them energy for sex and golf."

Sally rolled her eyes. "Now I know where the expression 'shallow advice' came from."

"All you need to know is this—men are simple creatures."

"I don't know about that, Mom. There's nothing simple about Jack."

Sarah held up her wrist. "Look at the time." She sprang to her feet. "That's good, sweetie, because no simple man would be right for you. I've said it before and I'll say it again—don't settle for someone who is one iota less than your equal."

Sally smiled as Sarah blew her a kiss and blew out the door. She didn't intend to.

An hour later, after she'd finally buckled down to work, Sally recalled Sarah's advice about food. All her life she had feasted on gourmet delicacies straight from Tilly's kitchen. On her own she could barely fry bacon. Come to think of it, she didn't have any domestic skills. Something told her Jack wouldn't care about that, but even so, it wouldn't hurt to cook a nice meal for him. He was coming over tonight to start their interview, and they had to eat something.

Yes, she would cook dinner. Something simple.

JACK HAD A BUSY MORNING—for an unemployed person.

At eight o'clock sharp he called the senior features editor at *Maclean's* magazine and left a message, being certain to mention that he was this year's Gobey winner. Might as well milk that for whatever it was worth. Then he placed calls to five other editors, ranking them in order of preference. Somebody, he knew, would bite.

With no option to call Marty, he then called Sheldon Crane, whose office was next to his at the *Satellite,* and asked him to check both his e-mail and his regular mail slot. There were no messages or letters, Sheldon confirmed. In other words, no job offers.

Jack didn't know if he was disappointed or relieved.

Next, he called Valmont Developments at its Kelowna head-quarters and booked an interview with some guy named Matt Caldwell. He sounded like your typical corporate executive: ed-ucated, slick and under the gun. Three o'clock tomorrow after-noon was the earliest time he could manage it. Jack had hoped for an earlier appointment, but it was no big deal. It left him the morning to get other work done.

Plan-related work.

As he was ending that call, his phone rang again and he made the mistake of answering it without checking the call display. Next thing he knew, he was at the Jackson house, replacing three washers and tightening up all their loose doorknobs.

Loose doorknobs. He was starting to feel like one himself.

After that he settled into a very pleasant midday with Sarah. He helped her catalogue her antiques, and she helped him to se-lect some new clothes at Morton's Men's Wear on Main Street. Jack didn't need help to buy clothes, but she got a kick out of it, so why not? They followed that venture up with lunch at Cora's Café. What a thrill it was when their togetherness raised eye-brows throughout the restaurant. Looking around, Jack thought, *I've been in town just three days and already I've been seen with its two most beautiful babes. Beat that!*

Sarah *was* beautiful. She was smart and quick-witted, too—like her daughter. If Sally was anything like her mother at that age... Well, there was no sense in going there.

As they were parting ways at her car, Sarah took his hand in both of hers and thanked him for everything.

"My pleasure," he told her sincerely. "Thanks for your help, too."

She bit her lower lip, a habit she shared with Sally. "Jack, I probably shouldn't be saying this, but Sally seems awfully fond of you. I just wanted to say that...please... Well, I can understand why, that's all."

From the look on her face and the way she'd stumbled over her words, it was clear to Jack that she really wanted to say: *Please don't hurt my daughter.* He mumbled something and nodded. Stupid.

Finally they parted ways and he headed for the *Post.* As he cruised slowly down Main Street, a few people waved hello to him and he waved back. Some of these folks he was starting to recognize. For sure, they all knew him.

As he eased into a parking space two doors away from the *Post,* Tawny Trubble approached the car. "Jack, I heard about what happened yesterday. Congratulations! Imagine getting those bone-headed farmers to talk civilly to one another. What a coup."

"Thanks, Tawny. Ah, where did you hear about it?"

"I got it from Ted Axton, who got it from Elvira Jackson, who got it from Trish Thomas. Before that, who knows?"

Ted Axton? Who was that? "It was nothing, Tawny. Really."

"Nothing? I heard you had to burn down a shed just to get their attention."

Jack chuckled. So it was true what Sally had said. Two storytellers, two stories. Stay tuned.

Without bothering to set the record straight, he wished Tawny a nice day and went into the *Post.* Charlie was standing on a chair, adjusting a crooked picture on the wall, high above his head. Upon seeing Jack, his eyes widened and his hand automatically flew to the middle of his back. "Oh, oh, the pain!"

Jack made the appropriate clucking noises. "Charlie, in your condition you shouldn't be doing that. Here, let me give you a hand."

Charlie frowned as Jack dumped the files from Peachtown Hall on one of the office's empty desks, then helped him get down. A worse acting job Jack had never seen. Good thing the faker had some reporting skills.

"A man can't just sit around and do nothing," Charlie grumbled.

Yeah, especially when there's nothing wrong with him, Jack thought as he helped him ease down onto a chair. Jack took his own seat and got right down to business. "Charlie, it's my turn to ask for a favor."

"Ah, sure. Go right ahead."

"I want you to let me work here on Sally's story—this afternoon, tomorrow morning and all day Thursday. But I want Sally to think I'm working for you."

The man who was never going to win an Oscar took a moment to digest that. "But...I thought you were in town to work on her story. I mean, isn't that what you're *supposed* to be doing?"

"Yup. And it's what I'm going to be doing. I just don't want her to know about it."

"May I ask why?"

"No. You wouldn't believe me if I told you."

Charlie rubbed his hands together and bared all three hundred of his teeth. Slowly he shook his head from side to side. "Well now, Jack, I don't see as how I could *intentionally* deceive a person that way."

Jack worked very hard to keep a straight face. "I understand perfectly, Charlie. You're a man with principles, a man with integrity. I wouldn't want to compromise you in any way. Let's just say that it would be our little secret."

"You wouldn't tell Sally?"

"No, and I need you to promise me that you won't tell her, either."

From the glint of his eye, Jack could tell that Charlie was busy working up a counterproposal. As the second sneakiest person in town, he probably felt obligated to come up with something.

"I've got a better idea," he said right on cue. "If you were actually working for me, there'd be no need for secrets, would there?"

"That's true, but then I wouldn't be able to get my own work done."

"Oh, I don't have anything big in mind. No, sir. Just one little thing. There's a meeting of the revitalization committee this afternoon at four. Shouldn't run more than two hours." Grimacing, Charlie leaned forward on his chair. "Frankly, I can't go more than twenty, maybe thirty, minutes with old Stone...er, with Elvira Jackson. So, if you could see your way toward covering it, I think I could do you that little favor."

Okay, that wasn't too bad. It was only one o'clock now. Jack would still have three hours to review the files and maybe even write a few paragraphs. At this point, they'd be out of context, but that didn't matter. He often worked that way. And he had planned to attend the meeting anyway.

"Charlie, I think we have a deal."

The men shook hands.

"Course, you might have to help out a little around here, too." Charlie added. "You know, with the phones and whatnot."

Jack dared not ask for a definition of whatnot. "I can help out a little, but that's all. Okay?"

As far as Charlie was concerned, that was perfectly okay. As he turned back to his own work, Jack opened a file and began to read.

Two hours later he wrote his first word.

12

STUPID, STUPID, STUPID.

She could have picked something simple, like she'd planned to do. But noooooo, Sally had to pick lasagna, a dish for which no recipe could be found in Tilly's Rolodex. In her teens she had helped the cook make her tasty version of the dish dozens of times, apparently from memory. Sally remembered the ingredients, but now she couldn't recall how Tilly had cooked them, or for how long, or in what order.

Confidence. Sometimes it got her in trouble.

Sadly, Tuesday was Tilly's night off, to attend her church group. And there was no point in asking Sarah for help. She'd refused to learn how to cook "on principle." As for Trish, she couldn't broil a steak without the fire department having to be called.

So, with Jack on the way, Sally stood helpless in her kitchen, up to her ears in ground beef and tomatoes and spinach and peppers and onions and mushrooms and cheeses and pasta, wondering what to do first. The sauce. Maybe she should make it first. Or the noodles. How long would they take? Did the veggies have to be cooked before they went into the casserole? Or did they cook inside it? Who knew?

Aha! The Internet knew.

Two years ago, Sally had installed a home computer in her living room, for those long, boring Friday nights when she didn't have a date. Heading toward it now, she paused to fluff up her sofa pillows and rearrange a few ornaments. Earlier she'd cleaned the room like never before. She'd even vacuumed under the sofa where, let's face it, no one ever went. The kitchen and bathroom had gotten a good scrubbing, too. The bedroom she'd left alone. Why bother?

No sooner had she called up a recipe than the Mustang pulled up at her front door. Darn. She barely had time to get off-line before Jack knocked, then let himself in anyway. Rising to greet him, Sally did a double-take. In leather sandals, baggy white cotton pants and a matching short-sleeved shirt, he looked like a Calvin Klein model.

What a hunk!

Amused, she looked him over as if she were considering purchasing him. "My, my. It seems all the women in the valley get their turn at dressing you."

He grinned from ear to ear, and Sally knew a zinger was coming. "It's true, but I'm only interested in the ones that want to undress me."

She nodded her approval. "Not bad, hotshot. Not bad at all. But you're not half the wit you think you are. Or is it the half-wit I know you are? Help me out."

They shared a laugh, then faltered. Jack was waiting for something, and Sally knew just what it was. She put her hands on her hips and issued a sigh. "You know what, Jack? I'm tired of hurling myself at you like some brain-damaged harlot. You could take the initiative, you know."

Laughing, he opened his arms and she walked into them. "Hey, you're good with words. I like that in a harlot."

"So kiss me then."

"Just one question. If I take the initiative, do you score a point? 'Cause I think I'm getting seriously behind in our little game."

Sally played dumb. "What little game?"

Jack shook his head and chuckled. "Sally, Sally, Sally."

They kissed then, sweetly, lightly. To say hello.

"So." Rubbing his hands together, Jack began to move

around the room. "Are you ready to... Wait a minute. Did you clean up in here?"

"As a matter of fact I did." Sally made a sweeping gesture, as if she were showcasing appliances on *The Price is Right*.

"It looks great, Sally, but I hope you didn't go to the trouble just for me."

Trouble? He didn't know the half of it. Sally eyed the computer. Would it be crass to call up that recipe again? Did a good wife need a search engine? Oops. Too late. Jack was in the kitchen, fingering packages.

"What's going on here?" he called out. "What is all this stuff?"

Maybe they could eat out. There were some very good restaurants on the road to Kelowna. "Nothing, Jack. Just some things I needed to stock up on."

Looking more than a little amused, he filled the doorway between the two rooms. "Were you by any chance attempting to make lasagna?"

Sally bared her teeth. "Do you think I could?"

"No. I'll bet my life savings that you can't boil an egg."

"Eggs are boiled?"

Jack squeezed his eyes shut and pointed behind him. "Get in here and help me. And be humble about it. A person who's never boiled an egg barely qualifies as a galley slave."

Relieved beyond words, Sally positioned herself at the big wooden chopping block in the center of her kitchen and awaited orders. Jack, who actually looked like a chef in those all-white clothes, set his cell phone down on the counter, slipped on one of Tilly's froufrou aprons and began to organize the various food items into categories.

Sally was dazzled. "Please tell me, Jack, that you are not, in addition to everything else, a gourmet cook."

"No. That would be my father. But you should be ashamed of yourself. Even a monkey can make a half-decent lasagna." He found a sharp knife and waved it in front of her. "Can you be trusted with this?"

"I honestly don't know."

"It's time you found out." He set the veggies down in front of her. "Slice these fairly thin, then wash them thoroughly. Did you buy garlic and onions?"

"Of course, silly." Sally looked around for them, but Jack found them first. While she eyed the mushrooms for some clue as to how they should be sliced, he placed the never-used wok she'd won at a county fair raffle on the big gas burner and fired it up.

Sally fell five degrees more in love. A man who knew his way around a kitchen was definitely her kind of man!

Jack looked over the food. "Did you buy olive oil?" His expression suggested that an omission of that magnitude would not go unpunished.

"In there." Proudly, Sally pointed toward a cupboard. She did have olive oil, thank you very much. She used it to condition her hair.

Jack emptied a little of it into the wok and set the bottle aside. "Okay, let's begin the interview. I've got lots of questions for you, but they're not in any particular order. First up, I know you have two brothers. Why are they so much older than you?"

"Uh-uh, not so fast, hotshot. I'm doing this only on one condition."

He stopped moving about and looked at her as if she were drunk. "Condition?"

"Yes, just one little condition." Sally grinned. *"Quid pro quo."*

When Jack's jaw hit the floor, a jolt of pleasure surged through her. Surprising him was too much fun. She could thrive on it for the rest of her life.

"I give you something—you give me something?" He shook his head firmly. "Ohhhhhhh, no, Sunshine, that's not how this works. I'm the interviewer here, and you are the interviewee.

Got it?'' He set about mincing the onions and garlic and motioned for her to stop dillydallying and finish her own task.

Slicing away, Sally considered her rebuttal. Under normal circumstances, Jack would be right. He, the reporter, would ask questions and she, the source, would answer them. But there was nothing normal about a reporter and a source who were involved in a story *and* engaged in negotiations to tear one another's clothes off.

"I beg to differ, Jack. You said we should get to know one another. What better opportunity will we have?"

He tossed the garlic and onions into the wok and cast her a presumptuous little smirk. "What's your hurry, Sunshine? We have all the time in the world."

Arghhh! "If you ask me that one more time, Jack Gold, I will throttle you."

He laughed. "I give. You're absolutely right. Now answer my question."

"Okay. Daniel is eight years older than me, and David is ten years older. Mom and Dad didn't plan for more children. Mom calls me her bonus baby, which is sweet, but really I was a mistake." Sally spooned the veggies she'd sliced nearly to death into the strainer, and took it to the sink.

Jack wiped his hands on Tilly's apron and, taking her by surprise, put his arms around her from behind. He kissed the top of her head. "Some mistake."

Omigod, who *was* this guy? Three short days ago she would never have believed Jack capable of being this open and playful. She nestled into him, loving the feel of his strong arms around her, and his warm, firm body against her back. "Tell me something. Since when do reporters kiss their sources? I heard there was no kissing in journalism."

"Yeah, well, there's no lasagna in it, either." Jack kissed her again, then released her. Sally watched him toss the veggies into the wok, then add the tomatoes and tomato paste. He lowered the heat. "Have you got any spices?"

"Spices?"

"Yeah, you know. Gritty looking things that come in little glass jars? They tend to be different colors."

Certain she had something somewhere that fit that description, Sally rummaged in several drawers and cupboards. Finally she found an unopened box of spices given to her by a former boyfriend. Poor fool. *He* never got to taste them.

"Hey, at least these will be fresh," Jack joked. He unsealed the box and peered inside it.

Sally clapped her hands. "Okay. It's my turn to ask a question now. I'll start with something simple."

"What do you mean by 'start with'?"

"Never you mind. Question—how come you're so handy? Frankly, hotshot, you don't look like the type."

"That's easy. I grew up on military bases. Those houses are old and mostly in poor repair. My father can't handle a screwdriver, so somebody had to learn." Jack opened three bottles of spice and, after sniffing them all, sprinkled some of each into the sauce.

"Okay. Next question. Do you have any siblings?"

"Hey, it's not your turn." Jack dug into a lower cupboard, coming up with a pot that Sally didn't even know she owned. He thrust it toward her. "It's time now for Princess to learn how to boil water. Fill this about half-full."

Sally drew a sharp breath. "I resemble that remark!"

"You're right. You do resemble it."

As a wonderful odor rose up from the wok, they locked eyes across the chopping block. Never had Sally been so comfortable with a man. And never had she allowed a man to take such liberties with her. Calling her a princess—what nerve! It was true, of course, and every man she'd dated knew it, but until now no idiot had risked her wrath by saying so.

She took a risk of her own. "I like you, Jack."

He shrugged in a boyish way. "I like you, too."

They froze. It wasn't much, but it was their boldest spoken

declaration of interest so far, and neither of them had a clue what came next. They had a growing intimacy, sure, but aside from the kissing rule its current boundaries weren't clear. *Did* they kiss now? Did they embrace? Did they clear the chopping block and replay that famous seduction scene from *The Postman Always Rings Twice?*

That would have been Sally's preference!

Instead, she filled the pot half-full with water, as ordered, and put it to boil on the stove. "I think it's your turn to ask a question, Jack."

He found a frying pan and dumped the ground beef into it. "Okay. Why are you serving on the town council? You're awfully young to be interested in politics."

"Sarah held that seat for twenty years, but she lost interest in it two years ago, so I ran for election. To be perfectly honest, Jack, I think I won mostly because I'm her daughter. I was keen, though. I mean, how else can you make a difference? Most people complain about politics, but don't bother to do anything about it."

Jack stirred the meat. "Good answer. I like a source who gives a good interview. But why aren't you shredding that cheese over there? You're the laziest galley slave I've ever abused."

Idly, Sally wondered just how many of those he had abused. But deep down she didn't care one whit about Jack's past. Her desire to know whether or not he had a girlfriend back home had subsided. Of course he didn't. If he did, why would he be kissing her?

"Okay," Jack said as she examined the cheese grater for buttons or levers or other complications. "Your turn. But keep it clean, okay?"

"Whatever. I repeat—do you have any siblings?"

"No. I had an identical twin brother, but he died."

Sally gasped. There were *two* of this man? Oh God, the world was a sadder place for that loss. "Died how, Jack?"

"Time's up. One question per person."

What an ogre!

Watching her shred—okay, mangle—the cheese, Jack shook his head sadly. "Pitiful, just pitiful. My turn again. Why do you care so much about this valley? I know why, but I need it in your words."

Sally had no trouble finding them. "This is my place. These are my people. What more can I say?"

"That's plenty. Okay, it's your turn again."

Blushing a little, Sally kept her eyes downcast and asked the one question she was dying to ask. "Did you do any work on my story today?" Out of the corner of her eye, she saw Jack smile.

"Not a lot, I'm afraid. I fixed a few things for Elvira and then I ended up working for Charlie again."

Arghhh! Charlie and Elvira—the two-headed monster of the valley. If she'd had any other choice, Sally would never have brought them into this!

She finished with the cheese and washed her hands. "What, pray tell, did you do for Charlie?"

"It's not your turn to ask a question, but I'll make this one exception."

"Thank you, Your Benevolence."

"No groveling, please. If you must know, I covered the revitalization committee meeting for him and, ah, whatnot. You know."

Sally didn't know. She didn't want to know. As much as she hated the prospect of losing Jack to the *Post* every day, she had no choice but to tolerate it. It was good for the long run—for Charlie and for her. But in the short run, what about her story? What about her libido? When, exactly, *were* they going to bed?

The water came to a boil and Jack slid the pasta into it. "This'll take about twelve minutes." He looked around. "Got any wine?"

Darn! Sally had forgotten to buy some, and lasagna without a robust red was just unthinkable. Hmm, it was seven-thirty. Tilly was off, but Andy might still be in the main house. Sally called, and sure enough, he was there, helping Sarah with the dinner dishes. He promised to bring a bottle down as soon as they were done.

Sally watched Jack drain the fat off the meat, then mix it in with the sauce. He stirred it and lowered the flame. "This can simmer until the pasta is ready. Why don't we take a short break?"

Wordlessly, they strolled out of the cottage and onto the patio. It was incredible, Sally thought, how much they enjoyed talking to one another, yet how little communication they seemed to need. Until now she'd never had a relationship with a man that wasn't all mixed messages and awkward pauses or, worse, long, excruciating silences. Dean and Sarah's easy love was the only thing that had sustained her belief in something better.

Oh wow, what a revelation! If their parents didn't have it, how could children expect to find happiness? Their children— hers and Jack's—would always know that joy was possible.

Their children? Whew, now *that* was confidence.

It wasn't extravagant confidence, though. With each passing day there was less likelihood that Jack would be leaving, even if he was offered a job in some exotic place. After all, what could be better than her?

He leaned against the patio rail. "God, it's hot. I don't know how you stand it."

Happier than she could ever remember being, Sally rested her back against his chest and drew his arms around her again. She'd liked that. A lot. "I truly cannot stand it anymore. I'd give everything I have for one day of rain."

Jack kissed her hair. "Okay. Next question. What's your favorite childhood memory?"

"That's easy." Sally gestured toward her digs. "I'm sure you've already figured out that this is the guest cottage. Anyway, Trish and I used to play house here. We kept our doll collections and all our little tea dishes and things here. I have fond memories of that.''

"Some playhouse!"

Sally rolled her eyes. "I know. Don't say it. Only a spoiled princess would have one this big."

"No kidding. Okay, it's your turn again."

"I meant to ask you this before. The other day, you said you were accused of bad behavior after winning the Gobey. What exactly did you do, hotshot?"

"Nothing, really. I asked for a raise. That's standard with Gobey winners. And I asked for a corner office. That's not standard but, hey, there was one available."

Sally was appalled. "That was it?"

"Well, I may have requested a few other little perks."

"Like?"

"Like deli delivery service at lunchtime. And a heated parking space."

Pickles on demand? Heat for the Mustang? Sally cracked up. "Oh, Jack, you're funny." She turned and put her arms around his neck. They kissed a little.

"Your turn," she reminded him.

His eyes traveled from hers to her mouth and back again. "Okay. Got a man in your life?"

"What's that got to do with my story?"

"Does that count as *your* next question?"

"Does that count as your next question?"

"I've already asked mine."

Sally sighed. "Jack Gold, would I be hurling myself at you if I had a man in my life?"

He shook his head. "I don't mean somebody serious. I just mean, you know, somebody you date casually, on Saturday nights. Somebody you go to the movies with, and to dinner."

Sally was a firm believer in not telling a man what he didn't need to know. But in this case, there was nothing to tell anyway. "Not right now."

They kissed a little more.

"It's your turn again." Jack tucked a loose strand of hair behind her ear. "But I'm warning you. I won't be impressed if you're predictable."

Predictable? There was no reason for Sally to ask if he had a woman in his life. Of course he didn't. "How did your twin brother die?"

"For a long time, we didn't know. Then it was diagnosed as sudden infant death syndrome. Not much was known about it at that time."

"Oh, how sad!"

Briefly, Jack closed his eyes. "Tell me about it. They named him Jason, and I can't explain it, but I've felt his absence my whole life. Something is missing." He cradled Sally's head in both his hands and looked deep into her eyes. "I needed...I need a soul mate."

"Me, too," she whispered just before his mouth smothered hers. Her stomach fluttered and a wild throbbing started between her legs. For the love of God, if they didn't make love soon, she would go mad!

"We should check on that pasta," Jack murmured into her hair.

Several kisses later, Sally floated back to the kitchen, hugging herself every step of the way. Life was wonderful! Until this beautiful man had come along, she hadn't really been living at all—just maintaining. Waiting, she now knew, for her real life to begin. And now that it was here, it was fabulous!

Humming softly, she stirred the sauce and checked the pasta. Hmm, it wasn't quite done. Good! There was time for more necking.

Jack's cell phone rang.

"Hey!" he called to her from outside. "Grab that, Sally. It might be important."

She flipped the thing open and pulled out its tiny antenna. "Hello," she said just as Jack appeared. She blew a kiss at him.

"Hello," a husky female voice replied. "Is Jack there?"

"Yes. May I tell him who's calling?"

"You can tell him it's Liz Montaine. If you like, you can also remind him that we had a date tonight."

"ANDY, TAKE THAT WINE BACK. We won't be needing it."

Once again, Tilly's kitchen helper stood wide-eyed and bewildered at the front door. Jack was starting to feel sorry for the kid. "Don't listen to her," he said over Sally's shoulder. "We will be needing it."

The boy glanced between them. Jack was still wearing Tilly's frilly apron. Sally's pink lipstick was smeared across his mouth, and hers. "If you don't mind, Mr. Gold, you seem very, ah, nice, but I work for her."

"Don't we all? I'll tell you what. Just leave it outside the door."

"Take it back!" Fuming, Sally brushed Jack aside and stomped off. He took the bottle from Andy and silently mouthed his thanks.

In the kitchen he found Miss All Steamed Up attempting to trim a layer of pasta so it would fit into the bottom of the casserole dish. Jack choked back a howl. He didn't know which was funnier—her utter lack of culinary skill, or her straight-from-the-gut reaction to Liz's untimely call.

Embarrassed, she refused to look at him.

"Sally," he insisted for the second time. "She is not my girlfriend."

She went on snipping. "It's okay, Jack. Honestly. I understand. The people I casually date always call me long-distance, too."

Oh, now that wasn't fair. "Gimme a break. We were supposed to go to a gallery opening tonight. I forgot about it, that's all."

"A gallery opening. How civilized."

"Yes, we go to openings. We go to the theatre. We go to parties. That's what she likes to do."

Sally almost nicked herself with the scissors.

"Here, let me help you with that." Gently, Jack took them away from her before she could hurt herself seriously—or kill him. She stepped aside and folded her arms, a defensive gesture if ever he'd seen one.

"Liz is not my girlfriend," Jack repeated. "She is someone I see once in a while. She's a nice lady. She's also a rich, spoiled trust-fund baby who likes to be seen with famous people. She thinks I'm going to be famous, and that's her only interest in me."

"Humph, and I suppose you have no interest in her."

"Hey, I'm thirty-four. I'm single. I date. That doesn't mean I'm committed to anybody."

Sally had no response to that.

As much as he wanted to be sensitive, Jack just couldn't take her seriously. First of all, he didn't have any feelings for Liz. He'd never had any. Secondly, he just couldn't abide a rupture in his relationship with Sally. Time wasted on this kind of nonsense? No way.

"Sally, Liz and I don't date exclusively. We are not an item. Got it?"

She sniffed in that snooty way she had, and looked out the window.

Now that he had the scissors, Jack took the risk of nudging her gently in the side. "I think you're jealous, Ms. Darville."

"I think you're full of yourself."

"I think you want me all for yourself."

"I think you're dreaming."

"I think jealousy is a stupid waste of time, Sally. People who care about one another never do or say anything to cause it. That's what I think."

Finally, she looked him in the eye. "Are you suggesting that you and I care about one another? Because to use your turn of phrase, the last time I checked, we didn't have a contractual relationship that included caring.''

Once again, Jack marveled at her particular genius. Nobody could fish with quite the finesse that Sally Darville could. He didn't bite, though. "C'mon, galley slave. Start ladling that sauce over these noodles. We're going to have a nice dinner, you and me, with wine, and we're going to continue our interview. Then I'm going to kiss you until your eyes turn inside out. After that I'm going to go home and have a cold shower, like I do every night. Okay?''

Silence.

"Okay, Sally?''

Grudgingly, she laughed. "A cold shower?''

13

IF THERE WAS one thing Jack knew for sure—and, let's face it, by Wednesday morning there *was* only one thing he knew for sure—it was this: he was happy.

Peering out the window of the *Post*'s office, he considered the lunacy of it.

He had lost a fabulous job. He had no job offers—at least none that Sheldon had found in his mail yesterday or again this morning. He had a terrific story on his hands, but so far no publisher. He was living in a one-vintage-car town, in someone else's home, with an alcoholic parrot. Against all odds he was back working for a weekly newspaper, like some pimple-faced apprentice.

If all that wasn't enough, he was also the harried, on-call handyman for a holy terror nicknamed Stonewall. He was afraid to lose sight of his car. He had a jealous blonde on his hands, and her friends were some of the most devious people he'd ever met.

And yet, he was happy.

Strolling down Main Street, chatting with people, made him happy—even if some of them thought he'd tied Evan Pratford to a chair.

Tooling around town in the Mustang made him happy—even if he had to keep an eye out for those pesky twins.

Hell, even those nightly cold showers made him happy—or, at least, relieved. A man couldn't go through life with a permanent erection.

The jealous blonde had a lot to do with it. Idly, Jack wondered if a man could fall in love with a woman in just a few days. He didn't believe in love at first sight. Lust, yeah. Always lust. But love evolved over time, didn't it? Frankly he didn't know. Right now he only knew what he felt.

He most certainly did not believe in jealousy. It was irrational and hurtful. But, say what you liked, it was also a reliable means by which to gauge a person's interest in you. People who didn't care deeply for one another didn't get jealous. That was a fact.

So, while he'd give anything for Liz's call not to have come at all, Jack was secretly thrilled by Sally's over-the-top reaction to it. It meant she had feelings for him, too. It meant that he wasn't, as he'd speculated earlier, just a pleasant diversion for her.

Not in the least did he blame her for being upset. The way they'd been carrying on these past few days—if he'd had a woman waiting for him back home, what would that have said about him? That he couldn't be true to one person? In point of fact, Jack didn't know whether he could or not. He'd never stuck around long enough to find out.

He was starting to think he could, though. Be true. To one woman. Forever. And not just because it was expected, either, but because with the right woman it would be perfectly natural. Sally, he was pretty sure, was that woman.

He also was starting to think she might change her mind about staying in Peachtown. Yes, she had family and friends here. Yes, this was her home. And maybe Jack didn't fully understand what that meant. As a kid, he'd lived all over the country. Home didn't mean a thing to him. But if Sally loved him, and he was confident she did, wouldn't home be wherever he was? Wherever they were together?

Anyway, it was way too soon to broach the subject. Hell, they hadn't even had a real date yet.

Sally Sunshine. She was the first thing he thought about every morning now, and the last thing he thought about at

night. As messy as things were, Jack couldn't deny the truth—
she made him happy like nobody before. Take last night. Once
they'd gotten past Liz, they'd had a great time. Eating. Drink-
ing. Talking and laughing. Sally hadn't been as affectionate as
usual, but that was okay. Their intimacy had been threatened,
and she needed time to reestablish it. Jack understood that.

They understood one another. Easily.

As for those devious friends of hers...

Jack closed his laptop—he couldn't concentrate anyway—
and eavesdropped as Charlie spoke on the phone to an adver-
tiser whose bill was overdue. Jack had forgotten how hectic a
weekly paper could be. Phones ringing off the wall. Couriers
coming and going. People dropping in just to chat. The dailies
had clerical assistants who formed a barricade against intru-
sions. Here, there was no shield.

"When are your staff reporters due back?" he asked when
Charlie, disgruntled and grumbling, was finally off the phone.

Charlie scratched his head. "Well now, that was sort of left
open, Jack. See, one's getting married, and the other's on, ah..."

"Vacation. Yeah, you mentioned that. I'm surprised you let
them go at the same time."

For some reason, Charlie was instantly nervous. Jack was
starting to recognize the signs. A tic. A clearing of the throat. A
rubbing together of the hands. A tendency to chuckle under his
breath while dodging eye contact. Without getting off his chair,
the man chewed up all the scenery around him.

Charlie shrugged. "Oh, well, summertime and all. You
know."

Okay, that made sense. Most people got married and took
their vacations during the hot months. Speaking of which...
Wiping fine beads of sweat off his brow, Jack went over to have
another go at Charlie's ancient, window-mounted air conditioner. The rusty old beater made a lot of noise in exchange for
very little cold air. He banged it a few times, then cursed at it,

like Charlie did. "I think this thing's had it. Maybe you should buy a new one."

"I'm afraid there's no budget for that."

Funny thing, every time Jack suggested an upgrade, which was once an hour, Charlie said there was no money for it. "I don't understand. Why don't you just requisition the chain for a new one?"

Charlie's bushy brows went up. "Chain?"

"Yeah. The chain that owns this paper."

"Son, I own this paper."

For a second Jack thought he had misheard the man. In all of Canada only a handful of newspapers were independently owned and operated, and those existed only because their owners were too proud or too stubborn to sell out. "You're kidding, right?"

"'Fraid not, son. I bought it in '78 and I've owned it ever since."

Jack looked around the office with new eyes. Wow, such freedom! With no big machine controlling it, a newspaper could be pretty much whatever it wanted to be.

Clutching his back and groaning, Charlie got up and poured himself a glass of filtered water. "Yeah, well, that freedom comes at a price. When things break down, the repairs come straight out of my pocket. Thanks to this damn economy, there's no new revenue coming in my door. And I don't have to tell you what's happened to the price of paper in recent years."

Energized suddenly—pent-up sperm, no doubt—Jack perched on the edge of his desk and picked up last week's copy of the *Post*. He flipped through it. "What you said the other day, about this being a good paper? You're right, Charlie, but it could be so much more. You ever think about going regional?"

"Sure, I have. But for that you need stringers. I haven't got the cash to hire them, and I'm too old to run around the countryside. In fact..."

Jack looked up from the paper. "In fact, what?"

"In fact, I'm retiring in a couple of months."

"Really? Have you got a buyer?"

Charlie grinned. "Yeah. You."

What? Jack shook his head. "Ohhhh, no, Charlie. I'm not your man. I won't even be here two months from now."

The look Charlie gave him then suggested that Jack was, if not the most naive fool he'd ever met, then a pretty close second. Come to think of it, everybody around here looked at him that way. On the drive to town this morning, he'd stopped in, on demand of course, to patch up a broken window for Elvira. When Jack had delicately suggested that she get herself a houseboy who didn't *mind* working with his shirt off, she'd given him the very same look. "Oh, Jack," she'd said with a dismissive wave. "You have no idea who you're dealing with, do you?"

Maybe Jack didn't know. Maybe these people were pulling the wool over his eyes, one blinding strand at a time. Regardless, he wasn't going to squander his career the way Charlie had done. Not for love or money or a ticket straight to heaven.

As if they'd just struck an agreement, Charlie said, "You know, this drought won't last forever, Jack. The economy will improve, and when the time comes to expand, you can always borrow money from the Jackson sisters. They've offered many times."

"Charlie, I am not..." Jack blinked. "The Jacksons have money?"

The worst actor in history reacted as if he might have just made a serious boo-boo, but wasn't sure. "Ah, yeah. Didn't you know that?"

"No. I thought they were poor."

The air resonated with confusion.

"Speak to me, Charlie."

"Well...they're not *exactly* poor. They have land holdings all over the valley—residential and commercial. They've got business investments here and in the states. Mineral rights. Oil and gas stocks. Canada Savings Bonds. Probably other stuff, too."

Jack closed his eyes and chuckled. Naive? He was the international poster boy for ignorance.

Two identical faces suddenly appeared in the window overlooking Main Street. "Jack," one of the Trubble twins shouted through the glass. "Can we take the Mustang for a spin?"

"No!" he told them for the second time that morning. "Get lost!"

"See, I told you so," the one who'd spoken said to the other. They got into a scuffle, then took off running.

Charlie picked up a photo and examined it. "Anyway, don't be hasty, Jack. It's a good opportunity. Think it over."

Ready and eager to work again, Jack flipped his laptop open and reached for the notes from Sally's interview. There was nothing to think about.

Nothing except her.

EVERY WEDNESDAY since they'd come home from university Sally and Trish met for lunch at Cora's Café. This time Sally was surprised to see her mom and Arlene Sacks at the table as well. Surprised and alarmed.

She slid into the booth, beside Arlene. "How nice to see all of you! I can't stay long, though. Jack and I are going to Kelowna to meet with whoever's in charge at Valmont these days."

"Mmm," Sarah said.

"How nice," Arlene intoned.

Trish said nothing at all.

Sally eyed them curiously. They were acting like a bunch of well-meaning but determined conspirators. "Is this another intervention, ladies? Because I told you, I've got that little chocolate problem under control. I haven't touched the stuff since April. I swear."

Trish cleared her throat. "This isn't about chocolate, Sal. It's about Jack."

"What about Jack? Is he okay? Is something wrong?" Oh God, if anything ever happened to him...

Arlene touched Sally's arm. "Jack is fine. It's you we're concerned about."

"Me? Why? I've never been better!"

"Sally," she began cautiously. "We'll come right to the point. We're worried that you're falling in love with Jack, and that you may be headed for heartbreak."

Sally glared at Trish. "Why do I think this was your idea?"

Trish didn't bother to contradict her. "Sally, we'd all like nothing more than for Jack to stick around here. Even me. I admit I misjudged the guy. But you're not leaving here with him. You told me that. So what happens when he leaves?"

These were the smartest women in town, Trish especially, and while she didn't necessarily act on it, Sally always considered their advice. But they were dead wrong about this. "Jack isn't going anywhere. I've got the situation under control."

The women clammed up as Cora set four caesar salads on the table—their usual. Sally looked up just in time to catch Cora wink at her. Duh, what was that about?

Oozing concern, Sarah reached across the table and covered Sally's hands with her own. "I'm sure you think you do, sweetie. Jack seems very taken with you. And heaven knows we..." She giggled. "Well, *I* am very fond of him, too. But Peachtown doesn't seem like his kind of place." She squeezed Sally's hands. "My personal fear is that you'll lose your head and run off with him."

"Don't be silly, Mom! I would never leave you. I would never leave *home*. And Jack's not leaving, either."

"Sweetie, I'm the neutral person here. I'm not sure what to think, but Trish and Arlene both think you're being overconfident."

"That's absurd. I'm not confident at all. I'm...optimistic."

Trish leaned forward and arched her brows. "Sal, Ghengis Khan was optimistic."

Sally sighed. This was sweet, but so unnecessary. "You don't understand, any of you. I know Jack will stay. He wants to be with me as much as I want to be with him." Ravenous suddenly, she dug into her salad. Only forty more minutes of this and she *would* be with him again.

Arlene tried reason, Sally's least favorite approach to anything. "Has he come right out and said he wants to stay in Peachtown?"

That gave Sally a moment's pause. Since dinner with the Jackson sisters couldn't be counted as a real date, Jack hadn't even asked her out yet. "Well, no, not in so many words."

The women exchanged a look.

"The reason I ask," Arlene continued, "is that Charlie talked to him this morning about the possibility of taking over the *Post* and, frankly, Sally, Jack wasn't interested."

What? Terrific. Charlie had already shown his hand. That was what happened, Sally knew, when you let rank amateurs into the game. Obviously she should have taken charge of that situation.

She shrugged. "So? Maybe he'll do something else." That was nonsense and she knew it. Jack was born to be a journalist. People like him didn't abandon their true calling for anyone— not even her.

Sarah dabbed at her lips with a napkin. "Sweetie, when is Jack supposed to go back to Vancouver?"

"I'm not sure. Sometime next week, after my story is written." Sally didn't care for this line of questioning. No one knew that Jack had lost his job, or that they didn't have a publisher. For now, they had agreed, that was best.

Arlene got the last word. "If he does leave, Sally, know that we're here to help you pick up the pieces."

Oh, how nice. "Thank you, ladies. I appreciate your support. But I promise you there won't be any pieces to pick up."

At Sally's insistence they talked about other things for a while, but she could tell they were consumed by worry for her.

Finally Trish looked at her watch. "I have to dash. The twins relocated someone's car this morning, then someone else actually stole it. There may be trouble."

Laughing, Arlene and Sarah also collected their purses to leave. Arlene needed groceries, she joked as Sally let her out of the booth, to help Charlie maintain his figure. Sarah was off to Cranbrook to look at more antiques. She kissed Sally's cheek. "We love you, daughter."

"All of us," Trish echoed.

Sally was touched. How could she ever leave friends like this?

After they were gone she lingered for a while, gazing out the window at Main Street. For the first time since meeting Jack a doubt penetrated her armor. Until this very minute the possibility of him bolting had been unthinkable. But if the people she loved and respected most in the world thought otherwise, what did that say?

Was she too confident? All her life, she'd gotten exactly what she wanted. Sometimes she'd had to work harder for it than other times, but that was life. Now Sally wondered if what everyone said about her was true, that she was a sweet but spoiled princess with no boundaries.

Before that silly notion could grab hold, Cora approached the table with a wise, knowing smile. She bent down and spoke softly. "Honey, I couldn't help but overhear. Don't you listen to them. I saw the way that young man looked at you the other day. You don't have a thing to worry about."

Sally's heart soared. "You know what, Cora?"

"What, honey?"

"I just changed my mind about something."

"What's that?"

"*You're* the smartest woman in Peachtown!"

CRUISIN' DOWN the highway in a candy-apple-red 1968 Mustang convertible, on a hot summer afternoon, with the top down and Bruce Springsteen full-blast on the radio, the sun blazing overhead, and a gorgeous, if slightly bonkers, blonde at your side.

Did it get any better?

No sir, Jack thought as he beamed sideways at the blonde. She was a vision in red today. Red mini-dress—very mini. Red high-heeled sandals. Red shades that curled up at the corners. And, of course, the bright red lipstick that made her look like a sexy starlet.

The lipstick was a problem. At the last tourist look-out they'd stopped at, the cheeky blonde had unbuttoned his shirt in search of new territory for kisses. Now Jack had telltale traces of Raunchy Red all over his upper chest. Some had found their way onto the collar of his white shirt. The blonde, of course, was unrepentant.

His own little demented dairy princess. That was how he thought of her now. With a smile.

Traveling with her was like traveling with a twelve-year-old. She'd loaded the Mustang down with *stuff*: corned beef sandwiches on rye, pickles, olives, tubes of cheese, gooey pastries, boxes of caramel-coated popcorn. And that was just the food. She also had dice, crossword puzzles, *Trivial Pursuit* cards, you name it. At an old mom-and-pop general store, she'd purchased a bottle of pink liquid soap and a little hoop, through which she insisted on blowing bubbles at him, then laughing as if it was a great joke.

Between stops, their interview continued. "So," Jack shouted over Bruce. "What's the most offensive thing a boyfriend has ever said to you?"

"Oh, Jack, what a horrible question!" Sally complained. "How's that supposed to help us get to know one another better?"

"Humor me."

She thought it over. "No one's said anything really offensive.

No one would dare. But... You know what, Jack? I don't think I want to tell you this."

"Get over it."

"Oh, all right. One guy said I was too much of everything. You know. Too smart. Too pretty. Too opinionated."

Jack cocked one eyebrow. "Too sneaky?"

"No, silly." She swatted his arm. "He didn't say *that*."

They passed a sign announcing City of Kelowna, just ahead. Jack stole a glance at the tanned legs poking out from under Sally's dress. Those legs had been driving him wild for two hours. His fertile imagination kept following them under her hem to the place where ecstasy lived. From there it wandered over her flat tummy and small, undoubtedly perfect, breasts to the nape of her neck.

It begged to be tasted, that body. And soon.

"Okay, Sunshine, what's the nicest thing a man has ever said to you?"

She fed him a pickle. "Uh-uh, wait your turn, hotshot. And since you asked, what's the most offensive thing a girlfriend ever said to you?"

"Someone called me arrogant once. Can you believe that?"

Sally laughed in the light fanciful way that always warmed his heart. "You? I'm shocked."

Jack chuckled, too. At the same time he marveled at how much he had loosened up in just four days with Sally. Until now, he realized, he'd never really been himself with a woman. Maybe he hadn't known who that was.

"My turn again. I repeat: What's the nicest thing you've heard?"

A wind came up and Sally gathered her hair into a knot. "Well, men always tell me I'm pretty. But I don't care about that. Pretty is a gift. You don't have to work for it. So, I guess... Someone once said I was a principled person. That's important, don't you think?"

"It is important, and I've always tried to live by that." Jack grinned. "But I don't know about you, Sunshine. It's pretty unprincipled, don't you think, trying to seduce a man when he has no choice but to behave?"

"Oh, and the fight he puts up!"

Talking nonstop, they passed through endless suburbs and into the old part of the city, finally stumbling into Kelowna's central business district. Jack asked his sexy sidekick to double-check the address for Valmont Developments. Matt Caldwell had given him directions, but neither he nor Sally, as it turned out, could follow a map. After a few wrong turns and one dead end, they finally found the place.

Jack parked across the street from the old sandstone office building and ran around to open Sally's door. She expected it, along with a million other courtesies. He was happy to oblige.

"Kiss me," she demanded as they stood beside the car.

He was happy to do that, too.

Traffic sped past them at a dizzying rate. When an annoyed driver honked and shouted at them to get a room, they parted lips and ran, squealing like kids, across the street and into the building.

In the elevator Jack went into work mode and began to question the need for Sally's involvement in the upcoming interview. "Listen, if you like, you don't have to stay for this. It'll take about an hour and I'm afraid it won't be very interesting."

Sally nodded as if she'd already considered that. "I'll go in with you, then maybe I'll take a walk. My legs are stiff."

When Jack tried to step off the elevator onto the third floor, she cried, "Hold on a minute!" Jack caught his sorry reflection in a hall mirror as she wet a tissue and dabbed at his mouth with it. His lips were lightly smeared with Raunchy Red—just enough to raise eyebrows. Sally freshened her own lipstick and they went quietly down the hall.

Valmont Developments had the sad, stripped-down look of a company in bankruptcy. Half-full boxes of books and office supplies littered the reception area, and a bank of file cabinets stood open and empty. Artwork had been removed from the walls and stacked in a corner. Even the receptionist, a fortyish brunette with a permanent scowl, seemed to have one foot out the door.

"Matt will be with you in a minute," she announced. "I'd offer you coffee, but the pot is packed."

Sally seemed surprised. "Matt Caldwell? I thought he'd gone to another company."

The receptionist nodded. "He is going, but they persuaded him to stay on here until the trustee has completed the paperwork. As you can see, things are in a state around here."

Jack and Sally sat down to wait. "Do you know Matt Caldwell?" he asked her. There was something about the way she'd said the guy's name. Something...ominous.

"Uh-huh," she answered vaguely. "Sort of."

Jack eyed her curiously. Sally never gave a short answer when fifty words would do. Before he could press her, a tall, handsome, blond guy with a thousand-watt smile emerged from the adjacent office. He was nattily dressed—Jack noted the five-hundred-dollar shoes—and impeccably groomed. Sauntering toward them, he had eyes only for Sally.

Something shifted in Jack's gut.

"Sally Darville," the guy said. "What a lovely surprise. I had no idea you were coming."

Sally and Jack got to their feet, and then—talk about slick—the guy seized her right hand, turned it over and *kissed* her palm. Sally blushed a dozen shades of pink. "It's nice to see you, too, Matt. I had no idea you were still here."

Wondering just how long Matt—what a dumb name—intended to hold Sally's hand, Jack thrust his own out. "Jack Gold."

"Oh, yes," Matt sniffed. "The reporter."

And the man who's with Sally Darville, Jack thought. Don't forget *that*.

"Your name's familiar to me. Didn't you win a goober award, or something?"

"Actually it was the Gobey Award."

"Oh yeah, right."

They shook hands, but Matt, whom Jack was already starting to think of as Hollywood, couldn't peel his beady eyes off Sally. "Are you joining us for the interview? I sure hope so."

Jack breathed a sigh of relief when she declined the invitation in favor of a shopping spree. "I don't get to Kelowna very often, you know."

"Tell me about it! Say, when...ah, Jack is it?"

Yeah, it was Jack.

"When Jack and I are through, why don't you join me for a drink? We can talk about old times."

Old times? What old times?

"Well..." Sally cast an uneasy glance at Jack.

"Thanks anyway," Jack said, "but we have other appointments. We have to meet with two of the company's small builders, and take some site photos. Then it's back to Peachtown before dark." That sounded bogus, but so what? He'd rather chew nails than spend another minute watching Hollywood here drool over *his* date.

"Actually, we could come back later for a drink," Sally said.

Jack wanted to strangle her.

"Great!" Hollywood puffed up his chest. "I'll be here until about six. There's a pretty good pub around the corner. We can get pizza and beer there."

"Of course, Jack will have to come along," Sally pointed out.

Come along? he thought. *Excuse me, but I don't ever come along.*

Hollywood looked crestfallen. "Ah, sure, why not? See you around six, then?" While Jack looked on, horrified, he kissed Sally's hand again.

Enough!

14

"PERSONALLY, I THINK jealousy is a stupid waste of time. Oh, wait! That's not an original thought, is it? Someone else said that. Hmm, I wonder who?"

Having the time of her life, Sally perched on the Mustang's trunk, shoes off and feet dangling over the back seat. Jack stood in front of the car, taking photos of an abandoned building site. He was a statue. Arms stiff. Back rigid. Nose all out of joint. It was the funniest thing she'd ever seen.

"Oh, stop it," he snapped. "I am not jealous of Matt Caldwell."

"Is that so? Then how come you keep calling him Hollywood?"

Without bothering to look at her, Jack shrugged. "Maybe I just don't like the guy. Maybe I think he's a pompous ass. Did you consider that?"

"Uh-huh, and maybe I'm going to morph into Madonna tomorrow." Sally pointed a shoe at his back. "You know what I think, hotshot? I think you just don't like Matt Caldwell liking me."

Squinting, Jack turned and smirked at her. His eyes were cold, his facial muscles tighter than a hamstring. "Why would I care if he likes you? That's none of my business."

Sally made a big deal of crossing her legs. She loved doing that when Jack's eyes were on her. It made him stupid with lust. "You're right. It is none of your business. But you're dying to know if I like him or not, aren't you?"

Snap. Snap. "I couldn't care less."

"Oh, c'mon, don't you want to know?"

"No."

"I think you do, Jack Gold. I *reaaaaally* think you do." Whew, this was tons more fun than a date with Matt Caldwell!

Jack strolled a few feet away from where he'd been and raised his digital camera for another series of shots. Sally drank him in, half-crazy with lust herself. In tan, pleated dress pants and a white—make that Raunchy Red and white—Ralph Lauren shirt, he was gorgeous.

And jealous. Hot dog!

Jack snapped a few frames, then dropped the camera to his side. While Sally took a short break from tormenting him, he pretended to be fascinated by the landscape. She could just see the struggle going on inside him. Dare he ask?

"Okay, tell me then. *Do* you like the guy?"

Ooh, he did dare. Tempting as it was, Sally thought it wise not to declare a victory by shouting *Aha!* It had taken a lot of courage for him to ask that question, and things were tense enough. "No, Jack, I don't like him."

He relaxed a little then—she felt that, too—but Jack was a guy and Sally knew he wasn't satisfied yet. The really-hard-to-ask question was still to come.

Snap. Snap.

"*Did* you like him?"

Ah, where jealous men dare to go. Sally hesitated. A direct answer would give everything away, and she wasn't quite ready to do that. "Maybe I did and maybe I didn't."

Snap. Snap. "What does that mean?"

"Why do you want to know?"

"Why don't you want to tell me?"

Wondering if the man could possibly be more childish, Sally scrambled out of the car and put her shoes on. "Because it truly isn't your business." She touched the Mustang's right front fender to determine how hot it was, then rested against it and crossed her arms.

Snap. Snap. "You're right. So let's just let the matter drop."

Oh please, why didn't the fool just admit that he was jealous, and that he was jealous because she was the best thing that had ever happened to him, and that he loved her fiercely, and that he couldn't imagine living the rest of his life without her? How hard would it be?

As if he'd just read her mind, Jack strode toward her with a no-bullshit gleam in his eye. He tossed the camera into the car and planted himself in front of her. Stunned, Sally unfolded her arms just as he took her head in both hands and smothered her mouth with a kiss that started out frantic, then slowed to become soft and sensual. It was a real macho kiss, a you-are-my-woman-and-don't-you-ever-forget-it kind of kiss.

Sally gasped when he brought her left leg up and ran his hand hard along it, from her ankle all the way to the hem of her dress. Then his hand snaked under the hem and across her lace panties, to the base of her spine. Then it slid around front, between her legs. While she moaned, Jack tortured her by caressing her inner thigh down to her knee, instead of up to the hot, instantly wet flesh that hungered for him every minute of the day.

It had never hungered like this. Ever.

"You don't want him," Jack whispered in her ear. His voice was husky, his breathing shallow and sharp.

"I don't want him," Sally whispered back. Frantically, she pulled his shirt out of his pants and ran her hands up his smooth, hot chest, under his arms, and around to his back. The freedom to do that was intoxicating.

Jack brought her other leg up and caressed it. At the same time his mouth was on her cheek, her eye, her ear, her hair, her neck. "You want me."

Sally could barely speak. "Yes."

"Me and only me."

"Yes."

"He's not the one."

The one? Oh please, Jack...

"He won't love you like..."

Love? "Like what, Jack? Like what?"

"Ma'am, are you all right?"

All right? Dear God, she was in heaven! She was... What?

As quickly as they'd joined, Sally and Jack separated and scrambled to compose themselves. A very tall, very imposing man in a blue uniform bearing the insignia of the Royal Canadian Mounted Police stood a few feet away. For some reason, he seemed concerned.

Oh...oh! He thought Jack was assaulting her!

"I'm fine, officer. Thank you." Mortified, Sally smoothed her dress down. What a sight they must be! Hair all poofy and tangled. Jack with red lipstick all over him. She, no doubt, was blushing scarlet from head to toe. With shoes to match, of course.

The officer nodded toward Jack. "This guy's not giving you any trouble then?"

Sally smiled. "I wouldn't go that far, sir."

"We're together, officer," Jack said as if that weren't obvious by now. "We're fine. Er, Sally's fine."

Momentarily satisfied, the officer trained his eyes on the Mustang. "Nice car. Is that the original paint job?"

While Jack gave him the short version of the car's long history, Sally slipped away to comb her hair and wipe the lipstick off her chin. The officer asked a lot of questions and Jack answered them all patiently, at the same time struggling to tuck his shirt back in. Sally giggled when it ended up crooked and he had to start over.

The second the officer left, she took her cell phone from her purse and called Matt Caldwell.

Jack frowned. "What are you doing?"

She motioned for him to wait.

"Matt," she said when he answered the call. "This is Sally.

Listen, Jack and I are running late, and we won't be able to make it for drinks. I'm terribly sorry."

Matt was sorry, too. He wanted a rain check. Sally danced.

Jack smiled sheepishly as she snapped the phone shut and put it away. "You didn't have to do that, Sally. I'm not your keeper."

"I know that, but someone also said that people who care about one another never do or say anything to cause jealousy."

Boyishly embarrassed, Jack shuffled his feet and looked around, at nothing. Sally smoothed her hair down, purely from nerves. They'd never gone this far before, sexually or emotionally, and with each new step they took, the door into intimacy opened a little wider. Words begged to be spoken: *I love you. I love you, too. I want to marry you. I want to have children with you. I want to grow old with you.*

Alas, it was too soon. "C'mon, hotshot, let's go home."

Halfway there, after a long, comfortable silence, Sally turned the radio down. She kept her eyes on the road. "We went out twice, Jack, when he was in Peachtown on business. I didn't sleep with him. I have no interest in him."

"It's okay. Really."

Ten minutes passed.

"I noticed, though, that you knew his phone number."

"Jack!"

WHAT A MAN IN LOVE DOES...

He panics.

But—does he panic because he's never been in love before? No. Does he panic because he's in love with a crazy woman? No. Does he panic because their love is complicated? No.

He panics because he's only got a thousand words on paper and he needs four times that many in order to finish. And until he finishes, he *can't* love the crazy woman.

Not like he needs to.

On Thursday morning at eight, Jack charged into the *Post* like a bull into a china shop. While Charlie looked on, baffled, he hastened to set up his laptop computer and organize his notes and photos. Jack pointed a finger at him. "Don't even dream of sending me out on assignment today. I'll help with the phones, but I am not leaving this room."

Charlie, of course, had a problem with that. "See now, I don't know about that, Jack. We had an agreement, you and me, and I can't imagine a man with your integrity reneging on an agreement. The police band says there's a car accident out on county road sixteen..."

Jack sat down. "Good. That'll be a nice drive for you."

"Drive? Oh, I don't think I can manage that, Jack. My back's giving me awful grief this morning."

"You don't have a back problem Charlie."

He blinked. "I don't?"

"No, you don't. Your only problem is that you can't say no to Sally Darville."

Defeated, and having the sense to know it, Charlie heaved a sigh of relief. "Do you know anybody who can?"

"No, and that includes me. Oh, and another thing."

"There's more?"

"Yes." Jack threw open all the drawers in his desk. Then he spun around on his wheeled chair and opened the drawers of the desk behind him. All were empty. "You don't have any staff reporters, do you?"

"*Wellllll.*" Charlie scratched his bald head, leaving a thin red mark. "I did have two..."

"Uh-huh, but one got married and the other one went on vacation, right?"

"If you must know, one eloped to California and never came back. I sent the other one out for sandwiches, and he never came back, either."

"Pity."

"I know. I'm still waiting for that pastrami on rye."

"My heart bleeds for you. Now, if you don't mind, I've got

work to do." Jack called up the document he'd started yesterday and scrolled through it.

"What's your rush?"

"Leave me alone, Charlie."

A hundred hard words later, Jack looked up to see, of all people, Dudley Morrison standing near his desk. "What the hell are you doing here?" Before the boy could deliver a speech, Jack spoke for him. "Let me guess. This is your Thursday job, right?"

Dudley nodded as if Jack had just made another brilliant deduction. "Yes sir. Thursdays and Fridays. See..."

Jack brandished a letter opener. "Dudley, do not even attempt to engage me in conversation today. Is that clear?"

"Very clear, sir."

"And one more thing. How old are you?"

"Eighteen, sir."

"Good. Call me Jack."

The boy reeled. "Oh, I couldn't! See, my dad says..."

"I don't care what he says. I don't want to hear another word from you, or from him. Got it?"

Dudley and Charlie exchanged a glance. Oblivious, Jack went back to work. A hard chore lay ahead. He couldn't afford to *think* about Sally today. He had to *write* about her—objectively. What a joke!

Five hundred painful words later, he looked up to discover he was alone in the office. Moments later he heard what sounded like a semitrailer truck roaring to life. That was followed by a series of clicks and bangs, then a whooshing noise and, finally, a loud but steady whir. A motor of some kind, obviously. Down below.

Annoyed, he strode to the back of the room and took the creaky stairs, one perilous tread at a time, to the basement. Hearing Dudley and Charlie's voices, he walked down a short hall, through a door and into a big, open room.

And blinked.

Running the full length of the room was the oldest and ugliest printing press he'd ever seen. It was as black as coal, and looked like an old locomotive train. Mixed odors rose up from it—stagnant water, ink and machine lubricant. Clad in heavy coveralls, Dudley and Charlie were hard at work, peeling freshly printed newspapers off its long conveyer belt.

"What is this?" Jack asked stupidly.

Dudley, who was closest to him, pinched his lips together.

Jack sighed. "It's okay, Dudley. You may speak. Briefly."

"Well, sir, ah, Jack, this here is the printing press."

"I know that, but why is it here?"

Charlie came around from behind the machine and wiped his hands clean with a damp cloth. "It's here because it was always here, and because it works. Needs a little TLC every now and then, though." He chuckled nervously.

Jack couldn't believe it. Typesetting the old way. Manually laying out the paper. Printing it on site. What century had he stumbled into?

Grinning, Charlie nodded toward the black beast. "Care to take a shot at this baby? If you're going to be in charge here, you'll have to know how to operate it."

"No," Jack huffed. "I don't want a shot at it. And I am not going to be in charge here, Charlie. You have to stop talking that way."

Having perfected selective hearing to precisely the same degree as Sally, Charlie brushed that assertion off and launched into a tedious dissertation on the inner workings of the machine. The only thing that saved Jack from death by exasperation was the ringing of the phone. Grateful, he sprinted back upstairs and took the call—from a woman wanting to know when they were running the story about that hunky reporter from Vancouver who'd plowed Jed Miltown under with his flashy car.

Jack set her straight on the car—she had the other part right—and went back to his desk. Three more calls and five hundred grueling words later, the front door flew open and, lo and be-hold, Jed himself lumbered in. Tawny Trubble was right behind him, along with the twins, Tilly McMahon and Elsa Jackson.

Jack's heart sank. It was nice to see them, but did it have to be today?

Aware that he was being rude, he explained straight off that Charlie was busy on the press. He prayed they'd take the hint.

Jed eyed the coffeepot. "No problem. We'll just visit with you until he's done."

Jack opened his mouth to argue, then changed his mind. Why waste the words? Instead he poured coffee for the adults. As they were rounding up chairs, the twins asked if they could sit in the Mustang for a few minutes. Jack okayed it. With Tawny present, he figured they wouldn't try anything. Nonetheless he warned them that "sit" meant "stay."

"Oh, don't worry about them," Tawny said as the boys bolted. "They're grounded for life. They're just lucky it's too late to cancel the caterer for their birthday party tomorrow."

He wanted to, but Jack didn't ask what kind of disaster the little imps had spawned. Asking would prolong the conversation, and he wanted these nice folks to drink their coffee, exchange a few pleasantries and then get the hell out of here.

Instead they settled in for a chat.

Elsa had nothing but good things to say about Jack. So hand-some! And so helpful! Jed thought the sun set in his right eye. He and Evan had actually had supper together last night. Imag-ine that! Tilly said how impressed she and the Darvilles were with Jack. So smart! And such an appetite! Embellishing some-what—you'd think he was Ghandi—Tawny said again how very sweet and understanding he'd been about his missing car.

For his part, Jack gave one self-deprecating shrug after an-other. He felt guilty, but he still wanted them gone.

No such luck. The conversation drifted to other matters and dragged on for another twenty minutes. Tawny remembered to ask if he was planning to attend the birthday party, and Jack mumbled something about checking with Sally. Providing these folks left before dark, he knew exactly what he and Sally were doing tonight. But tomorrow was wide open.

At one point, Tawny got up and peered at his computer screen. "What are you working on, Jack?"

He slammed the lid down and chuckled nervously. "Top-secret stuff. If I tell you, I'll have to kill you."

She flinched. That made him feel even worse, but what could he do? Tilly's eyes and ears were right there, ready to record and transmit.

Getting up to freshen his coffee, Jed asked how Sally's story was coming. For one heady moment, Jack thought Charlie had given him away. But it turned out that no one in the group knew anything. Relieved, Jack said the interviews had gone well, and that he wanted to start writing as soon as possible. That was a hint, but they didn't take it, of course.

Precious minutes ticked by. Jack cursed himself for even coming here today. It would have been so much more convenient to work at the inn. But what choice did he have? If his little plan was to work, he couldn't risk Sally calling—or worse—dropping in, and not finding him here.

And not for one minute would he chance leaving her alone with Charlie. Their history as co-conspirators went back a lot further than his own shaky alliance with the man. Jack was fairly certain that Charlie wouldn't intentionally give him away, but the man had a way of slipping up.

The guests lingered.

Just when Jack feared he might self-ignite, Charlie mercifully reappeared. Yes! Jack promptly excused himself and, ignoring the looks it generated, disconnected his computer and carried it to the back of the room. There he set it up on an old worktable, grabbed a chair, took a few deep breaths, and got at it.

Three hundred agonizing words later, he overheard Charlie refer to him as "the incumbent." Jack resisted the urge to bang his forehead on the table. There was no point, he knew, in contradicting the man. Within hours that juicy little tidbit would be all over town, and nothing he said or did now would change that. In fact, it might just make things worse.

He did, however, make a mental note—to kill Charlie.

The guests left midafternoon and Jack immediately commandeered Charlie for an interview. It didn't take long—as the official spokesperson for Peachtown, Charlie's part in the story was small. They talked for twenty minutes, then Charlie and Dudley called it a day. Jack marveled at that. If this were the *Satellite*, they'd be hard at it for at least another two hours.

Anxious and exhausted, he stared at his screen. It was five o'clock. He had a gruesome total of just twenty-eight hundred words down, every one the equivalent of a pulled tooth. He needed twelve hundred more. At, realistically, three hundred clean words an hour, he wouldn't finish until nine.

Nine o'clock. Dammit. Sally had made dinner reservations somewhere, and he hated to break their first real date. But it couldn't be helped. Tonight, come hell or high water, was the night.

As he reached for his cell phone to call her, it startled him by ringing.

WHEN IT CAME TO DATING, Sally had a few rules. Okay, she had a lot of rules. But they were all simple and easy to follow. The first was the simplest: *I am not available on a whim. If you want the pleasure of my company, you must promise to be here at a designated time, and you must keep that promise. If you are unreasonably late, you will not get the pleasure of my company.* Simple.

So when Jack called at five o'clock to say he might not make it until nine or later, she told him in no uncertain terms that nine o'clock was the cut-off time. If he'd said he might not make it until ten or later, she would have told him in no uncertain terms that ten o'clock was the cut-off time. Or eleven, or twelve. But he hadn't.

Sarah always said that men were like puppies. They needed

to be disciplined. Otherwise they would take liberties. Sally wanted Jack to take liberties with her. Lots and lots of liberties. But only in the bedroom. Elsewhere, a girl had to have some pride.

Wondering if she'd been maybe a little too proud, she checked the time. It was nine-thirty now, which meant that he wasn't coming at all. There was no way Mister Good as Gold would break her rule. He was too much of a gentleman for that.

Disappointment overwhelmed her. A whole night without Jack? What exactly had she done with her nights before he came along?

The sad part was that it wasn't really Jack's fault. It was that damn Charlie. Sally could just kill him! First of all, for interfering with her plans by pursuing his own half-baked agenda. Coming right out like that and asking if Jack wanted to buy the *Post.* What had he been thinking? It was too much, too soon. Sally just prayed he hadn't scared Jack off.

All day she had been itching to raise the subject with Jack, but she couldn't. It would have left the impression that she and Charlie were somehow in collusion. Which, okay, they were. But Jack didn't need to know that. He, much to her dismay, hadn't volunteered a word about it. What did that mean? That he was considering it? Or, that he'd dismissed it out of hand?

God, this was frustrating!

And making Jack work late tonight—what was that about? In all the years she'd known Charlie, he had never once worked later than 5:00 p.m. A man should be at home in the evening, with his wife and children. That was what he always said. So how come that didn't apply to Jack? He might not have a wife, but he had her. And Charlie, for all that he played dumb, knew exactly what was going on between the two of them.

The real mystery was—why had Jack stood for it? Why hadn't he put his foot down and refused to work late? Wouldn't he rather be with her?

Restless, Sally peeled her butt off the sofa and rifled through her collection of CDs. Jack might not be coming, but she was still in the mood to party, and nothing made for a better party than U2. She loaded the disk into her stereo and cranked up the volume.

As the distinct, opening notes of "Beautiful Day" came up, she drifted into her bedroom. Right after work she'd taken a long hot shower and assembled six of her prettiest dresses, every one suitable for a date where no one would be taking notes. Sighing with regret, she put them all away.

Then, with nothing better to do, she pried open her lingerie drawer and peered inside. At the bottom of the deep drawer lay a white box sealed with a pink ribbon. She opened it and removed its delicate treasure: a filmy white camisole with satin piping, spaghetti straps and little mother-of-pearl buttons down the front. There was a matching G-string and white stockings, too. Stay-ups with lace borders. Years ago she'd bought the ensemble with nothing more than a fantasy man in mind. She'd never even opened the box.

But now, why not? Being careful not to tear anything, she tried on the pretty things and appraised them in her full-length mirror. Hmm, something was missing. Shoes. Giggling, she fetched a pair of high-heeled cocktail pumps, white with thin straps, and tried those on as well. Hmm, very sexy. When she and Jack finally got around to real fun and games, this outfit would be perfect.

Someone rapped on the front door, loudly.

Sally froze. Who could that be? Trish, probably, bored and wanting her to go out for nachos and beer. But Trish always called first. So...

Panicked, Sally scrambled into her silk robe. There was no time to change. And the shoes, they were complicated. She bent down and tried to undo their tricky clasps.

A shadow fell across the floor.

Slowly, Sally stood.

Jack filled the bedroom doorway. His eyes were glassy and a

little wild-looking. His hair was wet, as if he'd just showered. In one hand he had a bottle of champagne, in the other two champagne flutes. A pink tea rose poked out from his jacket pocket. Amused, he looked her over. "Expecting someone, Sally?"

A slow burn started in her cheeks. "You're late, Jack."

"I know, and I apologize."

"Something wrong with your watch?"

"I know what time it is."

"Oh yeah?"

"Yeah." He grinned. "It's time to negotiate."

15

"WHAT DO YOU MEAN you don't *care* anymore? How can you possibly say that?"

With Sally frantic on his heels, Jack strode into the kitchen, smiling to himself. This was going to be even more fun that he'd thought. "I told you, I just plain don't care anymore. Who needs ethics anyway? I want you. You want me. Why should we wait?"

Sally gawked at him, horrified, as he poured a glass of champagne and handed it to her. Her eyes were so big, Jack figured they had to be visible from outer space.

"You can't mean that, Jack!"

"To you and me." He reached out and tapped his glass against hers. "Oh, by the way." He fished the rose out of his pocket and handed it to her. "I drove all the way out to the Jacksons' for this. I hope you like it."

Flower in one hand, flute in the other, Sally peered into his eyes, checking his pupils, no doubt, for dilation. "Have you lost your mind, Jack?"

"Aren't you going to try the champagne? It's top quality." Jack took a sip of the bubbly stuff and smacked his lips. "Mmm, good."

Sally set her own glass down on the chopping block and found a vase for the rose. She was past shock and headed for anger now. Good. Jack liked her all riled up. She had a certain charm when she wanted to slay him.

"Jack, I don't believe you're doing this! Yes, I want you. But not like this. What happened to waiting until after the story was written?"

"At the rate Charlie's got me working, I just don't know when I'm going to get it written. Besides, why do you care?"

She gasped. "I care because this isn't what we agreed on, and because it isn't right. I thought you had integrity. I thought you wouldn't compromise your principles for anything. I care because I thought *you* cared, that's why."

Jack treated himself to another look at those long legs in white. "Oh yeah? Then why have you been trying to get me into bed since the minute you laid eyes on me?" He moved toward her, but she took a few steps back, into the living room. She was hot now.

"You're over the line there, mister."

Jack eyed her robe. "What are you wearing underneath that?"

"None of your business." In the middle of the living room she stopped and pointed at the door. "Get out of here."

"Hey, you know what? U2 isn't quite right for this." Jack went over to her CD player and glanced through her mostly pitiful music collection. He'd have to do something about that. In the meantime, he found one gem—Marvin Gaye's *Greatest Hits*. Oh yeah.

"Did you hear me, Jack?"

The sad, soulful strains of Marvin Gaye's voice replaced U2's classic rock. "Hey, what's the big deal? Don't you want to spend the night with me, Sally?"

"Get out!"

"I don't think so." Jack tossed his jacket on the sofa and went over to her. While she stood there, spitting fire from those pretty blue eyes, he fingered the lapel of her robe.

She, of course, swatted his hand away. "Is there something about what I just said that you don't understand?"

"Hey," he groused. "How come I have to be good, but you don't?" It was a reasonable question.

"I am being good, in case you hadn't noticed."

"Mmm, you look good, Sunshine. I can attest to that." Itching to separate those lapels and feast his hungry eyes on what lay beneath, Jack opted instead to cautiously encircle her waist. There was no rush. They had all night.

Sally stiffened momentarily, then groaned and put her arms around his shoulders. Jack pulled her close. He'd guessed right. Something interesting was under that robe. If he didn't know better, he'd think she had another date tonight.

They moved to the music, and Sally sighed. "Oh, Jack, this is so wrong. I count on you to be good. I love your goodness. And I'm good, too, when you're not around. But when you are..."

His mouth was in her hair. "What?"

"When you're near me, I'm..."

"Say it, Sally. It's okay."

"I'm weak. I have...no control."

Against his will, Jack got an erection so big it threatened to tear his jeans apart. "Does that mean I'm staying the night even though the story's not written?" He braced himself. He knew exactly what was coming.

Sure enough, she pushed him away. "No, it doesn't. I meant what I said. Get out. You've disappointed me, Jack Gold, and I won't..."

He started to laugh.

"What's so funny about that?" she huffed. "You may not believe this, but I *am* a principled person. Yes, I want you, and, yes, you make me weak, but that doesn't mean I'm willing to compromise *my* integrity."

Enjoying himself way too much, Jack walked around her in a circle, looking her up and down. "Sally, Sally, Sally, who do you think you're talking to? You would have slept with me last night. You would have slept with me the night before. Hell, you would have slept me with me the first night. You're not just a harlot. You're a shameless harlot."

She got so hot then, Jack feared that flames might actually

shoot out of her head. In a flash, she was at the door, holding it open. "One word, mister. Out!"

Okay, that was enough. "Gotcha!"

"What?"

"Sally, the story is written."

"What?"

Excited, Jack started to gesture wildly. "It gets better. It's sold, too. Just before I called you this afternoon, I heard from the features editor at *Maclean's*. I pitched the story, then I faxed him what I'd written so far. He read it, he liked it and he called me back. They want it."

"But...but... Omigod, Jack!"

"It gets even better. He called me again an hour later. It's going to be their cover story, two weeks from today. They actually bumped another story for it." He paused for maximum effect. "Sally, you're going to be on the cover of *Maclean's* magazine."

"Omigod! That's incredible! But, I don't understand, Jack. When did you write the story?"

He told her.

"Charlie conspired with you on this?" She looked like she wasn't sure what to make of that. But whatever she made, poor Sad Sacks would be impaled on it.

"Actually I browbeat him into going along." Jack cleared his throat and tried to look serious. "As you know, Charlie would never lie."

The sexy little schemer blinked three times. "Oh no, of course not."

Heh, heh, just look at her, Jack thought. *She still thinks she's cleverer than me.*

An awkward silence fell and Sally blushed three shades of red. Jack watched, amused, while she downed her champagne in one gulp. She was nervous.

That was okay. He was nervous, too.

All day he'd thought about what he would say at this moment, scripting and rescripting and then rehearsing the final speech until it was a jumbled mess. Now he just said what felt right. "Sally, we agreed to talk about this, but I think we both know what we want. Do you have anything you want to say?"

"God, yes! But not now. Um, I mean, no."

"We agreed to negotiate, too. Do you have terms?"

"No. Just that…"

"What? What is it?"

She looked pained, as if she were about to say words he might not want to hear. Jack held his breath. If she'd had second thoughts, if she wanted out…

"It's just that I've never made love with anyone before," she said with heartbreaking vulnerability. "Do you understand what I'm saying, Jack?"

Relief overwhelmed him. "Yeah, and it's okay, Sally. Neither have I. But I want to make love with you. That is, if you'll have me."

Her eyes glistened. "If I'll have you? Oh, Jack, you're funny."

THUNDERCLOUDS ROLLED IN—dark, brooding beasts that would tear up the earth for miles around with great, shattering bolts of anger, then vanish without leaving a trace of rain. A wind came up and the sky went black.

In the living room, Jack and Sally lit candles.

"Take that off," Jack ordered. His tone was firm.

Facing him, Sally slowly slipped her robe off and tossed it on the sofa. With his greedy eyes all over her, every nerve ending in her body started to hum. Her nipples swelled and hardened and began to ache from nothing more than his gaze. A throbbing started in her womb. A steady pulse—the heartbeat of love.

Jack shook his head. "You're exquisite."

Sally trembled. To be admired by a man who loved and wanted you as much as you loved and wanted him—this, apparently, had no equal.

As "Let's Get It On" wafted through the speakers, she helped

Jack remove his T-shirt. At the same time her mouth found the sweet spot on his neck, near his collarbone. Moaning, he folded her in his arms and they began a slow, sensual dance.

Their love was a dance, Sally thought. The kind that's possible only for people who were put on earth for one another alone.

Halfway through the song, Jack pulled back and probed her eyes. "I love...Marvin Gaye."

Sally swallowed. "I love...Marvin Gaye, too."

Their mouths joined for a soft, sweet kiss. They were just mindless bodies now, mingled tongues, skin on hot skin, pulsing organs and muscles and tendons. Down below, Jack was rock hard. As he pressed against her, Sally grew wet between her own shaky legs.

They had drifted close to the wall between the kitchen and living room. Jack maneuvered her against it, clasped her hands and placed them flat against the wall on either side of her head. He kissed her long and hard this time. "Don't move."

Sally quivered as he undid the top three buttons on her camisole and brought his mouth down on the sensitive flesh he'd bared. His tongue teased the tops of her breasts, but refused to go farther.

"Please, Jack," she begged. "Have mercy."

"There's no mercy for the wicked, sweet thing."

Sally smiled. "Sweet thing?"

He ignored her and undid another three buttons. This time his tongue found the smooth valley between her breasts, and played there for a while. Sally was shocked by the sound that came out of her—a low cry fading to a whimper.

While she trembled with longing, Jack undid the final three buttons and gently peeled her camisole back. He watched with macho pleasure as her breasts swelled in anticipation of what he knew they wanted. "Beautiful," he whispered as his mouth finally, mercifully, claimed one swollen nipple.

His tongue...what he did with it...was incredible. Sally cried out as the first of what would turn out to be many explosions racked her body. Her head lolled back and her breath came in short, sharp gasps.

"I'll bet Hollywood Matt couldn't do that," Jack teased. He sounded more than a little pleased with himself.

Sally couldn't resist. "Mmm, probably not, but at least I wouldn't have to negotiate with him."

"Is that so? I don't recall you negotiating with me, sweet thing. Is this your idea of negotiations?"

"With you? Yes."

"With me alone?"

"Oh, Jack, do you doubt it?"

"No." Laughing, he slipped her camisole off and threw it away. Except for her G-string and stockings and shoes, Sally stood naked, but not vulnerable, before him. For this man, and this man alone, she revelled in being a shameless harlot.

While she murmured her pleasure, Jack caressed her sides, from the sensitive skin under her arms down to her thighs, and back again. He shook his head with wonder. "You are one hot woman, Sally Darville. You don't know how badly I want you."

Sally raked her hands through his hair as he cupped both breasts and taunted her nipples with light kisses. "Then take me, Jack. Now!"

"Not yet, sweet thing." Gently, he took her head in both hands and looked into her eyes. "I'm saying this first, and for as long as you and I are together I'm only saying it once. You're mine. Got it?"

"Are you mine, Jack?"

"You know it."

Frantic with desire now, Sally undid his jeans and helped him to step out of them. It was awkward, but they didn't care. When his Calvin Kleins were shed, and Jack finally stood naked before her, she burst into a smile. "Oh my, hotshot, I can see it's going to be a long hard night."

He chuckled. "This is just the warm-up."

Relishing the freedom, she took him in both hands and caressed the full length of him, becoming even wetter when he moaned with pleasure. Then she slid down the wall until her knees found the floor. She'd never been a fan of this—some men were crude about it. But this man begged to be devoured, every glorious inch of him.

There were a lot of those.

It was Jack's turn to cry out when she encircled him with her lips and set about teasing him the awful way he'd been teasing her. She made it agony for him, with light licks and gentle strokes that promised more, but didn't deliver. Then, little by little, she increased the pressure until he seized her head in both hands and begged her to stop before it was too late.

"You are delicious," she whispered against his throbbing skin. It seemed stretched to the breaking point, which excited her beyond belief.

"No more, Sally." Panting, Jack helped her to stand and they locked mouths with a savagery that frightened them both. As soon as they recovered, they were all over one another, making the frenzied love they so badly needed.

Jack's hands were on Sally's face, her breasts, her stomach, her thighs—everywhere but where she wanted them.

Eyes closed, she pressed against the wall, gasping for air. "Jack Gold, if you don't touch me soon, I'll go mad!" She parted her legs just in time for his fingers to slide under her G-string and start the torment she now knew to expect. Sure enough, Jack was in no hurry to satisfy her. While she writhed in near agony, his fingertips toyed with the soft hair there. Sally's quivers became shakes. "Jack, I'm begging you!"

Heartless beast that he was, he lifted her hair and brought his mouth down on her neck. At the same time, his fingertips skimmed over the wet tip that was so engorged with blood it pulsated. Sally cried out, but the beast just laughed.

His fingers slipped inside her.

Sally lost it. Totally.

By the time Jack rounded up a condom and carried her to the bed, she was a whimpering, salivating blob of flesh. She would do anything for him now, anything at all. Jack laid her on her back, removed her shoes and stretched out beside her. Sally automatically brought her leg up and over his, hoping, praying, that he would have the decency to end her misery. Instead he pushed it down and parted her legs. Gently he stroked her inner thighs. "What's your hurry, Sunshine?"

Sally shook. "Jack, please!"

"I love it when you beg." He kissed her lips lightly, teasingly, then tongued his way between her breasts and along her tummy. Sally convulsed when he tore her G-string away and used that same, magical tongue to part her other lips. "Mmm," he murmured. "Blond on blond. How sexy is that?"

The torture that followed was unspeakable. Clutching his head and pleading for relief, Sally cried out so many times, her voice went hoarse. "I can't take any more, Jack."

"Oh, yes, you can." He positioned himself above her and Sally automatically wrapped her stocking-clad legs around him. "You're going to take all of me," he whispered hoarsely. "Now."

In one hard thrust he was inside her all the way, and Sally instantly felt the most intense, exquisite pleasure of her life. There was no teasing—neither of them could have stood it. Instead, they quickly found their rhythm and made it perfect.

Jack kissed her, hungrily. Sally raked her nails across his back. They pressed together, hot skin on hot skin.

No man had ever looked into Sally's eyes when doing this, or perhaps she just hadn't encouraged it. But Jack wouldn't let her look away. "You're the sexiest woman alive," he told her. "I'll never get enough of you."

Sally could no longer speak. She shifted to take him in even deeper, not just into her body, but into her soul, where he belonged.

Jack's long, steady strokes quickened to become a relentless pounding. They both cried out again and again and again. Mouth open, eyes rolling back in his head, Jack became uncontrollable, and Sally knew he was on the brink. Her own final explosion came just seconds before he arched his back and let out one final, guttural groan. He collapsed on top of her, crying out her name.

For a long time they lay there quietly, almost frightened by the intensity of their passion.

Jack giggled first.

"Why are *you* laughing?" Sally asked him.

"It's Hollywood," Jack said. "I feel…sorry for him."

She cracked up.

Laughing along with her, he peeled a few strands of sweat-drenched hair off her face. "What's got your funny bone?"

"I'm not sure," Sally admitted. "I think it's because I just found heaven, and it's a happy place."

"I can go you one better, sweet thing. I just found home."

Sally's tears spilled forth. In her loveliest dream she had imagined only a simple declaration of love. "I have to revise something I said yesterday, Jack."

"Really? What's that?" He kissed her tears away.

"*That* is the nicest thing a man has ever said to me."

THEY SLEPT LIKE BABIES for two hours, then tumbled, bleary-eyed but refreshed, into the shower. Under the pounding torrent of hot water, they soaped one another down and made love standing up—erotic love that no dream could ever match. When they finished, Sally was as limp as a rag doll, and just about as daft.

She couldn't stop smiling.

Ravenous, they ambled into the kitchen, where Jack rummaged through the cupboards, griping about her "disgusting" lack of supplies. He did, however, dredge up a carton of Peach Paradise, a can of cling peaches, a bottle of chocolate syrup—

slightly past its best-before date, mind you—and a bag of slivered almonds.

"See," Sally joked. "I told you I had food."

Feeding spoonfuls of the messy treat to one another, they talked about the story. Sally was dying to read it, and Jack promised to run her a copy tomorrow. Like a good wife, she let him boast a little about his superior selling skills, but she also got him to admit that luck had played some part in their good fortune.

Jack had changed these past few days. He was more humble. So was she.

Between soft, lovely kisses, they talked about other things—their upbringings, their schooling, their hobbies. When Jack said he loved golf, Sally laughed, then couldn't explain why it was funny.

No matter what they talked about, she was faintly distracted. Her body was finally at peace, but her mind was a whirl of questions that needed answers, the biggest one being—what now?

"Jack," she asked instead. "Is it just my imagination, or were you testing me tonight, to find out if I really would sleep with you before the story was done?"

"A little, maybe. But don't worry, I'm not judging you too harshly." He grinned. "I probably would have slept with you that first night."

"Oh, how brave of you to admit that! You could have milked this forever."

He gave her a funny look then, and Sally wondered if she'd gone too far. Words of passion had been spoken, yes, but the L-word still hovered, and no one had said "forever."

Yet.

Awkwardly, she reached out and caressed the pink rose Jack had brought for her. "Please tell me that after working so hard all day, you didn't drive all the way out to the Jacksons' just for this."

"I did. And I wanted eleven more, too, but Elvira wouldn't give them to me unless I agreed to fix a leaky water pump."

Sally chuckled. "They don't call her Stonewall for nothing, you know."

Suddenly, Jack seemed amused. "One thing I've been dying to ask you, Sunshine. How did you arrange for Elvira's back step to give way? That must have been tricky."

Oh, darn. How did he know about that? Elvira herself would never spill the beans. "For your information, smarty-pants, I didn't arrange for that to happen. It was blind luck." Sally sniffed. "I had mentioned in passing that you were house handy."

Jack pointed his finger at her. "Uh-huh. And you know, of course, that I know that Charlie doesn't have a bad back?"

What? "No, I didn't know that you knew that he didn't, but, um, I guess I do now. Know that you...whatever." Mortified, Sally covered her face and groaned.

Jack reached out and caressed her hands. "Don't underestimate me, Sally."

Their eyes filled with love as they gazed at one another across the chopping block. Sighing, Jack took the rose from its vase and laid it down in front of her. "Let's get the awkward thing over with, shall we?"

Sally inhaled. "The awkward thing?"

"Yeah. In case you haven't already figured it out, I love you."

Sally exhaled. "Oh, God, I love you, too, Jack! So much!"

"I love you so much, I can't even find words for it." Jack came around to enfold her in his arms, and they kissed for a long time, the way people in love do. Not just to make contact, but to meld into a single person with one beating heart.

Afterward, they went back to bed, where Sally lay in Jack's arms, happier than she had imagined possible. They talked about ordinary matters for a while. Jack asked if she had to work tomorrow, and Sally confirmed that, like it or not, she had to go in by at least eleven, for meetings. They could sleep until then.

Or not.

"What will you do?" she asked. Until now every minute of Jack's time had been accounted for.

"I'll probably give Charlie a hand with the phones. He's on the press all day and could use the help. As for tomorrow night, I was thinking that you and I could, ah, negotiate a little more." Laughing, he caressed her breasts and tummy. "Maybe a *lot* more."

"I'm game for that! But first I have to help Tawny with the twins' birthday party. I'm the designated hostess—as in kitchen slave—this year."

"They're letting *you* in the kitchen?"

"Probably just this once."

"No kidding! Do we have to go?"

Sally laughed. It was such a husbandlike question. "Yes. Everyone in town goes. But we don't have to stay late."

"Hmm, and we won't, either."

A quiet, comfortable moment passed before Sally drew a calming breath and asked the question that was eating her alive. "When are you going home, Jack? I know you have to."

In the dark, he nodded. "I do, yes. The air conditioner is running full-blast in my house. My answering machine and mailbox will be full. Plus I've got personal things I need to get from my office at the *Satellite*." He paused. "I'm leaving Saturday morning."

"Oh."

A terrifying silence followed. Near tears, Sally feared she would die if Jack didn't speak soon. The ball was in his court, dammit.

Reading her mind, he adjusted their naked bodies so he could make out her eyes in the shadows. "I'll be back, and then you and I will talk. Understand?"

"Oh, Jack!"

"I love you, Sally Darville."

"I love you, too, Jack Gold."

His mouth found hers, and soon they were negotiating all over again.

16

By Jack's estimation, three hundred people were at the party.

Old folks, middle-aged folks, twenty-somethings, teenagers, kids and, of course, the requisite number of howling babies. The kids, all waving bunches of red and white balloons, were everywhere—in the house, the garage, the gardens, the trees. Jack was in such a good mood, he even let four of them play in the Mustang.

The adults mingled on the pretty grounds surrounding the Trubbles' sprawling ranch-style bungalow. It was a sweltering night, the hottest so far that week. Cooling his heels with Charlie in the shade of a magnificent old elm tree, Jack spotted familiar faces: Elvira, Elsa, Jed and Evan—who, much to his amusement, had arrived together—Dean, Sarah, Dudley, Arlene, Tilly, Andy, Cora and Trish.

And Sally. Sweet, sexy Sally.

Unable to wipe the grin off his mug, Jack watched her float through the crowd like an angel. She'd bobbed her hair and pinned it up with a feathered, black barrette, and she had on that cherry-red lipstick he dreaded and loved. Below that was a pale green flapper dress and black, low-heeled satin pumps—twenties vintage.

In a word, stunning.

She sought him out and blew a kiss. He laughed and blew one back.

Charlie shook his head sadly. "Boy oh boy, you've got it bad, don't you, son?"

Cradling a glass of wine against his chest, Jack kept his eyes on Sally. "Charlie, could a man ask a woman to marry him after one date? That is, without being judged insane?"

"Absolutely. I can perform the ceremony right here and now. We certainly have enough witnesses."

Jack chuckled. "I should have known better than to ask you."

A light wind came up, too light to provide relief from the heat. Jack's mind wandered into Sally's air-conditioned cottage, specifically into her bedroom, where a different kind of heat would be happening later tonight.

"I asked Arlene to marry me right after our second date," Charlie said. "I wanted to ask after the first one, but I figured I'd scare her off."

Sally sent Jack a dazzling smile, and he sent one back. "I doubt that would have happened, Charlie. Her feelings for you are obvious."

Charlie turned serious. "I never thought I'd say this, but are you sure you know what you're getting into, Jack? Sally's a handful."

"Terrifying, isn't she?"

"Scares the hell outta me."

They gazed out over the crowd.

Jack took a leisurely sip of his wine. It was from a local winery and was, frankly, superb. He planned to go easy on it, though. Another long, hard night lay ahead for him and his delicious, devious, demented little dairy princess.

Look at her. Wow. Very long, very hard.

"I'm glad for you, though," Charlie said breezily. "Things are working out pretty good all around. You and Sally will marry. You'll buy a house. You'll have a family. You'll take over the *Post*. Yes, siree, things are working out."

"Drop it, Charlie. I have no intention of taking over the *Post*."

Charlie chuckled. "Oh son, you have no idea who you're dealing with, do you?"

Why, Jack wondered, did everyone keep saying that? He was in complete control of his life. Well, except that he had no job and no idea where he'd be living a year from now. But those were just details.

"While we're on the subject, Charlie, how did you end up here, anyway? There are stories, but I don't know which one is true."

"Car broke down. Arlene was working the counter at Axton's Auto Shop. The repair was supposed to take two hours. Shall I go on?"

"Don't bother. One thing I'm curious about. Any regrets?"

"No, of course not."

Jack was surprised. It wasn't the answer he'd expected.

"Yes, I could have had the big career," Charlie explained. "But I've got something better. A wife who loves me. Kids and grandkids. I've got a life here, Jack, and I don't know that I would have been as happy somewhere else." He shrugged. "Course I don't know that I wouldn't have, either. That's the chance you take."

"Yeah, well, I won't be taking it," Jack insisted, and instantly felt guilty. Sometime between making fabulous love with Sally last night and hauling his tired but happy butt out of bed this morning, it had struck him that Peachtown wasn't such a bad place. Despite the weather, it was a beautiful town, and for all that they were a little slippery, the people here were among the kindest and most caring he'd ever met.

He *could* live here, he supposed. Maybe he could even be happy here, like Charlie. But that was irrelevant. Wherever he went from here, Sally would be going with him. Of that, he was absolutely certain. She loved him. They loved one another. Neither of them would ever find this kind of passion again. Sally had to know that. Who, after all, would love her like he did? Hollywood Matt might love her for a weekend, but once he got wind of one of her little schemes, he'd run screaming into the night. That blond hair went only so far.

And who else would have him? Women who didn't mind arrogance and self-absorption, that's who. Sally minded. She had higher standards. Meeting them would be one of the truly worthwhile challenges of his life.

What? Had someone just said something? Oh, right. Charlie.

"As I was saying before you drifted off there, Jack, I've never seen a more blatant case of lust in my entire life. The two of you have got the whole town hot and bothered. Drought's over, if you get my drift."

"Mmm."

"Do you love her, Jack?"

"Oh yeah."

"Watch your back, then," Charlie advised. "She's a hair smarter than you."

Jack shot him a questioning glance. "I beg your pardon?"

"Now don't take that personally, son, and don't worry about it. It's not much of an edge—though, heh heh, I must warn you, she can squeeze a lot out of a little."

She entered Jack's peripheral vision. He picked her up in all sorts of ways now, by her distinct, musky scent, her lovely voice, her laugh. He couldn't explain this at all, but he *felt* her presence even when he couldn't see her.

She walked up to him, smiling. "Hi." She looked fabulous. The others, trailing behind her, looked like a pain in the ass.

"Hi," Jack breathed.

With so many people watching, they weren't sure what to do next.

"Oh, go ahead and kiss!" Trish Thomas all but shouted. Obviously drunk, she had an entourage of friends with her, who looked in the mood to party hard. "Everybody knows you did the wild thing last night." That started them howling.

Sally had the grace to blush. "And just how do they know that, Ms. Thomas?"

"Ted Axton told them."

"And how did...?" Sally rolled her eyes. "Never mind."

Elvira, Elsa, Jed and Evan joined the group. Dean, Sarah, Arlene and Cora weren't far behind them. Charlie turned his back to them and spoke quietly to Jack. "About that kiss, son. If I were you, I'd be careful to read the politics of this situation."

Politics? Jack had no idea what the man was talking about. Baffled, he scanned the eager, sunburned faces before them. They all seemed to be expecting something, some ritual or local custom, but what? Surely they didn't need an okay to...

Oh. He got it. "Elvira, as the oldest, ah, as the eldest, ah, as the founding..."

"Move along, mush mouth."

Jack grinned sheepishly. "Do Sally and I have your permission to kiss?" It was the most bizarre question he had ever asked anyone, but it had a certain charm.

Elvira nodded her approval. "You're smarter than you look, Goldy, which is fortunate. Of course you have my permission. You don't think we came here for the cake, do you? And given that you've already done the..." She trained her terrifying eyes on Trish. "Are you lucid enough to repeat what you just said, dear?"

Trish burped. "The wild thing."

"Yes. The wild thing. Given that you've already done that, let's have a show, shall we?"

Blushing furiously, Jack and Sally gave them one.

Cheers filled the air. Jed and Evan slapped their thighs and whistled. One of Trish's inebriated pals flashed up a lighter and shouted, "Rock and roll!" Cora and Elsa linked arms, chiming, "Jack and Sally sittin' in a tree..." Dean seemed puzzled. "Wild thing? What are they talking about, Sarah?"

Laughing, Arlene took Charlie by the arm and led him away. Soon after, the others broke into pairs and dispersed as well. Slurring her words slightly, Trish confided to Jack and Sally that she and her friends had a case of tequila and "some very potent lemons." Were they interested?

"No, thanks." Jack drew Sally closer and she nestled against his chest. "We've got a date in heaven."

"Oh, puhleeze, get me a bucket." Teetering slightly, Trish

stuck a finger in her open mouth, a preview, Jack figured, of what she'd be doing later tonight. A wild-eyed woman from her group promptly dragged her off into the crowd. Befuddled, the others trailed after them.

Alone at last, he and Sally slipped behind the tree and kissed without the pressure of six hundred eyes on them. "Who were those people with Trish?" Jack asked. Not that he cared. He didn't care about anyone or anything but her.

Sally laughed. "Her old friends from law school. I recognize the bloodshot eyes."

"Mmm, I love *your* eyes. I love your smile. I love your laugh. I especially love your beautiful body. How soon before we can blow this pop stand?"

"Soon," Sally murmured as she kissed his ear. "Normally the hostess would help with the clean-up, but Tawny's letting me off the hook tonight."

Jack caressed her cheek and gazed lovingly down at her. They were so lucky to have found one another. And to think that Marty McNab had closed his eyes and fished her news release out of a big pile. What luck! "Good, 'cause there's something important I want to ask you, sweet thing."

Her blue eyes widened. "Why not ask me now?"

"No. I want to be alone with you."

"Um, okay. Right now I should go back and help Tawny. Have you said happy birthday to the twins yet?"

"Three times already."

"They really liked the video games you gave them. That was sweet of you, Jack."

He shrugged. Despite what everybody said, he *was* a sweet guy. Lately, anyway.

Blowing kisses over her shoulder, Sally walked away. Jack watched until he lost sight of her in the throng. He liked her in that dress, but very soon after they got home he'd be liking her a lot better out of it.

His pocket rang, giving him a start. The calls he got here were few and far enough between that he hardly recognized the sound of his own phone anymore. Sheldon Crane's home number showed on his call display. What could he possibly want on a Friday night at eight o'clock?

"Jack."

"Sheldon, my man. How's it hanging?"

"Same as always, unfortunately. You sound pretty good for an unemployed bum."

"Never been better. What's up?" Jack spotted Sally, spilling something off the side of a tray. He chuckled. Even when she was being a klutz, the woman was adorable.

"I took the liberty of opening your e-mail. You've got a few messages, nothing too serious. Oh, and a couple of phone messages, but the secretaries are handling those."

"Great," Jack said. "Anything else?" Oops, Sally dropped the tray. And hey, just look at all those guys scrambling to pick it up for her.

"Yeah. A letter. You might want to open it yourself."

ARMS LINKED, Arlene and Cora gazed across the lawn at the lovebirds. Arlene sighed. "Pitiful, aren't they?"

"Sad," Cora agreed. "How many more of those kisses will they blow before you start to vomit?"

"I'm approaching my limit. You?"

"I'm there. What's your take on the situation?"

Arlene didn't hesitate. "They were made for one another. What do you think?"

"Absolutely. She's a little smarter than he is, though. He'll have to buck up."

"He looks to me like he's up for it."

Cora let out a snort. "I sure hope so, for his sake."

"Consider this. Who else would have either one of them? I mean, for the long haul."

"I'd have him for a night."

"Mmm, maybe two."

They fell silent for a moment, then laughed.

Sobering, Cora said, "Here's the big question. Who do you think will win?"

Arlene had no doubt about that, either. "My money's on her. What's your bet?"

"How much money are we talking?"

"I'm in for fifty. Elvira will match that."

Cora cocked one eyebrow. "Any takers?"

"Believe it or not, a few fools are actually betting on him. Just enough to sweeten the pot."

"Good. Count me in for another fifty. The man who can resist that creature hasn't been born yet."

BY THE TIME Jack and Sally got back to her place, she was practically jumping out of her skin. He wanted to ask her something, in private no less. Yes!

Eager to get the mood just right, she put some soft blues in the stereo and cranked up the volume, then tidied her hair and freshened her lipstick. A woman had to look her best on an occasion like this.

Humming along with the music, she poured two glasses of wine and tried not to shake as she carried them out to the patio. It was a hot but lovely night, just perfect for a marriage proposal, she thought giddily. The air was fragrant, and the setting sun cast a golden glow across the patio. The man waiting there for her was beyond perfection.

She declared a toast. "To us, Jack."

"To us," he echoed. "We're an awesome team."

As they sipped their wine, Sally thought how cute Jack looked, all shy and nervous. It was no small thing, asking a woman to stay with you forever. Marriage was a serious commitment that carried big expectations and even bigger responsibilities. But they were up to the challenge. They were perfect together. Their love was perfect.

Everything was perfect!

Jack set their wine down and took both her hands in his own. Trembling with anticipation, Sally used her eyes to convey all the love and admiration and respect she had for him. Here at last was her fantasy man, in the flesh. Saying yes to him was going to be the highlight of her life.

"Sally."

"Yes, Jack?" She held her breath.

His eyes fairly glowed. "How would you like to live in New York?"

Whaaaaat? What...had he just said? "New York? But..."

Jack was beside himself with excitement. "Sheldon Crane called me from the *Satellite* a while ago. There's a letter on my desk." He squeezed her hands. "Sally, it's from the *New York Times*. Do you know what that means?"

"But...I thought..."

"I'll tell you what it means. It means I'm going to be an investigative reporter for one of the most revered newspapers in the world. What do you think of them big apples?"

Reeling, Sally sat down at the patio table and stared at him with openmouthed astonishment. He dropped into the chair across from her, grinning from ear to ear.

"How do you know that?" she asked reasonably. "Did Sheldon open the letter and read it to you?"

"No, it's none of his business. But I can tell you right now it won't be a letter of congratulations. It'll be an offer and, considering the source, it'll be a damn fine one."

"You don't know that for sure!"

"I will in a couple of days."

"Jack," Sally said quietly. "I can't go to New York."

His grin abruptly collapsed. "Why not? It's the opportunity of a lifetime for us."

"It's the opportunity of a lifetime for you! It has nothing to do with me."

"Hogwash. What are you worried about? That you won't fit

in? Look at you. You'd fit in anywhere—New York, Paris, Milan. You'd put 'em all to shame."

That was sweet—and pointless. "It has nothing to do with fitting in. I told you, Jack, I would never leave here."

"Yeah, but that was before last night." He gestured between them. "Before *us*. Surely things are different now?"

"For you, not for me!"

Bewildered, Jack shook his head. "Don't you love me?"

"Oh, Jack, you know how much I do!"

"Then come with me. We'll get married here—I know you'll want a big family wedding—then I'll sell my house and we'll buy a loft in Manhattan. Just think about it, Sally. We can get tickets for Broadway, visit the Empire State Building, the Statue of Liberty. It'll be a blast."

Near tears, Sally took a moment to organize her thoughts. "You don't understand, Jack. My career is here. My family is here. My friends are here. And it's not just a case of wanting to be near them. I'm morally obligated to these people, especially my parents. My brothers are die-hard bachelors, so Dean and Sarah are counting on me to produce grandchildren they can dote on. How can they do that if their grandchildren are thousands of miles away?"

That gave Jack pause for thought, and he stared off into the distance for a while. As she watched their horrible dilemma play out across his beautiful face, Sally's heart splintered into pieces—for him, for herself, for what could have been.

"I was confident you'd come with me," he admitted.

"That's funny. I was confident you'd stay here."

Jack grinned sheepishly. "I guess if you looked up confidence in the dictionary, both our pictures would be there, huh?"

Under other circumstances Sally would have laughed at that sad truth, but there was nothing funny about this situation. "What do we do now, Jack?"

Sighing, he got up, went to the rail and looked out over the valley. Standing there in his tight jeans and black jacket, he looked just like he had that first afternoon. Even as she sank into the depths of despair, Sally marveled at how far they had come since then. And shed a tear for how far they might have gone.

New York. He wanted to go. It was over.

"I've only known you for seven days," she said to his rigid back. "I can't give up my life for you, Jack."

Having learned to make eye contact while speaking to her, he turned around and perched on the rail. "I feel like I've known you forever, Sally. Don't you feel the same way about me?"

She nodded. "I do. But that doesn't alter my situation."

"I understand. So...I guess the decision rests with me, huh?"

The decision? Hope surged anew in Sally's aching heart. "Does that mean you'll think it over, Jack?"

He took a moment to do just that. "I'll make you a deal, Sunshine. *Quid pro quo.*"

Despite everything, Sally managed a smile. "Okay, what have you got in mind?"

"Here's what you need to understand, Sally. I love you more than I can say, but I've worked my whole life for this opportunity. Every decision I've made and every course of action I've taken has brought me straight to it. But..."

Please, Jack, make it a big but. "Yes?"

"If you'll give me a little time to think it over, I'll give you the benefit of my doubt. What do you say?"

On the surface it didn't seem like much of a deal, but it was huge, Sally realized. Not everything was about her. She knew that now, strictly as a result of loving this remarkable man. In just a few short days, Jack Gold had given her so much. Her story, soon to be published in a national magazine. More fun than she could ever remember having. A mirror in which to see herself, warts and all.

And his love, worth more than anything. As hard as it was, she owed it to him to at least try to understand his position. "Okay, it's a deal."

"Great!" He beckoned for her to come to him.

Sally didn't need prompting. The need to touch him was overpowering, especially now that their future together was threatened. No matter what Jack decided to do, the prospect of that future had been the greatest joy of her life. And if...well, if all she got in the end was two incredible nights, she would at least have the memory.

As the sun went down in a blaze of glory, they held one another tightly, fear and uncertainty adding a new, unwelcome dimension to their love. Jack buried his face in her hair. "Don't send me away tonight, Sally."

A dry laugh got stuck in her throat. "Send you away? Are you nuts? My whole life has become a quest to keep you here!"

"Make love with me."

"I'll do better than that. You and I are going inside now and you're going to tell me what I can do to please you—all night long."

Inside her arms, Jack shuddered.

THREE WEEKS.

Sally lived in a fog. Every day during the first two weeks she went from her cottage to her office, then sat at her desk, paralyzed for eight hours. She answered the phone, but couldn't recall who she'd just talked to, or what they wanted. She attended meetings where the faces around the table blurred together, along with the words coming out of those faces. Urgent work piled up on her desk, but she merely picked at it, as if it were food she didn't like.

On Monday of the third week, Dean declared her useless and sent her home. But that was no better. All she did there was wander from room to room, crying and muttering to herself like a crazy person. She couldn't eat, couldn't sleep, couldn't summon a single, rational thought.

Every night Sarah checked in on her. Sometimes she came alone, sometimes with Trish or Arlene in tow. Presumably they feared she might do something rash. But they didn't understand. She couldn't do anything except pace the floors, plumbing the depths of her misery—a well that apparently had no bottom.

Three weeks. He'd made his decision. He wasn't coming back.

On Thursday night of that week, all three women showed up together. They brought fresh flowers for her, and take-out food, and chilled wine. They were annoyingly cheerful, and noisy. Banging plates around. Chattering amongst themselves. Sally appreciated their thoughtfulness, but wished they'd just drop through a chute in the floor.

While they fussed about, she sat on the sofa, cradling her head in both hands and groaning. "I should have listened to all of you. I should have *known*."

Always a model of sensitivity, Trish snapped, "For heaven's sake, Sally, it's only been three weeks. Give the man his time." That earned her a harsh look from Sarah, but she merely shrugged and dug into her Moo Goo Gai Pan.

"How much time does he *need*?" Sally cried. Jack would have opened the letter from the *New York Times* long before now. Did he have to read it fifty times before realizing she was the better deal?

"Trish is right," Sarah said sensibly. "You just need a little patience."

"This is the best Moo Goo Gai Pan I've ever had," Trish announced. Arlene commented that she'd had better mushroom rice, though, and soon they were comparing restaurants around the valley like a couple of amateur critics.

"Oh God!" Sally wailed. "I feel so stupid. I actually had names picked out for our children. Can you believe that?"

Trish chewed and swallowed. "Really? Like what?"

Sally sniffled, then blew her nose on a used tissue. "Um, Annabelle for a girl, and Aidan for a boy."

"Annabelle. Nice. I like it. A girl could grow old with a name like that."

Murmurs of agreement followed, and Sally groaned. This party was getting old. Why couldn't they just leave her alone to die?

Arlene rearranged the flowers that Sarah had arranged earlier. "Three weeks or three months. It doesn't matter, Sally. Everyone knows how Jack feels about you."

"He loves you and he'll be back," Sarah quickly added. "You're worried for nothing, sweetie."

"Go ahead and say it," Sally told Trish. "I know you want to."

Trish blinked. "What? That I told you so? No way. I was wrong about Jack. I've already admitted that."

Baffled, Sally glanced at each woman in turn. What the hell was going on here? Just the other day they'd warned her that Jack would never consider living or working in Peachtown. This is not his kind of place, they'd said. He's not interested in taking over the *Post*, they'd said. So why the sudden change of tune?

Did they know something she didn't?

One thing she did know: No matter how much time he needed, the least Jack could do was call to give her an update. Or, even just to say, "Hi, how are you? I've been thinking about you." Was he planning to go straight from Vancouver to New York without so much as saying goodbye? After all they'd done together? After all they'd been to one another? Dear God, weren't they even *friends*?

A slow burn coming on, Sally got to her feet and started to pace again.

Alarmed, Trish looked up from her food. "Oh, oh, she's on the move."

"Sally..." Sarah began.

"How dare he!" Sally seethed.

The women abandoned their food and tripped over each other, trying to calm her down. But Sally got hotter by the second. No more Miss Understanding! They'd struck a deal, and

Jack, the straightest arrow she'd ever met—hah!—was reneging on it. If he didn't have the courage to face her, he at least owed her the courtesy of a phone call. He was arrogant, sure, but cowardly? Sorry. Not acceptable!

With all three women clutching at her heels, Sally stomped into the bedroom and pulled her small suitcase down from the closet shelf. While the others watched, horrified, she tossed mismatched items of clothing into it. "Trish, take me to the airport."

Sarah and Arlene both gasped. Trish reached across the bed and yanked the suitcase away from her. "Not a good idea, Sally. Steamroll, steamroll!"

Sally yanked it back. "On the contrary, it's the best idea I've ever had."

"Don't be too hasty," Sarah advised. "This really isn't necessary."

Sally stopped stuffing just long enough to gape at her. "Necessary? What has necessity got to do with this?"

The women exchanged a look, but Sally was too riled to interpret it. She went right on packing.

Wringing her hands and smiling faintly, Sarah urged her to sit down and think things through, but all Sally could think about was giving Jack Gold a piece of her mind. No way was he just walking out on her!

As usual, Arlene tried reason. "Sally, for all you know, Jack may be on his way here right now. Don't be a fool."

"Too late. I was a fool for love." Sally glared at Trish. "If you won't drive me to the airport, I'll drive myself."

Knowing all too well how badly Sally drove when on a rant, Trish caved. "Oh, all right. But this is too stupid for words."

Sally snapped the suitcase shut. "Let's go."

17

The real final showdown

"YOU KNOW WHAT, Charlie? I think we're really going to make something of this paper. I think we're going to win awards."

Charlie looked up from his desk and smiled. "I think you're right, Jack." He held up last week's edition of *Maclean's* magazine. Sally's beautiful, smiling face was on the cover, beneath the headline "My Place, My People: The Sally Darville Story." "If you can pull this off, you can do anything."

With Sally at my side I can do anything, Jack wanted to say. Only then.

"I just can't get over this." Shaking his head, Charlie dropped the magazine and picked up a list of real estate developers from across the country who'd called to inquire about building opportunities in the Okanagan Valley. "Thirty-two calls so far," he marveled again. "And more coming in every day. You did a hell of a job for us, Jack."

Shrugging the compliment off, Jack poured two glasses of water and handed one over. "To our partnership."

"To our partnership," Charlie echoed. They drank to their mutual happiness.

"Speaking of partners," Charlie said. "When do you think our cover girl will turn up? I sure don't want to miss it."

Jack was starting to wonder that himself and, frankly, to worry about Sally. "I can't figure what's taking her three days. There are six daily flights out of Vancouver."

Charlie shook his head and chuckled. "Imagine her going all

that way just to bust your balls. She's got balls all her own, that girl."

No kidding, Jack thought. He pictured her in the throes of a blind rage as she marched into the *Satellite*, only to learn that he'd already left for New York. It wasn't true, of course, but Sheldon was a convincing liar.

Jed Miltown stuck his head in the door. "Clouds are movin' in!"

Great, Jack thought. More thunderclouds. More lightning. More fires.

"Rain clouds!" Jed said and disappeared.

Together Jack and Charlie hastened to the window and peered outside. Sure enough, the sky was darkening, and the clouds amassing overhead were different than the others Jack had seen here. Rain. Imagine that! It was sort of...fitting.

After they resettled at their desks, the door flew open again and a tall, vaguely familiar man stepped inside. He had dark hair and a swarthy complexion, and wore a navy blue mechanic's uniform with the name Ted stitched across one breast pocket. He said hello to Charlie, then thrust his hand toward Jack.

Jack frowned. "Have we met?"

"We met a few weeks ago at the dairy bar. I'm Ted Axton."

"Oh, right." Jack didn't recall that meeting, but he'd heard the guy's name a few times since then. "What can I do for you?"

"I thought you should know that Sally is gunning for you."

"Hoo boy!" Charlie rubbed his hands together. "Show time!"

"How do you know that?" Jack asked stupidly. Everybody in this town knew everything about everybody, except for the people who needed to know what other people knew about them. But that was okay. He was getting used to it.

"I got it straight from Trish Thomas," Ted admitted. "She picked Sally up at the airport about an hour ago."

"What's her current position?" Jack asked—and laughed.

You'd think they were talking about a nuclear submarine in international waters.

Ted glanced out the window. "Three doors south and moving." No fool, obviously, he said a hasty goodbye and fled just moments before the nuclear threat herself sailed in. Ready to blow, she charted a course straight for Jack.

His heart leaped out of his chest. He hadn't seen this woman he loved so much for three long weeks, except from a torturous distance. Now here she was, looking fabulous in her little white tube top and white shorts, even with her skin all red like that. What the hell, she looked fabulous in any color.

He grinned up at her. "Hey, Sunshine, how are you?"

"I didn't come here to make small talk, Jack Gold."

"What? No hello? No nice to see you? No kiss?"

"I'd rather kiss a corpse." Breathing fire, she pressed her palms flat against his desk and glared at him. "Trish says you bought the Pittle house. How could you do that?"

"That's not all, Sunshine." Jack gestured around the office. "I bought fifty-one percent of this paper yesterday, just enough so I can keep my new partner here in line. He's agreed to stay on for a year, to help me get things rolling."

Fortunately for Charlie, Sally didn't so much as glance at him. "How can you do this, Jack? How can you just come back here and...and...*live* here? This is *my* place and *my* people, in case you've forgotten. Now give me back my house and get out!"

Slowly, Jack shook his head. He wasn't going to push this too far, but he'd waited three agonizing weeks for this moment, and a little fun seemed in order. "I'm afraid I can't do that. It wasn't easy getting that house. I had to promise the Pittles I'd marry you, or they wouldn't sell it to me." Jack was confident that would settle her down. Instead, she flew back out the door.

"Hey, wait a minute!" Laughing, he sprang to his feet and ran out after her. "We haven't talked about interior design yet. I'm thinking Mission style. What do you think?"

She ignored him and took off running down Main Street. Jack started to run after her, then changed his mind and hopped into the Mustang. Might as well be comfortable.

He cruised alongside her, trying to watch her and the traffic all at once. "You have no choice but to marry me, you know."

"I wouldn't marry you if you were the last reporter alive."

"Oh, yes, you would, Sunshine. You and I were made for one another, and you know it. We're two sides of the same coin, Sally."

"Get lost!"

"Oh, c'mon. You can do better than that."

Chest heaving, she slowed to a brisk walk and threw her arms in the air. "I can't believe I slept with you—twice!" A group of window shoppers turned and gawked at her as she flew past them.

The light at the intersection of Peach Pit Park turned green just in time for Jack to cruise on through. "That's funny, I don't recall much sleeping. Now be a good girl and get in the car. You're making a spectacle of yourself."

"Bite me, Gold."

"Mmm, maybe later, if you're good. Right now, Sally, I need for you to *get...in...the...car.*"

Tawny Trubble and the twins emerged from the park just as Sally passed the entrance gate. Tawny said a chipper hello, but Sally brushed her off and kept walking.

"Tawny," Jack shouted. "Tell Sally that she and I were made for one another."

She laughed. "Sally, you and Jack were made for one another."

"Hey, Jack," one of the twins called out. "Can we go for a spin?"

"No! Er, maybe later." To Sally he said, "C'mon Sunshine, get in the car. You know you love me."

"Leave me alone!"

At the dairy bar they passed a long queue of amused onlookers. Jack pointed to the building. "Hey, look, Sally. We finally made it here. If you're not busy, I'll take that tour of the dairy barn now, too. I never got that, you know."

She kept moving. "There are a lot of things you don't get, Gold."

"Ah now, that's harsh. Why don't you get in the car and we'll talk like grown-ups. You can't avoid me forever, you know."

She didn't have a snappy retort for that, and Jack realized she was running out of steam. Thank God. "Three weeks," she muttered. "Three weeks and not one phone call."

Jack spoke firmly. "I had to be sure, Sally."

She stopped cold then, and he quickly pulled over to the curb. Eyes full of hurt, she approached the car, gesturing wildly. "Sure that you loved me, Jack? How could you not be sure of that? You *said* you loved me, and I take a man of integrity at his word."

Savoring the moment he'd waited so long for, Jack reached into the glove compartment and fished out the letter from the *New York Times.* He held it up so she could see it clearly. "I was always sure I loved you, Sally. I needed to be sure that I didn't care about this."

Her eyes bugged out, precisely the reaction he wanted. "You didn't...open it?"

"No. I don't care what's in it." While she watched, stupefied, he tore the letter into several pieces and tossed them into the back seat. "Now, get in the car."

She sniffed and looked away.

"C'mon, Sally. Please?"

Muttering, she finally did as told, making sure to slam the passenger door as hard as possible. As she crossed her arms and burrowed into the corner of her seat, Jack pulled back out into the traffic, then turned left onto county road nineteen. It was time to go home.

"Three weeks, Jack."

"I had things to do before I could call you. Sheldon bought

my town house. He always liked it. I bought the Pittle house. I had personal business to attend to at home. And I had one very special thing I needed to get."

"A brain?"

"Don't be sarcastic. You'll see what it is in a minute."

They drove in silence for a while, the sky overhead getting darker by the minute. Jack could smell rain in the air—anybody from Vancouver could—but Sally was oblivious. Apparently one storm was all she could handle.

"How long were you in Vancouver?" she asked as they crested a hill and the inn came into sight.

"Two days. I've been back here ever since."

"Humph. Who in town knew that you were here?"

Jack couldn't resist the urge to grin at her. "Everybody except you." Her stunned reaction was priceless. She didn't like that one bit!

"I don't understand. When did you make your decision?"

"The second the letter was in my hand, I realized I truly didn't care about its contents. But I had to be sure I didn't care. And I am sure."

Sally gasped. "But that was three weeks ago!"

"I told you, I had things to do."

Moments later they arrived at the house—their house, Jack thought happily, where they would live and love. Where they would raise their children and play with their grandchildren. Where they would entertain their friends—and each other, every night from this day forward.

Jack parked the Mustang and hurried around to open Sally's door. Calmer now but still edgy, she slid out of the car, being careful not to touch him. The massive rock he'd had placed near their porch steps immediately caught her eye, and she walked over to it. Inscribed in its flat, rough surface were the words: *I promise to make Sally happy every day.*

His promise to her, carved in stone.

"I figured out what makes me happy," Jack said quietly.

"And it isn't the *New York Times*. Making you happy makes me happy."

Tears streamed from her eyes as she walked into his arms. "Oh, Jack."

Murmuring words of love and lifelong devotion, he crushed her against his chest and held her tightly. There were so many things he wanted to say. That he couldn't, no matter what kind of offer was on the table, imagine spending one more day of his life without her. That his true home was inside her and her only, and that while he could subsist somewhere else in the world, he could only truly *live* inside her heart.

One day he might even tell her that when he hadn't answered their letter soon enough, the *New York Times* had called him and reiterated their offer over the phone. And that it was the offer of a lifetime, but couldn't compare with one day of her love.

But Sally didn't need to know that now.

As they kissed, hungrily, desperately, the sky above them opened up and the rain, at long last, came down.

DRENCHED FROM head to toe, Sally snuggled against Jack. There were so many things she wanted to tell him, but they seemed redundant now. They were together and in love, and they always would be.

One day, just for fun, she might tell him the truth: that she had gone not just to Vancouver in search of him, but all the way to New York City. And, furthermore, that she had made a *real* spectacle of herself by storming into the *New York Times* and demanding to know in what office one cowardly Jack Langley Gold was hiding from her. Only to discover that Jack Langley Gold wasn't working for the *New York Times*. He hadn't even answered their letter.

She might also tell him that, if he had been in New York, she would have given up her life to stay there with him. In fact she would have gone anywhere to be with him, so much did she love and want and need him.

It would be the ultimate *Gotcha!*, well worth saving.

Grinning like the devil, Jack nodded toward the house. "The Pittles are in Grand Forks, signing the papers on their new condo. What do you say we go inside and, ah, negotiate for a while?"

Sally looked him over with smug satisfaction. There was only one question left to ask, and she already knew its answer. But why not? "So, hotshot, does this mean I win the game?"

"No, sweet thing. Only this round."

July 10: On the front page of every major newspaper in Canada

Gold Takes Home The Gold—Again

Jack Gold has made history by becoming the only journalist ever to win the prestigious Gobey Award two years in a row.

Gold, 35, was honored this year for the feature titled "My Place, My People: The Sally Darville Story," published last August in *Maclean's* magazine.

Three weeks later, Gold shocked the news community by giving up a senior position with the *Vancouver Satellite* to become owner-publisher of the *Peachtown Post*, in Peachtown, British Columbia. Gold has since expanded the weekly paper to cover news and features from across the Okanagan Valley.

In an interesting turn of events, Gold married Darville, 28, last month in a ceremony attended by more than a thousand people. When asked where they planned to honeymoon, the newlyweds said they weren't sure, but that it was "negotiable."

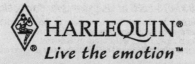

Harlequin Romance®

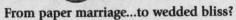

Contract Brides

From paper marriage...to wedded bliss?

A wedding dilemma:

What should a sexy, successful bachelor do if he's too busy making millions to find a wife? Or if he finds the perfect woman, and just has to strike a bridal bargain...?

The perfect proposal:

The solution? For better, for worse, these grooms in a hurry have decided to sign, seal and deliver the ultimate marriage contract...to buy a bride!

Coming Soon to
◆ HARLEQUIN®
Romance®

featuring the favorite miniseries Contract Brides:

THE LAST-MINUTE MARRIAGE
by Marion Lennox, #3832
on sale February 2005

A WIFE ON PAPER
by award-winning author Liz Fielding, #3837
on sale March 2005

VACANCY: WIFE OF CONVENIENCE
by Jessica Steele, #3839
on sale April 2005

Available wherever Harlequin books are sold.

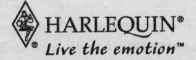